THE
COLONEL'S DAUGHTER

NANCY FOSHEE

Copyright © 2023 Nancy Foshee.

All rights reserved. No part of this book may be reproduced, stored, or transmitted by any means—whether auditory, graphic, mechanical, or electronic—without written permission of both publisher and author, except in the case of brief excerpts used in critical articles and reviews. Unauthorized reproduction of any part of this work is illegal and is punishable by law.

ISBN: 979-8-88640-743-3 (sc)
ISBN: 979-8-88640-744-0 (hc)
ISBN: 979-8-88640-745-7 (e)

Because of the dynamic nature of the Internet, any web addresses or links contained in this book may have changed since publication and may no longer be valid. The views expressed in this work are solely those of the author and do not necessarily reflect the views of the publisher, and the publisher hereby disclaims any responsibility for them.

One Galleria Blvd., Suite 1900, Metairie, LA 70001
1-888-421-2397

CHAPTER

Salt Lake City, UT, 1895

Her impatient right foot tapping seemed to echo in the nearly empty train station. Her fashionably green traveling suit was unrecognizable beneath the soot and grime from the steam engine. She wiped her face with a lace handkerchief and looked at the dirty cloth in her hand. This trip was not turning out to be what she had expected or hoped. The first time she would have seen her father in over 15 years and she looked like some hopeless beggar.

Abigail Randolph stood among her luggage at the train station gazing out at a crowd of strangers, scouring their faces to see if she could recognize the one person she hoped to find. Her handbag, parasol, and traveling case at her side, she held a tiny daguerreotype of her father dressed in his army uniform in one hand. With the other, she caressed her mother's locket, which she always wore about her neck. It always seemed to inspire courage in her, and she needed all she could muster today.

The cavernous hall of the Salt Lake City train depot in mid-August smelled of perspiration and stale cigar smoke. An infant's wailing reverberated across the expansive ceiling. In addition, there was a persistent hum in the room— various voices calling and greeting one another along with the constant shuffling of feet moving through the station to and from the platforms. People scurried about like so many insects while Abigail remained still, waiting for her father who was a colonel at Fort Douglas. Surely he wouldn't have forgotten that she was arriving today. She sighed, shook her head, and tapped her foot several times impatiently.

"Sir, can you tell me how to get to Fort Douglas?" she asked as she leaned toward a man who passed near her.

The stranger scowled menacingly and replied, "Fort Douglas, hmpf! Go back to your own kind, missy. We don't need you here." Then he turned and walked away with a woman and several children.

Confused by the man's attitude, Abigail pulled back erect and watched as the family group hurried away. Perhaps her voice had been too insistent, she thought. She had only been trying to be heard above the noise in the station. Besides, she was little used to waiting for someone else to do something. Both her upbringing and her education drove her to seek ways to actively help others. Grammy had always said that praying for someone wasn't enough if there was something specific you could do to ease their suffering. It was the main reason Abigail was here in this depot right now. Her father's letter had sparked that nerve.

The letter inviting her to come to Fort Douglas had arrived in Boston a little over a month ago just after she had completed her degree and she was considering what to do next. He suggested that she could work with the women in Salt Lake City to regain their right to vote. Abigail knew that women in Utah had voted almost from the beginning of territorial organization, so it was confusing to read about such a drastic change. Her curiosity both about the situation in Utah and a little about her father led her to make the trip clear across the country.

But on the train from Ogden, she learned about the problems that many Mormon women now faced since the end of polygamy. Like her great-great grandfather, Thomas Jefferson, Abigail was determined to oppose injustice and tyranny wherever it threatened anyone. Having originally thought she'd stay a month or so, she had now decided to remain as long as needed to free these women from the bondage of prostitution.

But where was her father? She had been standing here in this station for awhile. Right now, for the very first time in her life, she was glad her father was a soldier. It would make it easier to identify him from among the mass of other strangers in the depot. A flash of deep blue caught the corner of her eye, and she turned to see a much younger stranger in an army uniform.

"Miss Randolph?"

A clean-shaven soldier in a neatly pressed uniform stood before her. He removed his hat and politely bowed his head briefly toward her. She smiled politely, expecting any moment to be reunited with her father. She scanned the people who moved behind the soldier, but no one else appeared to be with him. Then she looked back at the stranger in front of her and frowned.

"Where's my father?" she asked.

He cleared his throat and moved a step closer, his body stiffly erect as if standing at attention. "I'm Captain Garrett Jackson Talbot, Miss Randolph. Your father asked me to meet you here and drive you back to the fort."

He reached for her traveling case while she stood silent. A tiny bit of irritation began to grow in her chest. She didn't know just what that meant.

<u>Does my father care so little about me that he would send a stranger for me?</u>

"Is my father all right?" she started. The noise in the room had all but muffled the soldier's voice.

"Colonel Randolph? He's fine. There was a meeting with the mayor and chief of police he couldn't miss. He sent me instead. I'm a little late, I know. I hope I haven't inconvenienced you, ma'am."

Abigail shook her head, feeling a little disappointed, though she didn't quite know why. Her father had been absent from her life for most of her twenty-one years. She'd been told her mother's health prevented the two of them from joining her father at the various forts where he was assigned. She felt she was the reason her mother died, and she wondered if her father blamed her as well. But as she grew older, she had come to believe something entirely different. Suddenly she was a little girl again, crying for her daddy. Anger, resentment, loneliness, and sadness battled for domination in her heart. She blinked back the small child, and the grown woman took control of her emotions again.

The captain picked up the other satchel on the floor beside her and ushered her toward the front doorway. "This way, ma'am. The wagon is just outside," he said, walking toward the door.

Abigail picked up her handbag and parasol. She had to admit she was surprised by this turn of events. She had fully expected to meet her father here in the train depot. She had even rehearsed polite greetings for the man. She sighed again and remembered her reason for coming to Fort Douglas—to help Mormon women who had been abandoned by their polygamous husbands. Her relationship with her father, or lack thereof, was another matter.

She quickly followed the soldier. Behind her, the porter pushed a cart with her trunks.

She watched while the two men worked to put her traveling cases aboard the wagon. The soldier climbed up into the flat bed and lifted one trunk while the porter guided it up to him. Together the two men managed to secure both of her trunks. After they finished, the soldier jumped down and latched the back of the wagon. He thanked the colored man, shook his hand, and gave him some change.

Watching this exchange amazed her. Back East, most coloreds were looked upon as second-class citizens. But here, this porter had been treated as an equal, at least by this captain. For the first time since she had arrived this morning, Abigail smiled.

"Ma'am, let me help you up," the captain said reaching to assist her.

She shook her head. "I think I can do that myself," she responded. "But thank you for offering." Then she edged up her skirt slightly, put her foot up on the metal step, found a handhold to pull on, and climbed the rest of the way up. Once there, she straightened her suit jacket and skirt, and situated herself primly on the wooden bench of the wagon.

The captain handed Abigail her parasol, then walked around to the other side, climbed up and took the reins. When he snapped the reins twice, the horses bolted forward suddenly and jostled Abigail from her seat and onto the wagon's wooden bed. As she fell, she reached for anything that would work like a handle, inadvertently grabbing the captain's arm.

"Whoa! Whoa!" he called as he pulled the reins. Turning toward her, he said, "Sorry, ma'am. Here, let me help you a bit." He wrapped the reins around the brake, and then he gently lifted Abigail back up onto the seat. "I've never driven this old freight wagon before, but Roger said it was the only vehicle we had that could accommodate all your luggage. I promise I'll be more careful."

Abigail felt her face grow hot and knew it must be bright red, maybe even close to the color of her hair. She took a deep breath. "It was my fault. I really am more accustomed to this kind of transportation, Captain. I spent most of my life on a Kentucky horse farm."

"Yes ma'am, so I've heard. Are you all right now?"

Abigail nodded, but this complete stranger seemed to know more about her than she did about him. She didn't know why, but a kernel of irritation began to grow, and she frowned as she looked away from him.

"Where is Fort Douglas?" she asked, reflexively touching her locket.

Without glancing in her direction, he pointed off to his left. "Up there on the Wasatch foothills, about six or seven miles from here. With any luck, we'll be there in less than an hour."

He shook the reins lightly, and the wagon began to lumber awkwardly down the dirt street. Abigail held onto the edge of the bench with both hands this time. A moment later, she glanced over at the man to her left. Was he laughing at her struggle to remain erect? No real gentleman would find her predicament amusing. But she wouldn't be terribly surprised if he did. She didn't have much regard for men in the military. They were all alike— all focused on themselves, leaving their families behind to chase after God knows what.

"You might want to use that, Miss Randolph," he said pointing to her parasol. "The August sun can really bake a person this time of year."

Abigail took his suggestion, and the shade beneath her parasol gave her instant relief. Within a few minutes, she realized she was embarrassed by her mood. This man is not responsible for my father's actions, she thought. She tried to think of something she could say. But she couldn't even remember his name.

"What did you say your name was again? I'm afraid in the confusion I didn't hear it."

"Captain Garrett Talbot, ma'am."

Abigail looked away from him again, scanning the scenery of what was to be her new home. "So, Captain Talbot, do you fight Indians or cattle rustlers out here?" she asked, turning to catch his response.

He laughed and shook his head. "No, ma'am. I'm legal counsel for your father."

"A lawyer?" she asked, surprised to learn he was educated.

"Yes, ma'am, though I mostly just advise your father on army contracts and a few other legal matters."

"Well, Captain Talbot, just what has my father told you about me?"

He shrugged his shoulders, never taking his eyes off the horses. "Just a little. You've been living back East, you've finished Smith College, and you've come to stay here awhile, ma'am."

"Is that all, Captain?"

"Pretty much. Of course, I could tell myself you're not originally from Boston. Your accent is definitely Southern."

Abigail knew she was blushing again at his remarks, but she began to relax with this soldier who was simply doing a favor for her father. The real source of her irritation was her father. He was as much a stranger to her as this captain. She guessed she had been around him less than two years' total time. She sighed again. Maybe things would have been different if she'd been a son instead of a daughter.

Abigail shook her head, and dismissed the conflicting emotions that always seemed to surface whenever she thought about her father. She decided to distract herself by surveying her surroundings. She couldn't help but be impressed with the scenery in downtown Salt Lake City. She hadn't expected it to be so modern looking. There were several tall buildings like those she had seen in Boston and New York. Though the streets were not yet paved, it was evident they were being maintained and kept swept of debris, especially near the impressive, cathedral-like structure.

"Is that the Mormon Temple?" she asked pointing to their left.

"Yes, ma'am," he replied matter-of-factly.

Abigail marveled at the sight of the Mormon sanctuary, positioned strategically in the center of the town. She'd heard about it from some of the passengers on the train from Ogden. It exceeded her expectations in grandeur.

"This street is South Temple, and over there is Temple Square," he said as he motioned. "The smaller building is their original meeting place. I guess they're keeping it for general meeting purposes. Only Mormons are allowed into the new temple. They completed it just two years ago, and last year they added the solid bronze angel on the top of it up there," he said pointing up to the spire.

Abigail gazed at the magnificent building. It was awe-inspiring, to be sure, but in her mind, it stood for a religion that permitted women to be cast aside. She turned her head away from the sight.

The captain guided the wagon easily to the right as he continued to describe the other sites for her. "This is Main Street. See, they got electric street cars running up and down the business district to Temple Square. There's even a stop up at the fort."

He gestured with his left arm, explaining, "This end of the street is Mormon-owned businesses. We don't shop down here."

"Why, Captain?"

"Don't question the Colonel's orders, ma'am. He doesn't want us to spend any time or money in Mormon businesses, if we can manage it. It's just better that way."

"Have you ever been around Mormons, Captain?"

"No, ma'am. I follow orders. Everyone at Fort Douglas does."

Abigail frowned. Her concern for Mormon women reemerged. How would she be able to assist them if she wasn't allowed to be around them?

"Well, Captain, I'm not in the army," she replied. Then under her breath, she added, "I won't be following anybody's orders."

Captain Talbot continued to drive the wagon down the noisy street. He gestured toward another row of shops. "South of here are non-Mormon businesses where most of us go shopping when we come to town. The Colonel will probably tell you himself he'd rather you stay on this side of the business district."

She turned her head again slightly toward him, curious about this man whom her father had sent in his place. Beneath the shade of her parasol, she cocked her eyes to the left to make as covert an appraisal as possible. His gray-blue eyes were intent on the road, only occasionally looking up in the direction of the sights he explained. He seemed unaware of her curiosity in him. He was an attractive man, clean-shaven so that his strong cheek bones and square chin were visible. There was the hint of a dimple in his cheek, too. She guessed him to be maybe twenty-eight years old. His sandy-colored hair was neatly barbered beneath his blue, wide-brimmed hat. Beneath his shirt sleeve, his muscles contracted with each move of the reins. He was certainly in control of himself and the animals. Maybe too controlled, she thought.

<u>He follows orders</u>, she thought sarcastically.

As he turned the wagon to the left, Abigail's eyes were drawn to a giant structure towering over the street. It was an imposing building in the center of what looked like a park.

"What's that?" she asked.

"That's the Salt Lake City and County Building. Just finished it last year. Inside are modern courtrooms, offices for judges and lawyers, and executive headquarters for the police. Had a little trouble getting it done because of the problems with money nowadays. But it got done. They dedicated the finished building last December."

She nodded again. The entire country had been experiencing economic difficulties. Back East, some banks and several railroads had closed. Factory workers had lost jobs due to reduced demand for some products. But she hadn't realized that areas as far west as the Utah territory were affected.

Abigail had been traveling for nearly two weeks now. Her body was achy and stiff from sitting in cramped places for long periods of time, and riding in this old freight wagon only intensified her discomfort. She was ready for this journey to be at an end. She had yet to meet her father, and she was still unsure what she was going to say when she did. She stared vacantly off in the distance, trying to rehearse words and actions that would be appropriate.

Despite her fatigue, a sense of excitement at her new home began to grow in her mind. Because it was a Western town, she'd not been expecting the municipal development here in Salt Lake City. The modern structures surprised her. Maybe modern facilities indicated a more modern attitude. She smiled as she considered the possibility of making a contribution here in Salt Lake City.

She glanced again at her companion whose bronzed hands continued to control the pace of the horses. Her mother had fallen in love with just this sort of man, and look what it had gotten her. She reached up to touch her locket briefly.

Abigail turned her head to stare absent-mindedly off to the right. They passed groves of orchard trees and small farms rich with grains waving in the breeze. The Mormons had truly made an oasis out of what must've been originally high desert country. After she'd learned her father had been assigned to Fort Douglas, she became curious about the Mormons. She had found several books about them, including one by Ann Eliza Young which was an expose` of polygamy. As she thought of the book, she became even more determined to stick it out here with her father, no matter how she felt about him.

<u>I'll just have to find a way to help them.</u>

"Why doesn't my father want you to talk with Mormons, Captain?"

"They're not particularly fond of us, ma'am. Been that way ever since the fort was put here back during the War."

"Why was a fort put here then?"

"It's common knowledge that Lincoln was concerned the Mormons would involve themselves in the conflict. He sent Colonel Connor out here to keep an eye on them. Must have worked because they never even considered participating in the War."

"So you've never spoken with a Mormon, Captain?"

"Can't say as I have, Miss. At least, not intentionally."

"But they're just people. Don't you ever want to learn about them?"

He shook his head. "Not really, ma'am. Their religion is their business."

"But what if their religion is a fraud?"

"Still none of my business. Constitution guarantees them the freedom of religion. They have the right to worship as they please."

Abigail frowned. Did he all of a sudden seem to act superior? Was it something in his voice, or had she only imagined it? She looked straight ahead in the direction of the fort. It must be orders or something. They traveled the next several miles in silence.

Awhile later as they rounded a curve, Abigail could see the gates of the post located just up a hill rimmed by dark gray mountains. Soldiers stood atop the stockade, apparently on guard. Realizing she would need both her hands, she closed her parasol. She grabbed the edge of the wagon seat again to keep from being thrown out of the wagon as the road inclined sharply up to the gate. In her struggle to remain erect, the wind caught the stiff brim on her bonnet, turning it to an odd angle and rearranging her hair. Trying to fix it, she pulled several strands of her coiffure loose. Still focused on bracing herself on the wagon, she snatched her hat off her head with one hand while still holding on to her seat with the other.

Up ahead, the road flattened out where two men stood beside what must be her father's house on the post. Her stomach seemed to quiver with a thousand little buzzing flies. Abigail Randolph was about to be face to face with her father after so many years apart.

Captain Garrett Talbot pulled the old freight wagon to a stop in front of the residence where the Colonel waited with Corporal Davis at his side. After securing the reins, Garrett turned toward Abigail. She readjusted herself after having nearly fallen on the ride up the hill and fussed with her hat, trying to put her bright copper-colored hair in place. Several stubborn strands of her hair dangled oddly from beneath her bonnet. She didn't seem pleased with the effect, although he had to admit to himself, the picture was quite charming. Even having seen her photograph in the Colonel's office, he hadn't been prepared for her to be so pretty.

He jumped down effortlessly before turning to assist his passenger. She tentatively took his hand as he guided her. He reached up and placed his hands securely at her waist, but as he set her gently down on the ground, she stumbled forward against him. Her hair was fragrant with the scent of lavender. For an instant, the warmth of her slender body against his took his breath away. But even this incidental physical contact was improper. They both quickly stepped back. Abigail straightened her skirts while Garrett instinctively moved to allow the Colonel to face his daughter.

"I hope you had a pleasant trip, Abby," the Colonel stated, "I know the trains can be a bit tiresome, but they do make transportation out here easier than the old covered wagons used to be."

The Colonel's eyes watered as he stood gazing at his daughter.

"I can't get over how much you look like your mother, Abby," he commented softly, almost under his breath.

She smiled weakly at her father, obviously a little uneasy with the attention. She extended her gloved hand toward him, perhaps to shake his hand. When he abruptly hugged her, Abigail stood stiffly in her father's embrace. Anyone could see she wasn't comfortable being with him. Moments later, the Colonel stood back and turned towards Garrett.

"Captain Talbot is my most trusted officer, Abby. Since I couldn't get away to meet you, I sent him to drive you here," he explained.

"Thank you, Captain," Abigail replied glancing briefly in his direction.

"You're welcome, ma'am. But you may call me Garrett."

She nodded and smiled up at him. Her green eyes glistened for just a moment before they were obscured by dark, thick lashes. He tried to think of something more to say, but she turned away. The Colonel led her toward the house, so Garrett moved to the back of the wagon to lend Corporal Davis a hand with the heavy trunks. When the Colonel and his daughter reached the bottom of the steps, a woman came out of the house and met them.

"Abby, this is Helen Davis, Corporal Davis's wife. She's been a godsend to me these past seven years. She and Corporal Davis agreed to occupy the back quarters off the kitchen. She's my housekeeper. Truth of the matter, I don't know how I would get along without her."

Helen beamed and extended both her hands in greeting. Abigail appeared to brighten up with the reception and smiled back at the Corporal's wife.

Helen grasped both of Abigail's hands in hers as she said, "I'm so glad you're here, Miss Randolph. Your father has been so happy since you agreed to come and stay with him. I've had a devil of a time trying to get the place ready for your arrival."

Glowing with hospitality, Helen wrapped her arms around the younger woman, embracing her as though they were long separated family members. Garrett watched as Abigail Randolph seemed to respond to Helen's friendliness. He realized the Colonel had been wise to ask the corporal and his wife to remain at the Colonel's residence, at least for the time being. Helen's presence would certainly encourage the Colonel's daughter to feel comfortable there.

"I'm sure everything will be just fine. I'm so glad to be off the train. Right now, I would just love to wash the grime off my face and get out of these traveling clothes."

Garrett watched as the two women strolled casually into the house. The Colonel grinned and shook his head before he turned around to face the captain.

"I know you're glad she's finally here, sir," Garrett said.

"Yes, indeed. Thank you again for bringing her here from the station. We'll have you over for dinner later in the week," he said before he turned to walk into the house.

As Garrett made his way back to his barracks, he felt a tremendous sense of relief that there would be a delay in his newest assignment. All he had to do was keep the Colonel's daughter out of trouble, and come spring time, he'd have his transfer to Army Headquarters in Washington, D.C. The Colonel had promised to provide him with a recommendation.

Now having seen Abigail Randolph in person, with her bright auburn hair slightly askew and those dazzling green eyes, Garrett realized this favor for the Colonel could be much more pleasant than he had originally thought. However, he would have to be very careful. He had been warned. The Colonel had said she was quite the crusader. She'd even marched with suffragettes back in Boston. No doubt she could be a handful. He'd heard her say she wasn't going to follow anyone's orders, and he was pretty sure she meant it. And he already knew she was much too interested in Mormon business. The Colonel wasn't going to like that one bit.

As he stood outside his barracks, he knew Abigail's arrival had also been observed by Edith Hempstead, Major Hempstead's wife and the self-proclaimed social monitor of the fort. He was sure that Edith would continue to watch her every move, just like she did everybody else. And the Colonel would get an earful whether he wanted it or not. There was little doubt she would be an obstacle for Miss Randolph. After just the ride back to the fort, he sensed Miss Randolph would not go along with Edith's way of doing things, which could mean trouble for all of them.

Garrett sighed. With all these potential obstacles, these next few months could be more difficult than he had first considered. And what if he failed? Would the Colonel be willing to assist him with his transfer anyway? With no immediate answers to his questions, Garrett stepped inside his barracks. He suspected Abigail Randolph was a tornado threatening to touch down, and he just hoped his career plans wouldn't be destroyed by it.

CHAPTER

After dinner with her father and the Davises, Abigail had retired early to the room that had been prepared for her. She'd plaited her waist-length hair, put on a clean white muslin night shift, and collapsed heavily into the crisply-made bed, with a prayer on her lips thanking God for safe passage across the country. She lay in bed still feeling the rhythmic motion of the steam engine, hearing the regular clackety-clack of the wheels on the iron rails, and the occasional shrill whistle of the train blaring its warning. Sleep came easily at first.

But then just at the first peek of sunrise, she was awakened by a blaring noise. Startled from a sound sleep, she spent several moments trying to recall where she was. She rushed to the window in time to see a flag being raised as soldiers stood to salute. Remembering her arrival at Fort Douglas, she climbed back into her bed. She pulled a pillow over her head to obscure both the noise and the light. Then exhaustion returned, and she drifted back to sleep again.

Her mind wandered comfortably back in time to her childhood home in Kentucky. She sat astride her favorite mount. Grammy scolded her, "It's not ladylike." Poppy smiled and urged, "Ride on, Abby girl. You know your horse, and you know the path." Her mother waved from the porch. Abby felt her hair blowing loosely behind her, the wind on her face, the sun lighting her way. She looked over her shoulder to see if her mother was still watching her, but no one was there. She wrapped her arms around the horse's neck and leaned forward feeling his mane against her face. It was a sweet sadness.

Abigail continued luxuriating in restful dreams until the mid-morning sun rays reached in through the open window and gently caressed her face. As she opened her eyes, it seemed the whole room was bathed in a golden haze. She could hear muffled voices, not close, but in the distance, it seemed. The curtains suddenly waved in the air as they permitted the August breeze to drift unheeded into the room. She blinked several times lazily. The memory of last evening and the end of her journey slowly emerged. Abigail reached for her locket still around her neck just beneath her night clothes.

She lay in the bed recalling the evening's conversation and glanced curiously around her new bedroom. It was spacious, more than she had experienced while living in the dorm at Smith College. In addition to the large bed, there was an oaken dresser, a large oval mirror, and a gigantic chifforobe. Near the window was a royal blue overstuffed chair with a small lamp table beside it. This room was warm and inviting just like the one she had left in Kentucky.

Then her eyes were drawn to an object on the wall near the chair. She could smell its fragrance— a crisp, fresh cedar aroma which seemed to permeate the entire room. She pulled herself to the side of the bed and stared intently at the empty bookcase.

The fragrance pulled her from the bed to examine the smooth wood with her hands. The wood had been sanded smooth and had a soft, almost talcum powder feel to it. Then as she stood there, she saw a piece of paper folded neatly on one shelf. Opening it slowly, she saw an eagle in a circle at the top of the page. Below it she read "Thought you would like a place for your 'treasures.' You won't have to stack them in the corner here." Though she hadn't seen it often in her life, she instantly recognized her father's handwriting.

Chill bumps covered her arms. How could he have known she would bring books with her? How did he know she called them her 'treasures'? She ran her hands along the newly sanded furniture and smelled the fresh scent of cedar shelves which waited to be filled with books. She was instantly reminded of Grammy's cedar chest where she kept her own 'treasures.' Abby remembered fingering delicate lace hankies and finding pressed flowers within the pages of a small Bible. She smiled as that precious memory of times long ago drifted away with the growing morning light. Then, in an instant, she began unloading books from her trunk and placing them on the bookcase. She had carefully arranged nearly half of them when she heard a knock on her bedroom door.

"Miss Randolph? It's me, Helen. I brought some biscuits and milk. May I come in?"

As Abigail opened the door, the aroma of fresh biscuits preceded Helen into the room. Helen placed them and a pitcher of milk on the table in the corner. Abigail quietly thanked her for the welcomed breakfast while putting on her robe and sinking into the chair.

"I heard you stirring around up here, and thought you might be hungry," Helen replied looking over at the half-filled bookcase. "I see you found it. Your father had it made special for you. He hoped it would make you feel right at home."

Abigail stopped almost frozen in place. Her amazement must have shown on her face as she turned to face Helen.

Helen laughed lightly. "Guess you didn't know he was so concerned about you, did you?"

Abigail shook her head in disbelief. "My father and I have not talked much over the years. He's been gone most of my life. When I was a little girl, my mother often told me why my father was away, but it didn't keep me from wondering if he regretted having only a daughter and not a son." She reached to touch her locket out of habit. Just the memory of her mother was reassuring. She reached for a biscuit, took a bite, and instantly recognized how hungry she was.

"Well, from all he's said these past weeks, I can safely say that isn't the case at all, Miss Randolph."

Abigail quickly swallowed a mouthful of biscuit. "Oh, please, call me Abby," she replied. "Since we are living here in the same house, there is no sense in any kind of formality. Besides, I want to be on a first name basis with anyone who can bake biscuits which taste this good."

"Yes, ma'am, Abby," she replied sitting on the edge of the unmade bed.

"You think you could teach me how to do this?" Abby asked pointing at the plate of diminishing biscuits.

"Maybe. We'll see," Helen added winking with merriment.

Abby finished the last bite and swallowed the milk gratefully. She was beginning to feel more awake now. The breakfast helped, but the company supported her even more. Nodding her head, she asked, "Helen, if my father is so concerned about me, why did he send a stranger to meet me at the train?"

Helen smiled as she answered, "Well, that is a fair question, I'll give you. But if I had to guess, I think your father felt you might be uncomfortable driving the long distance up to the fort with him. And your father really did have a meeting scheduled."

"Still, a stranger?"

"Captain Talbot's no stranger, Abby. He's the Colonel's right hand man nearly every day. Major Hempstead may be next in rank, but Garrett Talbot is the one the Colonel relies upon for counsel. He sent no stranger. He sent you the most trusted officer on this post. Besides being the best looking," she added with a smirk.

"Best-looking?" But she did blush slightly as she remembered his eyes and that barely perceptible dimple.

"Aw, c'mon. You must've noticed. He's so tall and handsome, and he really has the most fabulous smile. If I wasn't already married to the man of my dreams, I'd certainly swish my skirt at him a time or two."

Abby felt her jaw drop in shock. "Shame on you, Helen." Almost as an afterthought she added, "Well, even so, he's a soldier. I could never consider someone in the army."

Helen giggled as Abby flopped on the bed beside her. They both laughed heartily rolling on the bed like little girls. After several minutes, the two women were chatting as though they had grown up together.

"It must have been wonderful, going to college back East," Helen said.

"Yes, I learned a lot. But it was a bit lonely, too. With my grandparents and my mother gone, I felt really alone."

"So why'd you stay?"

Abby felt a sense of recognition all of a sudden. "That's who you remind me of."

Helen looked totally puzzled at Abby's comment.

"My first weekend at Smith College I met Katherine Hampton. She was a senior. She came to my room and announced I was to be her little sister for the school year. You don't look very much like her, but your mannerisms remind me of the friendship she gave me back then when I felt so alone."

Helen smiled appreciatively and then asked, "Did you go to many parties and dances when you weren't studying?"

"Some, well, maybe more than a few, now that I think of it. And I did travel to New York a time or two to shop. Katherine knew all the best places to shop. Do you have any dress shops in Salt Lake?"

Helen lay comfortably on the bed and rolled her head from side to side. "Some, I think, though I don't go to town very often. I've only got one fancy dress that I wear to the Harvest Ball each year."

Abigail got up from the bed and sat down in the large chair by the window. "Well, I have several, Helen, and I just bet there's one that'll fit you."

Helen grinned broadly, her eyes sparkling with delight. "You remind me of someone, too. My baby sister. She's redheaded like you. I sure miss her."

"You have a big family?"

"Yes, both Roger and I come from large families, lots of children," Helen sighed. "The day he came to visit and rolled in the dirt with my brothers playing, I knew we were meant for each other. We always thought we would have a brood of little ones by now, but it . . ."

Abby thought she saw Helen's eyes tear up, and she felt immediate concern for someone she had just met. "I'm sure you'll get your wish in no time, Helen."

Helen got very quiet and seemed to be searching for the right words. Then she turned toward Abby and asked, "Maybe it's none of my business, but how did you lose your grandparents?"

Abby sat up straight in the chair and sighed heavily. She pursed her lips and then nodded her head before beginning. "I was away at Lexington negotiating on the sale of some of our thoroughbreds. Poppy wanted me to use that money to pay for my college. While I was away, there was a lot of rain in the area, and there was concern that the levees might be swamped. Poppy and Grammy left our farm, which is on high ground, and drove into the low-lying areas to help some of the poorer families to get out of there. On their way out, they must have gotten stuck in the mud or something. The sheriff told me they were swept away by a flash flood—that there was nothing anyone could have done to save them. At least they died the way they lived: working to help other people who needed them."

Helen smiled back weakly at Abby. She reached and patted Abby's knees in a gesture of understanding. Then she sat up and changed the subject. Pointing at Abby's collection of books, she asked, "Which one is your favorite?"

Abigail reached over to the bookcase from the chair and withdrew her copy of <u>Pride and Prejudice.</u> "This one, I think, because the main character, Elizabeth Bennett, is so outspoken and independent. She doesn't really allow customs or conventions to keep her from doing or saying whatever she feels. And yet, it is a love story. Though they don't really get along at first, she does end up with the richest and most handsome bachelor, Mr. Darcy."

"Oh, I'd like to read it myself. Have you really read all these books here?"

"I'm afraid so. These and several others that I didn't have room to bring. I thought I might one day be a teacher and would need my own copies of these books. Now I'm not sure what I am going to do. Like I said, we haven't spent much time together, at all, in my life. My father's been away leading the life of a soldier, while I lived with my grandparents after my mother died. I had a very good life, and I wouldn't change much about it; but it does make moving in with him a trifle strange. We really don't know much about one another. I am totally surprised he knew of my interest in books. Or that I used to stack them in the corner of my room."

Helen laughed. "Oh, yes, indeed. He made quite a fuss about getting this bookcase ready for you. Insisted it be made from cedar wood. Even gave extra leave to the two privates who finished it for him last week. You should have seen his face when it was finally put in place there."

Abigail sat somewhat amazed. "So where is my father now?" she asked.

"This is Saturday, Abby, and Colonel Randolph always goes riding on his horse around the post, a kind of inspection, of sorts. But I think he just likes the opportunity to get outside," she responded with a broad smile. "He's quite attached to his horse, Grant. Won't let anyone else ride him."

Abigail glanced out the window to see people scrambling about, some, obviously children, running and playing. There seemed to be a purpose in their busyness, but she couldn't discern it.

Helen, too, looked out the window to the dirt streets below. "Oh, I should tell you he has arranged a welcome for you tomorrow after post chapel. It will be a dinner on the church grounds, like I remember from back home in Springfield. Several of the women are setting things up today. If you like, I can take you around the fort a bit after I finish in the kitchen area," she offered.

Abigail nodded back at her new found friend. "While you're working downstairs, I'll just finish putting things away up here . . . in my bedroom," she answered as she looked around the room in what was to be her new home. She liked this new environment. Maybe she had been wrong all along, she thought.

After Helen took the tray from the room, Abigail quickly put her clothes and other belongings in their proper places. Then she washed her face, arranged her hair neatly on top of her head, and, after selecting an appropriate afternoon dress, she freshened up for her first walk around Fort Douglas.

※

"Garrett, what're you doing here? It's Saturday, and there's a game over on the east field," asked Lt. Morgan from the door of the captain's office.

Garrett nodded, "I know, Chet, but I just wanted to get these last two reports finished before Monday. Would've had them done if I hadn't gone to the city yesterday." He shuffled some papers together and stuffed them into a file.

Lt. Chester Morgan strolled into Garrett's office and over to the window which faced the Colonel's residence. "So how'd that go?"

"Fine, it went just fine. Found her at the station, drove her home to the Colonel, and left her with Helen." He looked over at his friend and sometime-confidant. "You know, I rode all the way back from the city with her, and we talked a bit, but I'm not even sure she looked at me once. It was like I wasn't even there."

"Stuck up, huh. Most officers' daughters are like that."

"No, I think it was something else. Maybe it's cause she's from back East."

"Yeah, they can be right snooty, too, I hear. But being the Colonel's daughter, she's probably not much to look at anyways," Chet added matter-of-factly.

Garrett shook his head vigorously. "You are definitely wrong there."

Lt. Morgan swung around from the window to face him. "What? Tell me."

"She's quite fine looking. A beautiful redhead with green eyes. Almost takes your breath away. Too bad she's the Colonel's daughter. She's definitely off limits."

"But didn't the Colonel ask you to kinda chaperone her?" Lt. Morgan asked.

Garrett shrugged. "In a manner of speaking, I guess you're right. He as much as said if I do this favor for him, he'll approve my transfer."

"That's what you want, isn't it?"

"Yeah, but I still can't believe he knew I wanted to transfer to Washington," he answered. "He didn't even flinch when I told him what I was thinking. I thought he'd be upset or something."

"But he promised to write a recommendation, didn't he?"

"Sure did. But he asked me to wait until spring. And in the meantime, he asked me to watch out for his daughter."

"So, maybe he's trying his hand at matchmaking?" Chet laughed when he saw Garrett's reaction to his comment.

"That's not funny."

"But he asked you to keep her away from the Mormons in town and act as a buffer between his daughter and Edith."

"Oh, yes, I know what he asked, but I'm sure, given the way he's talked about her, he has no inclination to let anyone touch his daughter. No, she's off limits, for sure. Besides, I think she's going to be a handful. She didn't seem much interested in me, but she's already interested in the Mormons. You know what could happen."

"Uh oh. That won't sit well with the Colonel. What're you gonna do?"

"Don't know yet. I'll just have to tread softly with this assignment. I really want to transfer to Army Headquarters, and the Colonel can make it happen for me. Finished," he said standing up and pushing in his chair at his desk. "Now let's go watch that game. Sgt. Mullins has an arm on him. I bet he'll strike out Mason, don't you think?"

And the two men exited the building with their minds on baseball.

"Here are the parade grounds, Abby," Helen said as they strolled outside. "This is where the soldiers practice marching, and over there is where the respect to colors is given at sunrise and sunset each day. You'll hear the bugler, just like this morning. But you'll get used to it in a few days, maybe. Roger is up before sunrise each morning anyway, and I have to be up to make the Colonel's breakfast, so it's not a problem for us. If you want to sleep in, you might need to put a pillow over your head again." Then she pointed toward flagpole with the stars and stripes waving briskly in the warm Utah breeze.

Abby beamed taking in the beauty of the grounds. The large grassy area was encircled by a semi-paved drive which connected to the houses lining three sides of the commons. Majestic ponderosa pines and fir trees were intermingled with aspens and maples along the outside area of the parade grounds. Children played on these grounds happily, running in and out from the base of the trees, their sounds of merriment evident. Two small dogs barked and chased each other in the midst of the children. One mother called for an errant child to come home immediately, and Abby watched as a little boy reluctantly turned from his playmates and stomped home to his mother.

As the two women strolled down the wooden walkway which lined the commons, the sky overhead blazed with the heat of the afternoon sun, bathing the area with a warming glow. The gentle cooling breezes traveling down from the mountains above kept the whole area comfortable. From out of one of the houses nearby, Abby caught a whiff of freshly baked bread, and she was instantly reminded of Grammy baking something to take to their neighbors. She was surprised to realize she was beginning to feel at home here in this place. Life on an army fort was totally different from what she had expected.

"Over there are where the enlisted men live with their families," Helen remarked pointing to a row of single houses to their right. "And over there are the houses occupied by the officers and their families," she added, gesturing toward a semi-circle drive of houses to their left. An inviting gazebo stood in front of the row of officers' homes as if to announce their prominence.

"And over there are the barracks for officers without families on post. The single enlisted men's barracks are farther back on the east side of the fort," Helen added. "About a thousand soldiers are stationed here."

Abby surveyed the fort and smiled. Fort Douglas seemed to be a pleasant place to live. She might have enjoyed living here when she was younger, but it was decided she should remain in Kentucky with her grandparents. Now her father was all the family she had left. If only she could learn more about her father and develop a relationship with him, she might be just fine here.

Hearing more about the fort and its people would be a good start, she thought as she studied the natural beauty which surrounded her. She would just have to be vigilant to find the opportunity needed to intervene in the lives of Mormon women. No doubt, an opportunity would be presented in time. As Abby mused on her newest cause, a large magpie floated effortlessly down from the air like a kite gently falling to earth and landed gracefully at the base of a solid cedar tree. She realized this scene had brought her unexpected joy.

"Well, you must be Colonel Randolph's daughter, the one we have heard so much about," came a voice from behind her.

Abby and Helen turned to face three women who were strolling behind them. The one in the center was larger and taller than her two companions who were both quite petite.

Abby smiled and nodded to greet the three women. "Yes, ma'am, I'm Abigail Randolph," she announced politely and extended her gloved hand as if to shake their hands.

"I thought as much," the larger woman replied, ignoring the gesture. "I am Edith Hempstead, and," turning to each of the two women who walked at her side, "this is Carol Randall and Ruth Johnson."

"Pleased to meet you," Abby replied nodding her head in the direction of each of the ladies.

"I see that Helen is showing you around our fort. I know you must appreciate that she is willing to take the time away from her duties," Mrs. Hempstead replied haughtily, her stony face revealing a disdain for people she considered to be her inferiors. "However, I should tell you it is bad form for you to mingle with her outside of the Colonel's residence. She is, after all, just your father's housekeeper and the wife of an enlisted man. I am sure one of the officers' wives would be glad to assist you, Miss Randolph."

Abby frowned at the woman's patronizing tone. Edith Hempstead was a stout, imposing woman with narrow eyes which quickly communicated her sense of entitlement. She had a broad forehead, dull gray hair pulled back from her face, a face which had little practice smiling, Abby surmised as she studied her.

Suddenly not sure if she should be intimidated, Abby stepped back a bit and reached for Helen's arm. Then the impulse to defend her new found friend caused her to square up her shoulders and reply to this woman. "Thank you very much, ma'am, but I'm quite satisfied making my own decisions and choosing my own companions. It is very kind of you to offer, nevertheless," she added, accentuating her Southern drawl to appear polite.

The two women on either side seemed shocked that anyone would challenge the woman's authority. Edith Hempstead's face pinched up like a prune as she scowled her disapproval. The silence was deafening as everyone waited for a verbal reaction from the hateful woman. She shook her head, and 'hmpfed,' before the three of them marched away in the opposite direction.

"What, on earth, was she talking about, Helen?" Abby asked as soon as the three women were out of earshot.

"I'm sorry. I probably should have warned you. Mrs. Hempstead considers herself to be the unofficial social monitor of the fort, I guess because the Colonel is a widower, and Mrs. Hempstead's husband is the major who is second in command here. She doesn't approve of the officers' wives associating with the rest of us women."

Helen paused, turned away from Abby, and started to walk back toward the Colonel's residence. "I should never have offered to take you around the fort," she added shaking her head. "I should have known she would object."

"What? You can't mean that. What is this nonsense all about anyway? What's the difference between enlisted men and officers?"

Helen stopped, sniffed, and heaved a sigh before replying, "Officers are in charge; enlisted men, like my husband, take orders."

"I still don't understand. I thought everyone on the fort takes orders from someone."

"True, but enlisted men never give orders. Oh, it's confusing to me, too. But Edith Hempstead doesn't want us enlisted men's wives to fraternize with officers' wives. We should just go back home now."

"So what. She's not in charge of me. I certainly have no reason to adhere to her code of conduct," Abby stated defiantly. "Look, Helen. From the instant we met yesterday, I felt I had found someone whom I could trust, and nothing what's her name says makes any difference to me."

"But you really don't want to make an enemy of her, Abby. She can be very mean." Helen looked up at Abby apologetically, as if she were to blame for the unsettling scene they both had endured.

"Don't you worry about me. I can take care of myself. There's nothing she can say or do that is going to change my mind," Abby asserted. "As far as I'm concerned, she's just some old windbag."

"I'm serious, Abby. She's not someone to ignore around here. You don't know the power she has."

"Oh, poppycock! I'm not letting her tell me who I can be seen with anywhere."

Helen sighed. A moment later, she grinned broadly and slipped her arm around Abby's. "C,mon, then," she said with a hint of mischief in her voice. "I'll show you some of the places Mrs. Hempstead would never think to take you."

And they wandered off giggling like two schoolmates on the playground at recess, neither one realizing battle lines had been drawn which were every bit as dangerous as a mine field.

CHAPTER

Garrett had never seen the chapel so full, not even at Christmas services. It seemed everyone wanted to welcome the Colonel's daughter. He stood at the back with several of the other single men, giving room for entire families, especially the women and children, to occupy the wooden pews. The post chaplain recognized and welcomed Abigail Randolph at the start of the Sunday service, and mercifully realized the majority of folk in attendance had come to support the Colonel's efforts to make his daughter feel welcomed. The chaplain's sermon on the lost sheep was appropriately short, but meaningful. The congregation sang and prayed, then hurried out the doors to the waiting celebration on the grounds.

Standing out of the way of the hustle and bustle, Garrett was amazed at the efficiency of the women setting the tables with a multitude of homemade dishes. The children scattered about, some trying to snatch a taste without being caught, but the watchful eyes of their mothers prevented any major intrusions. The chaplain had already blessed the meal at the conclusion of the service inside the chapel, so upon the Colonel's command, whole families sat at the tables and began serving themselves from the variety of meats, vegetables, and baked goods which were available. Several of the women, including Helen Davis, moved from table to table serving up fresh squeezed lemonade. Garrett chose to sit at a spot occupied by several of the bachelor soldiers where the conversation lent itself to a possible game of baseball after lunch. Jovial and light-hearted, they challenged one another and offered mock wagers on the outcome. Then their easy banter was interrupted as Colonel Randolph stood to address the gathering.

"I want to thank all of you for coming out today to welcome the arrival of my daughter, Abigail. She and I have been separated by many miles for many years, and I was concerned she wouldn't want to travel all the way out here. She does, after all, have a mind of her own. But here she is, and I am so very proud that she has agreed to stay here with me, at least for the present."

The Colonel paused a moment and checked his daughter's reaction to his introduction. He beamed at her and continued. "I haven't officially asked her as yet, but I'm hoping she will consider filling in at the school until the new headmaster arrives at the end of September. Perhaps she will provide tutoring for some of our older children."

The Colonel glanced again at his daughter who was blushing modestly. "Perhaps some of you can persuade her yourselves," he added with a gentle laugh. "I may be the commanding officer here, but I know she won't take orders from me."

The crowd chuckled their response, and several clapped in appreciation. A few of the women began nodding their approval of the suggestion, and Garrett could see that the offer of the Colonel's daughter tutoring their children was well received. However, observing the sudden somber look on Abigail's face, Garrett was fairly certain she didn't appreciate this public suggestion. Colonel Randolph stepped aside and began moving around to greet the wives of his officers and some of the enlisted wives, as well. Just after the Colonel left her side, a swarm of anxious mothers surrounded Abigail. Garrett realized now would be the time to provide her with an escape, and at the same time, make a start on his assignment for the Colonel.

Garrett edged his way into the middle of the crowd and took Abigail's arm. "Excuse me, ladies, but Miss Randolph and I have a prior engagement. She's promised me a walk around the chapel glen. You'll have to talk with her later. Right now, her time belongs to me." So saying, he led her out from among all those women, and escorted her directly to the other side of the chapel where the large spruce trees and aspens offered welcome shade from the midday sun.

"I thank you, Captain, for rescuing me," Abigail said quietly as they trekked along the paths among the trees. Magpies clucked their disapproval and chickadees seemed to snicker in the trees, but Garrett and Abigail continued to stroll quietly through the glen until they came to a wooden bench parked strategically between two massive spruce trees. Garrett stopped, and gestured for her to sit.

When Abigail frowned, Garrett said, "Don't worry. It's totally proper. Your father and the rest of the entire post are within eyeshot."

Abigail blushed and smiled. She sat down and adjusted her dark blue jacket over her matching skirt. Garrett took off his hat and sat beside her, making certain there was a proper distance between them. He intended to do everything possible to make her feel comfortable in his company. His career depended upon it.

"I guessed from the look on your face that the Colonel didn't tell you what he was going to say."

"No, he didn't, although I think he might have said something about filling in at the school until the regular teacher could come." She frowned as though she were scouring her memory. "I think he said something about a teacher coming from back East, but there was some problem so he can't be here until the last week of September. Everything is a bit hazy. I don't think I've completely gotten used to things out here yet. I feel a little bit like I'm still traveling to get here."

Garrett cleared his throat, pausing before replying, "Yes, but it should pass in a day or two. But as for your father volunteering your services, I'm sure he just wants you to feel at home here. I know he has gone to a great deal of trouble these past few weeks trying to get everything ready for your arrival."

He paused to observe her reaction. "Tell me, have you seen the bookcase yet?"

Her mouth fell open slightly, and, as she turned to face him, her eyes were wide with surprise.

Garrett nodded as he continued. "The Colonel told everyone he wanted that bookcase done in time for your arrival. He visited the carpentry shop several times each week to check on their progress. He was very exact in the specifications. Believe me, I know what I'm talking about. He really does want you to be happy staying here."

Garrett turned to look at her, sitting prim and proper on the bench. Then he decided to reveal what else he knew. "To tell the truth, Miss Randolph, your father has been quite lonely here. If Corporal Davis and Helen hadn't agreed to share the Colonel's quarters with him, I don't think he would have made it these past several years. It's good you agreed to come."

She was obviously reflecting upon the information he had just provided her about her father. When she glanced up at him, he noticed again her bright green eyes and her porcelain complexion. For a moment, he forgot his true purpose. She really was quite lovely.

"Captain, thank you for giving me just a little clue about my father's feelings. I confess, I don't know exactly what I'm going to do now that I'm here. But I know whatever it is, I want to make a contribution like so many other women I've read about."

Garrett chuckled reflexively. "Miss Randolph, you needn't worry about anything. You are Colonel Randolph's daughter, and a fine lady. You'll be well cared for, I'm sure. Your father will see to it."

She frowned, and there was just a hint of danger in her eyes. "I know you mean well, Captain, but I don't need to be taken care of," she replied matter-of-factly. "It may not seem so, but I'm perfectly capable of taking care of myself. I've been doing so for the past several years."

"I only meant there's nothing for you to fret about now that you're here. The Colonel will see to everything, ma'am."

It seemed a shadow had come across her face, hinting of a darker mood. She breathed a heavy sigh before breaking the momentary silence. "I hope you're not one of those men who think a woman's only function in life is to be a wife and mother. I want to do more. I want to make the world a better place. That's why I agreed to travel clear across the country."

He turned his hat in his hands wondering what he should say next. "I didn't mean to offend you, Miss Randolph. I know there are many women who have dedicated their lives to the betterment of us all."

Abigail nodded and seemed to speak meditatively. "Women like Elizabeth Blackwell, who became a doctor in spite of all obstacles placed before her because she was a woman. Helen Hunt Jackson, a soldier's wife who studied and wrote about the atrocities against the Indians. Jane Addams who has worked in Chicago for years working with the less fortunate there. And Abigail Adams, my namesake, who encouraged and counseled her husband, the second President of the United States. I want to be just like these women. I didn't go to college so that I could be cared for like a fine lady. I want to make the world a better place so that someday my father will be proud that I'm his daughter."

Garrett was stunned by this admission. Did she really not know how much her father loved her? How could something so clear to him be such a mystery to her?

"Still, there's no reason for you to be worried, Miss Randolph. That's all I meant."

She shook her head slowly. "Before I heard from my father, I actually thought I might focus my efforts on helping children in Boston and New York who find themselves having to work at such a young age in order to survive. It was a cause I could support and still work with suffragettes. I have my inheritance, so money wasn't a major concern. Even after I got his letter, I very nearly chose not to come. Women already had the right to vote here, but when I found out that suffrage had been taken away, I decided to come to Salt Lake City to work to get it back. Then on the train I heard about something else more serious. I don't know how yet, but I know the cause I want to fight."

"I know, women's suffrage," he responded.

"Not just suffrage," she said louder than previously. She paused as if considering her words carefully and then continued, "but problems faced by Mormon women and their children."

Garrett sat confused by her comments. "Personally, I don't know anything about these problems that have gotten your attention. I am fairly certain that the Mormon church will take care of their own. They always have. And I know that your father will not appreciate anyone from the fort sticking their nose into Mormon business. That includes you, Miss Randolph."

Abigail brushed her skirt before she stood up slowly. Garrett, too, rose from the bench, still fumbling with his hat in his hands nervously. In the quiet between them, he heard chickadees giggling above them in the pine trees.

She took a few steps away, and kept her back to him as she spoke. "Captain, you seem to be a very nice man, and I appreciate your concern for me. But I assure you, the Mormon church is most certainly not helping these women. And I am determined on this course. If my father objects, then so be it. I have a mind of my own and will not be dictated to."

Garrett was startled. Something in the tone of her voice disturbed him. Was she upset with him? All he did was tell her the truth. He waited to see if this reaction was a momentary one.

Abigail turned and extended her hand to him in a gesture of goodbye. As they shook hands, she said, "Thank you for your candor, Captain. You've been a gentleman, and I will tell my father so. I think it would be best if I were to rejoin the others before they consider me to be ungrateful. I can find my way back on my own."

Garrett watched as she strode away leaving him dumbfounded, standing alone. What had he said that had upset her? And how was he ever going to accomplish the Colonel's request now? He shook his head ruefully. He was beginning to see what the Colonel had meant. He had just witnessed her independent streak, and he was completely baffled by what to do next.

Abby continued to reflect on her conversation with Captain Talbot as she made her way back in the middle of the celebrating crowd. While he may have given lip-service to the contributions of women, he still acted as though all women just wanted someone to take care of them. This attitude brought out her stubborn streak. She felt angry, frustrated, and confused, all at the same time. Captain Talbot had the uncanny knack of drawing out information from her that she wasn't quite ready to reveal. She frowned. Why did this man's opinion seem to matter?

As she stood in the midst of the spectators, people around her began clapping. Abby turned around quickly to see Mrs. Hempstead moving toward an elevated platform beside a piano.

The audience settled and hushed respectfully. Edith Hempstead seemed to glow in the attention. After the musical introduction was played, she began to sing a rendition of "Amazing Grace." Everyone stood silently, but Abby winced as the woman screeched inharmoniously. Looking around, Abby wondered what their reaction would be, and was surprised that no one seemed to object to her distortion of this religious favorite. Perhaps they knew better than to challenge her. When Edith had completed the final verse of the song, Abby watched as everyone applauded. There was obviously much Abby would need to learn about the politics of this little community.

"So what'd you think?" asked Helen who had found her way to Abby's side in the crowd.

"Honestly? Are you sure you want my opinion?"

"I think I share that thought," Helen said grinning. "But no one is brave enough to say it out loud. Why don't we wander back to the house and get out of this sun? I bet you've had enough of all this attention for one day."

Helen led the way across the chapel grounds to the Colonel's residence. They hurried quietly away from the congregation that still surrounded the lunch tables on the chapel grounds. Children were running and playing happily, while a group of soldiers and some of the older boys had retreated to the commons to play a rowdy game of baseball. Abby was relieved when she glanced back over her shoulder and saw that no one had taken notice of her leaving.

Once inside the house, Abby collapsed on the settee in the parlor while Helen sat across from her in an overstuffed chair. With the windows wide open, the breeze was able to cool the room unhindered. It was a pleasant retreat for the moment.

"I hope you weren't upset by Mrs. Hempstead's performance," Helen offered. "Unfortunately, it's somewhat of a tradition here. I don't think anyone has the nerve to suggest that she can't carry a tune. To tell the truth, the magpies sound sweeter."

Abby giggled her agreement. "That woman really does think that she's in charge around here, doesn't she?"

"Yes, and I'm afraid there's no one other than your father who could take that position away from her. But Colonel Randolph is too kind, and probably too busy to get involved in such things," Helen offered. "Still, she's the main reason we need a new school teacher here."

Abby sat up and looked questioningly at her companion. "What do you mean? What happened?"

"Poor Hannah. She was a sweet girl, about twenty-five years old. She made the mistake of contradicting Mrs. Hempstead. From what I heard, Edith was visiting in the school and began talking with the children as they were reciting state capitals. She announced that Philadelphia was the capital of Pennsylvania. When Hannah corrected her in front of the children, saying that it was Harrisburg, Mrs. Hempstead argued with her. Edith was so embarrassed that she demanded the girl be fired immediately."

Helen leaned back into the chair. "When your father refused to allow that to happen, Edith set her sights on destroying the girl. Poor Hannah found herself alone with no one to speak up for her. I guess that's when she started going to town regularly. She met some people who invited her to one of the Mormon churches. But then Edith began spreading lies about Hannah around the fort. Several of the mothers kept their children home from school because they felt Hannah was going to teach Mormonism in the classroom. Finally, Hannah left to marry a farmer in that church this past March, and the children have not had a teacher since."

"That's awful, Helen. How could my father let that woman get away with such behavior?" Abby asked.

"It's not his fault, Abby. He tries to stay out of the petty issues created by her group. He's arranged for a new teacher, a man, to come here late in September. I guess he figures she will not be able to bully a man as easily as she did Hannah."

When the women heard the front door close, they both sat up and waited to see who had entered. Then Helen, recognizing the Colonel's stride, stood up. "Sir, can I get you anything?" she asked respectfully.

Colonel Randolph inclined his head toward her and said, "I think I need to talk with Abby."

Helen nodded her understanding and left the room quietly. Seeing his daughter on the settee, the Colonel cleared his throat to catch her attention. Abby stood up and turned to face him, struggling to sort through the conflicting emotions that swarmed within her.

"I wish you had spoken to me before you made that announcement today, Father," she said with a mixture of hurt and annoyance in her voice. "I've barely gotten my things unpacked. I don't have any idea what I want to do just yet. Why did you do that?"

Her father smiled, and started to put his hands on her shoulders, but stopped abruptly. "Abby, I apologize if I overstepped. It's just I am so glad you agreed to come out here. I want to do anything and everything to insure that you are happy to stay. I hoped having a job, something important that needs doing, would encourage you to remain here with your tired, lonely old father."

Abigail sighed and looked up into her father's kind face. His neatly groomed salt-and-pepper beard reminded her of her beloved Poppy. The silver and gray streaks in his dark hair were the perfect complement for his bright hazel eyes. The sincerity she saw there melted her resolve. Still he was nearly a stranger to her. She flashed a smile and nodded, before she moved to the other side of the large room, and sat in an overstuffed chair that invited her. "Apology accepted," she said softly.

The Colonel strode to the desk across from her, opened a drawer, and retrieved a bundle of envelopes carefully tied with a white ribbon. Then he moved toward her and handed them to Abby. "These are the letters your mother wrote to me all those years that we were apart. Each page is filled with descriptions of you when you were a baby up until you were ten years old. She wrote of your learning to ride, your love of books. Then after your mother died, your grandmother begged me to let you remain there with her because she felt you needed her support. I was a stranger to you even then, and she knew you would need the guidance of a woman. I only agreed because she promised to continue your mother's practice of writing to me. In these letters, I read all about the helpless kittens you found in the barn, about your stacking books in the corner, and about your interest in the women's suffrage movement."

He walked back over and leaned against the desk while she began gently handling the delicate pages gently tucked within each envelope. Then he continued, "Your mother was so very proud of you, as am I. But I lived for these letters, Abby, for moments that I could experience vicariously. These were all the family I had. I know I made a choice to be a soldier. I wanted so much to overcome the shame placed upon our family's name by my father's support of the Confederacy. I thought that if I dedicated my life to the army, somehow the stigma would be erased."

His voice seemed to trail off with the sense of the loss he spoke of. Abigail stared at her father, and for perhaps the first time in her life, she was beginning to understand why he had chosen the army over his family. Being raised in Kentucky, she knew first hand the turmoil people had experienced there following the War. Confederate officers had been ridiculed publicly after Lee's surrender. Even when the shooting had stopped, there was so much unresolved animosity. Then afterwards, many families lost their land and all they had to carpetbaggers.

Recognizing her father's distress somehow eased her own sense of loss. Her father actually had placed honor and duty ahead of his own personal needs. She could almost understand that. At that moment, she could glimpse in him the same heart that she had. She sensed they had something rare in common—a desire to make a difference.

Abigail stood up and strode over to her father's side. She hesitantly put her arms up around her father's shoulders to offer him the first hug she could ever remember giving him. He had always been like a stranger to her the few times he was around when she was a little girl. He returned her embrace with his own, and she could feel him sighing with relief. She felt compelled to offer him some measure of comfort as tears welled up in her eyes. These were not the words of a man who was disappointed that his only child was a daughter. Nor did he seem to hold her responsible for her mother's death. But why, after all these years, now that she was a grown woman?

Her father laughed softly and stroked her hair. "You know the very first time I tried to hug you, I got a mighty slap instead."

Abigail stood back and frowned. "What are you talking about?"

He grinned and nodded his head. "You were not quite three years old. I came back to Kentucky on leave for a month before heading off to the Dakota Territory again. You were in the kitchen with your mother, and I couldn't help myself. I raced into the room and tried to pick you up, but you didn't know me. You reared back and slapped me in the face so hard I thought I'd been hit by a brick."

Abigail's jaw dropped in amazement. Then she couldn't keep from laughing at the thought of a little toddler striking her father. "Father, I don't remember slapping you. I'm so sorry that happened." Then a vague memory drifted up to her conscious mind.

"I'm not. From an early age, you knew how to defend yourself from strangers. But, it did hurt my feelings just a little that my only child wouldn't let me near her for a few days. You seemed to get over it though when I took you riding on my horse."

Again Abigail was amazed by the memories which began to flood her mind. That was the first time she rode on a horse— it hadn't been with Poppy, but with her father. She was beginning to see this man had more to do with her life than she previously thought.

She moved closer to him and took his hands in hers. "Father, if I am going to teach these children next month, I will need to get some different books and other supplies from town. Perhaps I can go into Salt Lake City later this week and see if I can find what I need there?"

Her father nodded warmly. "I'll talk with Corporal Davis. He can drive you into town. Perhaps Helen can go with you; you two ladies could spend the day in town with Corporal Davis providing escort to you both."

Her father cleared his throat, put his hands on her shoulders, and looked her squarely in the eye. "But, Abby, please promise me you will be careful. The Mormons in Salt Lake City are not inclined to welcome anyone from Fort Douglas. Helen and Corporal Davis can guide you away from the Mormon businesses. Mormons still do not really like to do business with outsiders. And sometimes there is conflict between the non-Mormons and the Mormons in the business district. You will have to be watchful," he asserted. "Promise me, Abby. I won't be able to relax unless I know that you will behave yourself in town."

Abigail beamed. If anyone else had said this to her, she would have been offended. But just now, hearing the warmth and compassion in his voice, she agreed to his request and answered, "I promise." She hugged her father again, an embrace that was genuine affection for a man she had never really known.

"And, Abby," her father continued, "there's one more favor I have to ask of you."

She stepped back, still facing her father. He appeared to be slightly uncomfortable which caused her to frown. She waited impatiently, not sure what price this favor might cost her.

He cleared his throat and began again, "I need you to agree to attend Mrs. Hempstead's tea party she is having in your honor tomorrow afternoon."

Abby knew the look of shock on her face was the only reason her father would have for chuckling at that moment.

"I know, I know, she can be quite overbearing at times, but she is the major's wife, and as such, she is due the respect of his office. I'm not requiring you to like her, or even socialize with her regularly, but I do need you to be polite and courteous to her. Can you do that for me, Abby?"

Abby continued to pout, her brow furrowed deeply. She glanced up at her father who stood patiently waiting for her affirmative response. She nodded her head as she replied, "Well, if it will make you happy, Father, then I will go. But I don't expect that I'll enjoy myself much there. She did speak to me yesterday near the commons, and she wasn't very nice to me or to Helen."

"I know how she is, Abby. You have my permission to ignore most of her directives, but I need to keep peace here at Fort Douglas, and I'm afraid if you don't consent to attend her party in your honor, I'll never hear the end of it. So please, for me?"

Abby nodded her consent again.

"Thank you," he replied and put his arms lovingly around her again. For the moment, Abby allowed herself to feel safe and protected. As she remained there in his arms savoring the experience, she uttered a silent prayer of thanksgiving for this opportunity to get to know her father. And she followed her thanksgiving with a prayer for assistance in dealing with bossy Edith Hempstead. She knew she would need divine intervention to keep her from confronting the woman and making things at Fort Douglas miserable for her father.

CHAPTER

4

The sun on Monday afternoon was mercifully shining along the path as Abby trudged to Mrs. Hempstead's home. Glancing down the street to her left, Abby noticed how the officers' quarters were all uniform, like well-dressed soldiers standing at attention. Each house in the row was dark red brick with white-washed framed windows, a small covered stoop, and an interesting white-washed design at the front gable; it looked like a cross between a concave triangle and a fancy letter capital "A" suspended just below the roofline of each house. She smiled to herself as she mused whether that letter stood for "Army" or something less attractive for Mrs. Hempstead.

Straightening her gray tea jacket and smoothing her blue plaid skirt, Abby gently knocked on the front door which was opened by Carol Randall. Both women exchanged greetings, and Abby was led into the front parlor where five other women were seated busily chatting and complimenting one another.

"Ladies, I'm sure you all know this is Abigail Randolph," Carol Randall offered to the small crowd. Pointing to each lady in succession around the room, Carol continued with introductions, "Miss Randolph, this is Millie Reid, Sarah O'Connor, Martha Jennings, Kathleen Harris, and Ruth Johnson whom you've already met."

Abby nodded to each woman as they were introduced, knowing all the while that she was terrible at remembering names. Then a nervous young lady came into the parlor carrying a silver tray with dessert plates and a cake. Behind her strode Edith Hempstead with a menacing scowl on her face. The tray was placed clumsily on a center table in the room, and the housekeeper/servant girl quickly exited. Abby's eyes followed the girl wishing she could change places with her at this moment.

"Well, I see that Carol has introduced you to all the ladies here, but I'm sure she didn't include their husbands' ranks which I think as the Colonel's daughter you should know. Ruth's husband is Major Johnson, making him third in command at Fort Douglas. Carol and Martha's husbands are both captains, and Millie and Kathleen are married to lieutenants. Kathleen is actually still a newlywed, having married Lt. Zachary Harris just last October, right after the Harvest Dance, wasn't it, dear?" she asked, looking at Kathleen and receiving a confirming nod.

"See, Miss Randolph, I'm informed about every important detail on this post as befits my station here," she smirked as she asserted her rank in the room. Abby noticed that immediately all of the other women present gave respectful ear to whatever Edith had to say. They all seemed to nod obediently as if to join in a chorus of affirmation.

"So, dear, please be seated here. All of these ladies are here to meet you formally. We all want to make you feel quite at home while you're visiting Fort Douglas. The Colonel has been so consumed with plans for this occasion, and we certainly want to do whatever we can to welcome you."

Abby started to express her thanks, but felt that perhaps she shouldn't interrupt Edith's monologue. Instead, Abby flashed a smile of gratitude to the other women in the room, hoping that she wouldn't inadvertently communicate her discomfort.

While Edith continued with her remarks, Abby glanced around the room to see that each table, buffet, and chest was topped with white lace crocheted doilies or scarves. The sun rays could barely creep in through the layers of heavy draperies that hid the windows. Though well lit artificially, the parlor seemed oppressively dark and dusty. Air didn't seem to circulate in the stuffy room. The entire parlor had the aura of tight structure as if everything was under this woman's control. Abby sighed; it must be her imagination.

"Would you like some pound cake with your tea?" Edith asked, offering Abby a delicate china cup and saucer.

"Why, yes, m'am, I would, thank you," Abby said. "I apologize if I seem a little distracted, Mrs. Hempstead. I confess I'm still not quite settled from my long journey to get here."

"Quite all right, dear," Mrs. Hempstead offered magnanimously. "We all understand that you must be tired from your trip. However, I simply couldn't wait to offer you hospitality since none of us knows how long you will be visiting here with us."

Abby took a dainty bite of the cake, then cleared her throat. This was the second time that Mrs. Hempstead had made reference to her visiting rather than staying. "Well, my plans aren't certain, as yet, but for now my father is encouraging me to stay a while. By the way, this cake is delicious. My father would just love this. Could I have your recipe so that I could surprise him?" Abby asked, trying to change the subject.

Mrs. Hempstead sneered broadly, but then leaned back in her chair, "Oh, dear, I'm so sorry, but the recipe for this cake is an old family recipe that I would never share with anyone. I'm sure you understand."

Stunned, Abby fumbled for some appropriate response, but could only summon, "Oh, I understand. I shouldn't have asked." She knew she was blushing and turned away.

The other women in the room seemed oblivious to her discomfiture as they continued to chat busily with one another. Abby concentrated on drinking her tea and tried to enter into their conversations, but felt like a total outsider. Finally, she turned to Martha Jennings who was nearest her and asked, "I know women had the right to vote here in Utah until just recently. Have you lived here long enough to vote?"

The look of shock on Martha's face caused the entire room to silence completely. Martha blushed, but didn't offer an answer to Abby's question. Almost instantly, Mrs. Hempstead cleared her throat and offered a reply on her behalf, "Women are no longer allowed to vote here, Miss Randolph, not that a proper lady would engage in such foolishness anyway. Voting is the responsibility of men; we women have other more important things to do with our time."

"But surely, you realize that voting is a right which women must be allowed to have. After all, we are part of this country, just as men are. We work alongside our husbands, fathers, and brothers, and as such, we should have the same rights they have in our country. You can't possibly believe that voting is the sole province of men."

The other ladies in the room sat frozen, waiting for Edith's reply. Instead, Edith scowled furiously and stood up as if to command attention. "Voting *is* the sole province of men, Miss Randolph. No proper lady would question that. Besides, all suffrage has accomplished here in Utah is to provide each man with multiple votes. Everyone knows that these heathen men simply told their wives how to cast their ballots. No, with women no longer allowed to vote, it's rightfully back to one man, one vote, the way it should be. Women have no business being involved in such things."

Abby carefully set her empty tea cup back inside its saucer on the center table. She stood up, held her head high, and after pursing her lips, spoke quietly, "I'm afraid I must disagree with you, Mrs. Hempstead, but as this is your home, I will not engage in any further discussion of the topic. As I said earlier, I'm still not quite rested from my travels across the country. With your permission, I'd like to thank you for hosting this get-together in my honor, but I think I really should leave now before I say something that would offend you any further."

Mrs. Hempstead smirked victoriously. Abby nodded her gratitude to the rest of the women who remained seated in the parlor before she slipped quietly out the door. Once outside the house, she took several deep breaths and enjoyed the crisp, clear Utah air. Glancing back over her shoulder, Abby felt very much like an unwary insect which had just luckily avoided a treacherous spider web. She quickened her steps unconsciously as she approached her father's residence, relieved that she had been able to comply with his wish and survive the ordeal.

Captain Talbot paced to and fro in the Colonel's office. Somehow he knew he had failed to complete the task his commanding officer had given to him. And even if it was a bit outside the line of duty expected for a soldier, he desperately wanted to prove to the Colonel that he was worthy of any assignment given to him. He berated himself internally, continuing his pacing until the Colonel entered the room. Then, as if a bullet had whizzed by, he froze in a saluting attention.

"At ease, Captain," the Colonel stated as he moved behind his desk. "What seems to be the problem?"

Garrett cleared his throat several times before answering. "Sir, I'm not sure I'm the right man for the assignment you've given to me. Miss Randolph is a fine lady, sir, make no mistake about that. But it seems I've said something to offend her."

The Colonel chuckled at the captain's obvious discomfort. "Sit down, Garrett," he urged gesturing to the chair facing his desk. "I'm aware that Abby's had a few problems already. But I assure you, nothing you said compares to my requesting that she attend Mrs. Hempstead's tea party yesterday. When she came back from that fiasco, she made me promise I'd never volunteer her appearance again."

Garrett grimaced, and replied, "Well, sir, I doubt seriously she'll be interested in my company anymore either. I came to report that I failed to complete the favor you requested."

Colonel Randolph glanced at his adjutant, and grinned. "Garrett, I told you she had some character traits that would make the assignment difficult. She's head-strong and very independent. What on earth happened that makes you think you failed?"

"Well, sir, I thought I was doing the right thing," Garrett began, mentally visualizing the scene with the Colonel's daughter. "I pulled her out of that crowd of women at the church supper. She did say she appreciated that. We went strolling in the park beside the chapel, and we were talking about a variety of things. I'm not sure what, but I must've said something that offended her, because she got up and thanked me and left."

Colonel Randolph's jaw dropped in amazement. "So what did you say?"

"Well, sir, she was talking about women who've made contributions, and I told her that she didn't need to worry about making any contribution because you'd see to it that she was provided for. I'm not sure what upset her, but I'm fairly certain that she won't take kindly to my coming over for dinner or the like."

The Colonel nodded his understanding. "Abby is quite the independent woman, Garrett. She's taken care of herself for quite a while, and she's not inclined to accept someone else taking over for her, and certainly not me." He paused scratching his head appearing as if he was trying to come up with an idea. Like a bolt of lightning he said, "Riding, Garrett. Take her riding. She's an excellent horsewoman. Can handle just about any mount. She can ride my horse, Grant. That's it, Garrett. Offer to take her riding. She won't be able to resist it."

"Thanks for the help, Helen. My hair's so long now that I can hardly manage to wash it by myself anymore, and I sure didn't want to try to do it in the bathtub upstairs," Abigail said while Helen poured another pitcher of cool water over her head to rinse off the lather.

"I'm glad to, Abby. This reminds me of times when I would help my sisters wash their hair. Sometimes we'd throw soap bubbles at each other," she answered.

"Oh, like this?" Abigail replied tossing a handful of soap lather at her. Helen squealed with delight. The room resounded with peals of laughter as the two women played out a childhood game in the kitchen. Dodging and tossing soapy water at each other, neither of them noticed that they were no longer alone in the room.

"Ladies? I knocked on the door, and heard all the commotion in here. Is everything all right?" asked Captain Talbot.

Startled, Abigail looked up at him, her wet hair jumbled all about her, a towel in her hand. She was wringing wet from the spontaneous game she and Helen had been playing. Helen, too, looked disheveled and soaked, but was grinning widely at the experience. Now seeing Abigail caught by the captain in disarray, Helen broke into uncontrollable laughter. When he ventured farther into the room, Helen pelted him across the chest with some of the remaining soap lather. Enjoying the startled reaction of the captain, Abby joined in and both women almost simultaneously tossed handfuls of lather and water toward the interloper. He dodged the next soapy wet mixture that was tossed his way, and quickly retreated from the room.

"I'll wait in the study, ladies. When you're finished washing the kitchen floor, I'd like to speak with Miss Randolph about the possibility of going riding later this week."

Abigail's head shot straight up at the mention of riding. She immediately wrapped her hair with the damp towel and followed Garrett out of the kitchen to a much drier location.

"Did you say riding, Captain?" she asked as if she wasn't sure what he had suggested.

Captain Talbot grinned and nodded. Abby was suddenly aware at how strange she must look with her hair wrapped carelessly in the towel. She glanced down and saw some soap lather that lingered on the blue gingham apron she wore over her morning dress. She felt a little uneasy with the appearance she must have presented just now.

"Your father's informed me that you're an accomplished horsewoman. He even suggested that you could ride his preferred mount, Grant. I asked his permission yesterday, of course, and he was only too happy to oblige. What'd you say, Miss Randolph? Are you interested in accompanying me on horseback later this week?"

"My father told you?" she asked, curious as to why her father would discuss information about her with someone she had just met.

Garrett nodded. "If you're not interested, that's fine. I just thought that maybe you'd appreciate a guide up on the Wasatch Mountain trails."

"It's been awhile since I've been able to ride, Captain. However, I think I'd like to give it a try again. When?"

"What about day after tomorrow? I have several reports to work on tomorrow. I'll get them done, and plan to see you Friday morning around nine." So saying, Garrett bowed his head in greeting to both Abigail and Helen, who had just come into the room. He replaced his hat and closed the door behind him as he left.

Helen looked at Abigail and winked with amusement. Both women laughed again as they returned to the kitchen to clean up their mess.

Later, while combing her hair in her room, Abigail mused about the prospect of riding with the captain. If he thought she would need his assistance, he was much mistaken. She'd show him. The idea of riding out here in such beautiful country was intriguing. And perhaps spending time with Captain Talbot would prove to be enjoyable as well. She would just have to be careful what they talked about. She grinned at her reflection, a glint of mischief surfacing in her eyes as she contemplated the proposed outing. And at the same time, she began to suspect that something else was going on with this military man.

CHAPTER

Salt Lake City's Main Street was busy on Thursday with shoppers and folks on their way to conduct their business for the day. Corporal Davis had dropped off Abigail and Helen, then headed to the local feed store before going to the depot to pick up the week's mail for the fort. The two women had already located a store that contained several copies of the books Abigail wanted for the students on post. Abby had been pleased that the bookstore was so amply stocked.

Now they were enjoying a respite sitting outside at a local café sipping lemonade. Pleasant breezes fanned the valley streets, and Abigail luxuriated in the sunshine that gently warmed the afternoon. Though she had heard that the summer weather here could be very hot, today the heat was not oppressive. Looking around her, she was beginning to feel that she could call Salt Lake City home from now on.

They were taking their packages to the corner where Corporal Davis had pulled up the freight wagon, when Abigail spied a dress shop. Handing the bundles up to the Corporal, she returned to the shop and entered. Something in the window had caught her attention, and she was determined to examine it herself. She quickly checked in her purse to verify she had brought enough money with her. The sale of her grandfather's horse farm had enabled her to have a small inheritance. (She was glad not to have to ask her father for money, though she suspected he wouldn't hesitate to give her a generous allowance.)

"I saw a split riding skirt in your window," she said to the clerk as she pointed in the direction of the window. "I'd like to see it up close. Will you get it for me please?"

The clerk nodded and quickly provided the requested item for Abigail's inspection. It was a dark brown split skirt made much like those worn by Argentine gauchos that she had read about in a copy of <u>Harper's Bazar</u>. Abby held it up in front of her to see if it might fit her small waist. "We'll be glad to provide alterations if needed, m'am, but just looking at it now, I think that'll be a perfect fit for you, don't you?" the clerk suggested.

Abigail nodded and smiled broadly. Her mother had made her a pair of riding pants to accommodate her insistence upon riding astride when Abby was only about six years old. With Captain Talbot inviting her out to go riding, she had wondered how she would manage to do it with the heavy skirts she had. But here was the answer to her problem.

"There's a matching Basque jacket, if you like," announced the clerk. "Sally Barber is our dressmaker. She saw a picture in a magazine and decided to copy the style. We even found a hat to match," she continued parading both items on the wooden counter for Abigail to admire.

"The jacket might be a little larger, but it will allow you to comfortably wear a blouse with it," she remarked watching as Abigail slipped the jacket on. Then guiding her toward the large oval mirror in the corner, the clerk said, "See how lovely it is?"

Abigail fingered the jacket delicately. She noticed that the dressmaker had included some fine cream-colored embroidery on the edges. She admired her reflection and turned to ask the price for both the jacket and the split skirt. When she determined that the price was more than fair, she added the Spanish style brown hat to complete the wardrobe, and sauntered out of the store pleased with her latest acquisition. In the back of her mind, she considered the effect of this outfit on Captain Talbot. She expected him to be both shocked and intrigued. Suddenly going riding with him held even more interest for her than it had previously. She grinned mischievously in anticipation of the event scheduled for tomorrow. She'd show him now, for sure.

Abby rejoined the Corporal and his wife who were sitting on the wagon talking. She handed her bundle up to Helen, and started to climb up to the seat, when she heard women's voices calling out loudly across the street. Curious, she turned around and moved to see a gathering of people, mostly women, beneath the shade of the tall sheltering trees on a corner of the property attached to the City and County Building. She strode across the dirt street with Helen and the Corporal tagging along behind impatiently. Corporal Davis appeared to object to the delay, but his wife shushed him, and the two caught up with Abigail as she stood at the back of the crowd.

"We women must unite to provide for our Mormon sisters who've been cast aside like last year's clothing. They are suffering abuse at the hands of strangers, lustful, sinful men who prey on fallen women. All because some Mormon men no longer want the responsibility of providing for the multiple women they took to be their wives. Now that the Mormon Church no longer sanctifies polygamy, what's to become of these women? They have no skills beyond that of being wives and homemakers. How are they to provide for themselves and their children? And with work for men so scarce, who's going to offer jobs to these women?"

The woman paused briefly, then continued with her answer, "It's up to us, ladies; we must step up to provide an answer that doesn't include working in the brothels of the Red Light district. That's what the Women's Housing Association is all about; women helping women. Join us in the fight to provide rescue homes for these women left on the roadside by the Mormon Church in its struggle for statehood."

Abigail glanced around at the mostly female crowd as they applauded and cheered the speaker. She then asked a bystander who the speaker was. "Why that's Mary Grant Major. She belongs to the Women's Housing Association. We're here to show our support for this cause. We meet each week at First Methodist Church, just down the road over there," she replied pointing in the direction where Abigail could find the meeting place. "You should come join us every Wednesday afternoon at three. Cornelia Paddock will be there to advise us on the next steps we can take to clean up the abomination of prostitution."

Abigail thanked her for the information before she responded to the tugs on her elbow. Reluctantly, she agreed to leave with the Corporal and his wife. However, here was the answer she had sought to her own question. Here were women who concerned themselves with the plight of others. She was determined to come back next week on Wednesday to learn more about this organization and what she might do to support it. And she had just the person in mind to enlist in this scheme.

Garrett arrived promptly in front of the Colonel's residence riding his horse, Pepper, and leading Grant for Abigail to ride. He dismounted, tied the two sets of reins to the post, and dusted off his riding trousers in anticipation of greeting the Colonel's daughter. He pondered for a moment how he would assist her onto the big horse knowing that she would have to somehow arrange her flowing skirts and petticoats in order to sit astride the horse, the way Colonel Randolph said she would insist on riding. If she wasn't riding side saddle, there would be some adjusting that would have to be done. But since the Colonel was the one to suggest taking her riding, he must know what he was talking about, so maybe there wouldn't be as much difficulty as Garrett had previously imagined.

Then he laughed quietly to himself at the possible scene, Miss Randolph sitting atop the horse with her skirts bundled on either side of her, not leaving her much room to maneuver. It would probably be a short ride. He could spend the rest of the day with the other bachelor officers, maybe a baseball game even.

"Good morning, Captain," came a cheery voice from the porch.

Garrett reflexively removed his hat to respond, but words got stuck in his throat. His lower jaw dropped in amazement and shock. He was totally unprepared for the scene in front of him.

"Like it?" Abigail queried. "I bought this outfit yesterday in town. I knew it would be perfect for today." She stood gracefully above him on the porch, wearing a dark brown split riding skirt that fell just below her knees. A starched white blouse was tucked in at her slender waist which was accented by a shiny, wide black belt. It was the same color as the polished riding boots which clearly reached up to her knees. The matching Basque jacket with the bouffant shoulders and tapered long sleeves served to accentuate most of her well-developed feminine curves.

When she turned slowly in front of him to give him the complete effect, he could see that her wavy red hair cascaded loosely down her back, restrained by a single black ribbon tied at the back of her neck. Then she pointed to her riding gloves and the Spanish style hat.

"See?" she asked again seeming to enjoy his shock at seeing her displayed in something other than the usual multiple layers of fabric women of the '90's wore.

Garrett cleared his throat trying to maintain some sense of dignity. He nodded to her to acknowledge that he had heard her, but as yet he still had no appropriate words to cover his shock. Though he had seen other women wearing men's clothing, seeing the Colonel's daughter dressed in this fashion was startling. But something else seemed to be rising up within him. Something he didn't quite recognize yet, but realized he was in some sort of daze.

Then, as if to add insult to injury, Abigail strode the distance to her father's horse, took the reins from the post, put her left foot high up in the stirrup, and pulled her body erect onto Grant's back. She quickly found the stirrup for her right foot and adjusted her frame into the saddle. She leaned forward to caress the horse's mane and pat the side of his head affectionately. When she gently tugged Grant to the right to turn to the dirt road, the horse obediently followed her lead, and ambled slowly in the required direction. Then, Abigail twisted slightly to look over her shoulder, and called, "Are you coming, Captain?"

Still in a daze, Garrett quickly roused, replaced his hat, and with the reins in hand, leaped to Pepper's back. He urged the horse to quicken his step in order to catch up with the Colonel's daughter. Abigail continued to guide Grant slowly toward the front gates of the fort. Once outside the post, she stopped and turned to Garrett now just to her right. Once he had indicated the best trail to take, she was off in a modest gallop leading Grant eastward towards the Wasatch foothills with Garrett working to keep up with her.

How in the world was he going to be able to tell the Colonel about this? But he had an idea that someone else would be reporting his activity to the Colonel long before they had even returned from their ride.

At a grove of maple and aspen trees near an irrigation trough, Garrett dismounted Pepper and beckoned Abigail to do the same. Pepper seemed grateful for the fresh mountain water and slurped eagerly. Abigail led Grant to get his share, and the two horses nudged one another playfully as they rested. Garrett withdrew a blanket roll and his canteen from his saddle, and pointed to a shady spot in the grove. Abigail followed, casually removing her riding gloves and hat.

"It's so beautiful up here," she announced as she took in the scenery to the west of them. The valley below looked like an oasis. Even from this distance, she could easily see orchards and small vegetable gardens that dotted the landscape. And the city was visible, too, with its streets set at right angles and the granite face of the Temple towering majestically above the other buildings.

Up here in what some folks called the East Bench, the air was crisp and cool, even with the late August sun beaming down upon them. The mountains rose behind them, dark gray and barren with just a trace of brilliant snow that looked like whipped icing on a cake.

"I think I can understand what would have impelled the Mormons to settle here," she offered admiring the scene in front of her.

Garrett nodded and turned to remove his canteen from his saddle. Walking over to where she surveyed the valley, he unscrewed the top and offered it to her. Hesitating just a moment, Abigail took a drink of the cool liquid. She poured just a dab onto a handkerchief and began to gently wipe tiny beads of sweat from her forehead. The water felt so refreshing against her warm moist skin.

After gulping from the canteen himself, Garrett replied, "Yes, it is quite beautiful up here. You know, the Mormons celebrate what they call the "Days of '47" each year with parades and parties. It's a regular Fourth of July event out here," he said matter-of-factly.

"'Days of '47'?" she repeated. "What's that all about?"

"When the Mormons originally came here, you know, in 1847. They say that their leader, Brigham Young, brought them over the Wasatch Mountains and when they entered the valley below, he decided they weren't going any further. Now they celebrate that event every year on July 24th."

Abigail looked at him with a new found appreciation. He seemed to be more intelligent than she had originally thought him to be after that initial conversation last Sunday afternoon. <u>At least he knows something about the history of this place.</u> Maybe he's something more than just a pretty face, she thought. Indeed, he was a handsome man by her estimation, tall, strong, and masculine. But he was a soldier. Then she remembered something that had been puzzling her lately, and figured he might be able to clear up the mystery for her.

"Captain, I saw a seagull in town yesterday. Aren't we a long way from the ocean here?"

Garrett laughed and nodded as he replied, "Yes, we are, Miss Randolph. Some think the gulls are attracted to the lake, but there are no fish there because it is so salty. Nevertheless, the seagull is considered by some around here to be almost a guardian angel of sorts."

Abby dropped her jaw in disbelief, "What're you talking about?"

"Well, when the Mormons first settled this valley almost fifty years ago, their first crop was just beginning to grow when an army of gigantic crickets began eating everything in sight. Being religious people, as the story goes, they prayed for deliverance from God, and thousands of seagulls showed up to devour these locust-like insects. Like I said, some people think those birds came in answer to prayer, and so when they see them flying around town, they feel a sense of God's presence all over again."

She nodded and then continued questioning him, "So what else can you tell me about the Mormons, Captain?"

He had moved away from her side and was sitting on the red and orange plaid blanket he had since unrolled in the shade of the trees. He looked up at her and beckoned her to sit across from him. When she moved to join him, she realized how sore her muscles were. It had been almost a year since she had been able to ride. Her legs ached as she strode the short distance to the blanket. Riding this morning had been wonderful, but now she knew there was a price to be paid for this foolishness. Nevertheless, she was determined that her companion would not know of her discomfort. She eased down and prepared to listen, waiting for the opening she hoped he would provide.

"From what I can tell, they're not a whole lot different from other folks. Their beliefs are a bit different from what most of us believe, but they don't sacrifice babies in the town square, so I don't exactly think they can be called heathens. I've read where they experienced a great deal of mistreatment in other towns where they tried to live before coming out here. I think I can understand why they would want to get as far away as possible so they wouldn't have to always be afraid, don't you?"

Abigail frowned as she considered this information. She was intrigued to learn that he had read about the Mormons. He seemed to know about more than just army rules and regulations, which made him a bit more interesting. She decided to probe further. "What'd you mean mistreatment, Captain?"

He scanned her expression carefully as if he did not really believe that she would be interested in what he had to say. "Well, I know that ever since the Mormons began their religious practices, they've experienced opposition. They've been run out of towns from New York to Illinois. I think it was in Nauvoo that some of them were killed, or at least seriously injured in a mob."

Garrett hesitated briefly before he continued, "At least, out here, they can expect to live their lives peacefully. And just look what they've managed to do in nearly fifty years of farming and settling the Salt Lake Valley. They are basically good people wanting to worship God the way they see fit. Some folks object to the Temple; they say it's too showy. But I've read about huge cathedrals built back East and in Europe. I don't see a problem with their wanting to build something unique for their own worship practices. I guess I'm just tolerant of other folks," he stated taking another swig of the water from his canteen.

Abigail turned toward him frowning just a bit. "So what about polygamy? That's not just a religious difference, Captain. The United States government has declared that practice to be illegal. What'd you say to that?"

"Yeah, I know lots of folks were up in arms over that. Personally, I can't think of a legitimate reason for a man to marry more than one woman. In fact, I think having one wife would be about all I could handle. But their church eliminated that practice five years ago. They knew statehood depended upon that," he answered matter-of-factly.

"So what about the women, Captain? What'd you think happened to all those women who were in plural marriages?" she asked waiting to spring her trap for him.

"What women? I just told you, they don't do that anymore, Miss Randolph."

"I know they don't perform any more plural wedding ceremonies, Captain, but what about the women who were previously the multiple wives of important Mormons? What'd you supposed happened to them?" she asked waiting for the expected response. She knew in the next moment, he would step both feet into her waiting trap.

"I don't know, Miss Randolph. I haven't given it much thought actually. I guess legally they're no longer married which makes them, unmarried? But whatever their circumstances, why should that concern you? You planning to convert?" he asked hesitantly.

"You don't really know about those women, do you, Captain? Like most men, you just assumed that someone would take care of them, like you said fine ladies should expect. But many of these women have no one. No one is taking care of them, or at least, no one in the Mormon Church is."

She paused briefly to allow him to realize how serious she was about this issue. He frowned like he was definitely paying attention to her argument. But she knew he had no idea how passionate she was on this issue.

"But the Women's Housing Association in Salt Lake City has recognized the suffering of these women, and is doing something about it. They're providing rescue homes for these women, Captain, because these women, who were formerly married but now cast out of their homes and families, are winding up on the streets of Salt Lake without any provision whatsoever. This organization is working to help these women who otherwise would have no other choice but to work in the brothels of the Red Light district in order to support themselves. And I want to be a part of it, Captain, and to do so, I'm going to need your assistance," she announced.

Garrett leaned back, his eyebrows raised in amazement. "I'm afraid that won't be possible, Miss Randolph. Your father . . ."

"Yes, my father wouldn't allow it, would he, Captain? You do seem to know what my father would and wouldn't allow me to do, don't you, Captain? Is that because my father has arranged for you to supervise me while I am here? To keep me out of trouble?" she asked, continuing to tighten the noose around his neck.

Garrett appeared to struggle for the appropriate words. Moments ago he had been in control. Now he stuttered and coughed. He had been caught unknowingly, and he seemed desperate to keep her from knowing the truth about his arrangement with the Colonel. But Abigail had already figured it out, and she intended to use that information to her advantage.

"That's the reason you offered to take me riding, isn't it, Captain? My father suggested it, didn't he? Even suggested that I ride his horse. You know, the horse he won't let anyone else ride?"

Garrett studied her carefully. He appeared to be trying to figure out what his next move should be. He frowned and nodded a reply. There was no need to try to hide what she already knew.

"I thought so, Captain. There were just a few clues, but I guessed he didn't trust that I would be satisfied staying out here unless I had something important to do. He must have thought that you could steer me away from mischief. The kind of mischief that the Colonel's daughter definitely shouldn't be connected to."

Garrett nodded, before she continued. "He knew me well enough to know that I wouldn't respond well to a command, so he engineered this little arrangement where he could keep an eye on me, and still let me think that I was independent. Clever, but quite transparent, I'm afraid," she said as she laughed musically.

She stood up and wandered over to a nearby tree, then turned to face the captain. "I know that he'd do just about anything to keep me here. You're right, he's lonely. The army has been his family these past many years. He made choices that have left him feeling regretful, and I understand him better now that I've come out here. I always thought that he preferred the army to his own family. Now I think he made difficult choices out of honor and duty, and I respect him more now that I've seen for myself."

She sighed as she thought of the years she had been without her father. "All these years he's been trying to live down the shame of his father and grandfather supporting the Confederacy during the War Between the States. I know that's the primary reason he will never be promoted to general, though with his years of service and loyalty, he should've years ago. I think I understand him now, Captain, and that's why I'm not upset that he asked you to watch over me. However, I do intend that you'll assist me in maintaining this little arrangement. I'm determined to go to a meeting next week on Wednesday in Salt Lake. It's at the Methodist Church there. I'd like you to drive me into town, and to bring me home, safely afterward."

"Now, Miss Randolph, I know your father wouldn't allow me to do that. He wouldn't want you to get involved with anything that could prove embarrassing to him or the fort, and what you're talking about is sure to offend the Mormons in town," Garrett offered, hopelessly entangled in this web of deceit.

"Captain, I need you to take me this one time because I don't yet know my way around the city. I'm afraid that if I go by myself on the street car, I could get lost. If that were to happen, my father would be upset, and he'd most certainly blame you."

She paused to see that her words were having the desired effect on him.

"Whatever arrangement you've made with my father can remain our secret. He won't hear from me that I know he's asked you to keep an eye on me. He'll be happy, I'll be happy, and you'll get whatever it is that you bargained for. So what's it going to be, Captain? Do we have an appointment on Wednesday?" she asked with her eyebrows raised waiting for his inevitable assent. He nodded and closed his eyes in defeat.

"Thank you, Captain," and with his unspoken response, Abigail put her riding gloves back on, adjusted her hat, and strolled over to Grant to begin the trip back down the hillside to the fort. She was triumphant because now she knew of a way that she could help those unfortunate women. She could achieve her purpose, and that was more important than anything or anyone else. She'd just have to come up with some sort of plausible story for her father, something that wouldn't upset him as much as the truth might. She wasn't quite ready to challenge his authority or her budding relationship with him just yet.

CHAPTER

6

Captain Talbot forced himself to focus his attention on the documents that lay before him. Colonel Randolph had requested that he brief him on these deeds at a meeting scheduled to begin in the next few minutes. With all his aggravation over the situation with Abigail, he had not really been able to concentrate on any of his assigned duties. He sighed, and tried to think of how he might be able to explain Wednesday's excursion into Salt Lake City, even as resentment tightened the muscles in his chest. Several times during his sleepless night he'd actually considered telling the Colonel the truth and let the consequences fall. But his transfer to Army Headquarters was still uppermost in his mind. He didn't want to risk it while there was still a chance.

"Well, Captain, I guess I've no one to blame but myself for the mess my daughter is about to step into," came his commanding officer's voice as he stepped into the captain's office. "I'm the one who wrote her that women don't have the right to vote here anymore. I'd hoped that bit of information would lure her out here, and I guess I was right. Now she's Hell-bent on that ill-fated crusade, short-lived as it may be," he continued as he slid into the vacant chair by Garrett's desk. "I never told her that women will get the right to vote as soon as the new state constitution is ratified. And I just as soon she doesn't know. I'm sure you can guess why."

Garrett was stunned, and his amazement must have been etched on his face. *How is it that the Colonel doesn't hold me responsible for this?* "Sir?" he asked hoping to get a clarification before he revealed information that he really didn't want Colonel Randolph to hear from him.

"She told me all about it last night at supper, Captain, so you needn't be concerned. Abby wants to go to that suffragette meeting at the Methodist Church in town Wednesday. She said she would take the streetcar, but I'm concerned that she could still get lost in town. I appreciate that you offered to drive her in the carriage. That way, I know she'll arrive there safely, and more to the point, someone will know exactly where she is. I couldn't stand it if something happened to her."

Garrett cleared his throat, and loosened the collar around his neck. Abigail had apparently decided not to tell her father the entire truth of her intentions, and Garrett wasn't inclined to clarify the situation for him. As far as Garrett was concerned, that was between the two of them. He was just the innocent bystander in this disaster in the making. He only hoped that when the smoke cleared, he would still have the rank of captain in the army.

"Did you finish reviewing those documents I gave you from last year?" the Colonel continued, obviously finished with the subject of his daughter's plans. "Those land deeds concern the sixty acres that were granted to the college last year. We need to be certain the language is clear enough. Also, I've received word that Congress will consider giving them additional land down the road. Have you reviewed them yet? Will that language stand?"

"Yes, sir. I'm quite confident that the wording used last year is sufficient. And we can use these deeds as examples for future land grants."

"You know, Garrett, on another note, I've received word that when Utah achieves statehood next year, Fort Douglas is likely to be designated as the Regimental Headquarters within the next year or so. In fact, I have to travel to Cheyenne some time this fall to discuss the details with the regimental generals along with some of the Senators who're most involved with the Department of War. I'll need these deeds, as well as other documents about our troop strength and involvement with public safety, when I attend that meeting."

The Colonel stood and walked over to the window as he continued giving Garrett the information. "I'm not sure of the exact dates for my trip just yet, but it'll probably be around the first week in October. And while I'm gone, Major Hempstead'll be in command of the post, but I'll be counting on you to keep Abigail out of mischief." The Colonel turned, smiled, and extended his hand to shake rather than accept a salute from the junior officer. "Hope that won't be a problem." He started out of the doorway, but stopped and turned to face Garrett again.

"Oh, and by the way, you and Abby were seen leaving the fort Friday, and my daughter was sitting a horse the way a man does. Edith Hempstead was here in my office not twenty minutes after you left riding. She's convinced that it's her responsibility to keep watch over my daughter's comings and goings. I swear, not much escapes Edith's interest on this fort. Just so you know, I mean it when I say you're the only person I trust to protect Abby."

Garrett nodded his understanding. He knew that the Colonel's request, while unofficial, was just as binding as if it were a formal command.

Wearing a blue skirt with a short waistcoat with large lapels, Abigail entered the meeting room at the Methodist Church with a faked air of confidence. Her hands trembled and her heart raced as she quickly slipped into the first available seat. Fashionably dressed women were milling around the room. They all appeared to be older than she which added to her nervousness. Shouldn't there be other women her age involved in this struggle? Then a woman in a skirt with a fitted blazer suit jacket and a short blue tie at the collar of her white shirtwaist moved to the podium to call the meeting to order. Abigail found herself suddenly surrounded by other women nodding and agreeing with one another. Because she did not know anyone by name, she preferred to sit quietly and learn.

With a pounding of a gavel, the woman said, "I call this meeting to order. Today's date is August 25, 1895, Mary Grant Major, presiding officer." She grinned broadly and as she shuffled some papers in front of her.

"Ladies, I want to thank you all for coming to this meeting today. We've quite a bit of good news to share, and much more to discuss by way of strategies in our quest to salvage the dignity of the fallen women of our community," she began.

"First, let me announce that the city has agreed to continue its contribution of $100 a month to the support of our rescue homes." At that, several women expressed their delight with a ladylike applause.

"Yes, the mayor has agreed to give us that money from the fines collected from the 1st District Court. It is our hope that soon those fines will no longer exist because there'll be no one to continue the practice of prostitution in Salt Lake City." Again the women answered her remarks with a round of applause.

"In addition, Dr. Helen Ritchie has agreed to continue serving as the matron of her home so that the women who find a retreat there will have a suitable example to follow." The ladies on either side of Abigail nodded their approval, as did several other women in the room.

"And now finally, we need to discuss the proposed strategies for reaching more of these unfortunate women who've fallen into this shameful occupation." With that introduction, several different ladies raised their hands to offer ideas. Abigail listened intently. Though she wanted to contribute, she felt reluctant to offer an idea just yet.

Then all of a sudden, the woman at the podium paused. Frowning just a bit, she looked directly at Abigail and posed a question, "What do you think we should do, young lady?"

All at once every woman in the room turned to stare in Abigail's direction. She felt her face turn its typical shade of scarlet. However, she had an idea that was beginning to take shape, and since she had determined that she would make a contribution to this cause, she stood up and said, "Well, m'am, I was quite impressed with the speech you made last week in the city. I think you and others of your organization should plan to make more such presentations in the parks of the city. Perhaps, you could try to set up a rally at a park area that is close to the area where these women currently reside."

Taking a deep breath, because she suddenly realized that she hadn't done so in a few moments, Abigail sat down in the midst of muttered affirmation. Looking around, she saw several of the ladies nodding in agreement with her idea, and the woman at the podium smiled in response.

"I'm so sorry. Where're my manners? Would you introduce yourself to those of us in the room who don't know you, dear?" Abigail bowed her head briefly, and stood again to introduce herself. "My name is Abigail Randolph. I'm a graduate of Smith College in Massachusetts. I've just recently come here to stay with my father, Colonel Randolph."

"Colonel Randolph at Fort Douglas?" the woman asked. When Abigail nodded, the room burst into applause. The women sitting on either side of her extended their hands to welcome her immediately, and several of the ladies who were just in front of her turned around to utter their pleasure at her attendance.

"Thank you so much, Miss Randolph, for that excellent idea. We'll consider just how to do this when the strategy committee meets again next week. Would you like to be a member of that committee, dear?" she inquired looking straight at the Colonel's daughter.

Abigail's assent was clear. With a sigh of relief, she felt that she was on her way to making the contribution she so wanted to make.

As the meeting concluded, the women present began milling around making it a point to welcome the newcomer. Mary Grant Major was one of the first to shake Abby's hand. Others followed her example, and Abby found herself feeling at home with this group of women.

Then a charming matronly woman approached her. "Miss Randolph, let me introduce myself." Pausing a moment to make eye contact with Abby, she continued, "My name is Rachel Porter; my husband is the pastor of the church here. I'm so glad you could come to our meeting, but how did you know about us?" she asked.

Abby beamed her acceptance and replied, "Someone at the rally in the park last week invited me to come. I didn't catch her name, but I did remember the place and time."

"Well, I'm so glad you could make it, my dear. There are so few young women willing to take on the challenge of this nature. I suppose it has more to do with the fact most of them are busy with young families and the responsibilities of a household. I assume you're not married," she suggested nodding and smiling warmly.

"No, I'm not married. I'm committed to doing whatever I can to make other people's lives better. I've marched with suffragettes in Boston, but I think this issue is of much more importance just now. I want very much to make a contribution to such a noble cause. In fact, I believe that's the real reason I've come to Fort Douglas," Abby replied sincerely.

Mrs. Porter led Abby to a table where another lady had placed a cup of tea for her. As the two women sat down, Abby gratefully sipped the refreshing beverage while Mrs. Porter began to advise, "You know, my dear, these Mormons are not real Christians as far as I'm concerned. I know they'll tell you that they believe that Jesus Christ is the Son of God, but the rest of their doctrine is heresy. The whole issue of polygamy is only the tip of the iceberg, if you ask me."

Mrs. Porter paused to gently wipe her lip with her napkin before continuing, "My husband has expressed several concerns for the salvation of these people who've been horribly misled by their so-called prophet. I want you to be very careful in your goings and comings in and around the city. I don't want you to be another victim; so many people who don't have a strong faith to guide them are easily swayed to believe what the Mormon missionaries tell them. I myself have been approached by them, and I can tell you they can be quite persuasive with their arguments."

Several of the other women seated and standing nearby nodded their agreement. Then they turned the conversation to other topics including the fine weather and the members of the strategy committee. As Abby considered the pastor's wife's warnings, she suddenly felt a bit more concerned about her safety among the Mormon citizens of Salt Lake City. She was very glad that she would be returning to Fort Douglas with the protection of Captain Talbot.

They had ridden in silence for what seemed an interminably long period of time. Captain Talbot kept his eyes straight ahead on the road, but inside he was steaming. Abigail fidgeted with her gloves and purse on her lap. Finally she said, "Thank you so much for taking me today. That meeting was just what I needed. Those women are making a difference here, and I'm definitely a part of it now."

Garrett sat frozen in place, staring straight ahead. He felt that if he were to make any comment, even to acknowledge her presence, he might explode with the pent up anger and resentment he felt. He continued driving the horses in silence, the muscles in his forearms clenched rigidly.

"I met several of the most influential women of Salt Lake at that meeting today," Abigail continued.

She seemed to ignore the fact that he had yet to respond to her. She prattled on like an excited child, and that was really getting on his nerves. He gritted his teeth so hard he thought his jaw might break.

"Sarah Reed was there. She's the wife of the Presbyterian minister in town, and she's an officer in the WCTU, you know, the Temperance Union. I also met Mary Grant Major; she's the lady that I heard speaking at the park just last week. And I met Dr. Helen Ritchie, too. She's the matron at one of the rescue homes that this organization provides. And Mrs. Porter, the wife of the Methodist minister, was extremely kind to me. She made me feel so very welcomed there. And now I'm on the strategy planning committee. Most of the women there were much older than I am. They seemed surprised that someone my age would want to participate. But I assured them that I was serious."

Garrett could stand it no longer. He jerked the horses to an abrupt halt, nearly tossing Abby to the floor of the buggy. With all the restraint he could muster, he twisted his upper torso to confront her, "You have no idea the mess you've made, have you? You've dragged me into this little deception of yours, against my will, and you are oblivious to how your actions could affect me."

Abigail's face registered amazement. "What deception, Captain? I don't know what you're speaking about."

"This 'suffragette' meeting, for one. You lied to your father about exactly what you were attending today. He thinks you might get involved in handing out some pamphlets or marching in a parade. He has no idea the real danger you've put yourself in."

"What danger, Captain? That was a perfectly safe meeting with a group of older women in the Methodist Church. I was in no danger there."

Garrett was so angry he could have spit nails at the incredulous woman who sat beside him in the carriage. "Are you so naïve that you don't know how dangerous it can be to tamper with someone's business?" he asked.

"What business?" she replied, obviously unaware of his point.

"Miss Randolph, those women are talking about removing prostitutes from the Red Light district. Whether we like it or not, prostitution's a business, and a very shady business, at that. There are some very unsavory folks connected with prostitution in Salt Lake, many of them powerful businessmen who finance the business as silent partners. They won't take kindly to a bunch of Protestant women interfering with their profit margins. And when you remove available prostitutes from the brothels, you'll definitely be affecting their profit margins," he spat out, enunciating the final two words as if he were nailing a lid shut.

Abigail's mouth fell open and her eyes registered shock. "So, you want me to respect prostitution as a legitimate business, and treat these poor fallen women as livestock or other business commodities? I can't believe you! I want to help these women, and all you can talk about is profit margins. What kind of person are you, Captain Talbot? And exactly how'll my being involved with the Women's Housing Association threaten you?"

"Well, how about this: you lie to your father, and your insistence that I be a part of it, may cost me my rank! If your father ever finds out what you've been up to, he'll blame me. He trusted me to keep you out of trouble while you're here at Fort Douglas. He asked me to befriend you because he knew that your high and mighty ways wouldn't go well with the other women on post. And I only agreed as a favor to him so that I could get his recommendation to Army Headquarters back East."

Garrett paused to catch his breath, then continued, "To make matters worse, you've managed to get Edith Hempstead's undivided attention. She's watching every move you make, and coincidentally now, every move I make. And now, I'm caught up in this mess with you, and I'm furious. I've worked my whole life to get to this stage of my career, and it could all vanish in a moment when your father finds out that I knowingly took you to this meeting today. He was particularly concerned about you involving yourself with the Mormons in town. If you continue with this nonsense, there's little doubt that there'll be repercussions for all of us. Your desire to make a contribution may well contribute to putting me in the stockade!" he said.

Then he snapped the reins, and the horses shot forward at a full gallop toward Fort Douglas, causing Abigail to fall against the carriage back. Garrett determined he would deliver her safe and sound back to the Colonel's residence and that would be the end of it. If he ever saw this troublesome woman again it would be too soon for his liking.

CHAPTER

"Oh, there you are, Garrett," announced Colonel Randolph. It had been a two weeks since Garrett's argument with Abigail when her father came looking for him. At the recognition of their commanding officer's voice, the two privates and Captain Talbot immediately stood at attention and saluted.

"At ease, gentlemen. What's going on in here?" he asked.

Captain Talbot beckoned the Colonel over to the desk where the private was demonstrating the use of a new machine. "Colonel, Private Jenkins was showing me how to use this new contraption called a typewriter." Then speaking directly to the private, he said, "Write today's date, September 13, 1895."

The private followed the direction and Colonel Randolph uttered a satisfied <u>hhmm.</u>

"It's slow going, but using this will make it possible for us to have machine written reports rather than having to send handwritten reports to a printer. He's typing up the reports about our troop strength for your meeting next month," Garrett answered pointing at the handwritten reports the private was using. "I'm told that once they get the hang of it, these reports will be done more efficiently and neatly than even our usual typesetter could do."

With eyebrows raised, the Colonel nodded his admiration for the new equipment and the effect it would have. He continued to watch for a few minutes as the private pecked away on the keyboard with his two forefingers. Even so, Private Jenkins seemed to know exactly where the right keys were located. "That's some fancy new toy there, Private. Keep up the good work."

Then turning back to Captain Talbot, the Colonel said more softly, "Garrett, I was looking for you. Let's go to your office."

The two men turned and walked down the short hallway to the well-lit room where the captain regularly completed his daily assignments. The Colonel closed the door, and Garrett began to feel somewhat anxious. Had the Colonel learned the truth about his daughter's meetings in town? Rather than sit behind his desk, Garrett decided to take one of the chairs against the wall and offered the other to the Colonel. Garrett hoped that this arrangement would help him to feel more at ease, but he remained in a state of fixed anxiety when Colonel Randolph spoke.

"Garrett, I wanted to invite you to a formal dinner party at my house a week from this Saturday evening. Major Hempstead and his wife and several of the other officers and their wives'll be coming, and I'd like you to be there for Abby."

Garrett frowned and hesitated before responding, "Sir, do you think that's such a good idea? Abby's already had problems with Mrs. Hempstead. And you know how that woman likes to gossip around the fort. Are you sure you want to invite her into your home?"

"I know Edith has been a problem, but I'm hoping that with my supervision and in my own home, I can correct that for Abby. I can't allow any slight to Major Hempstead just because his wife is such a gossip. Besides, maybe by inviting her to my home, she'll soften some in regard to Abby, and certainly, if you're there, perhaps Edith'll accept that your relationship with my daughter is appropriate."

"Well, sir, your daughter might become suspicious of our arrangement. I wouldn't want that to become a problem between you and Miss Randolph," Garrett continued hoping to persuade the Colonel against including him at this occasion. He didn't really want to be involved with her anymore if he could prevent it. And she probably would prefer it that way, too.

"Don't fret, son. I told Abby of my intentions for the dinner party, and she's the one who suggested I invite you."

Garrett's jaw dropped in utter amazement at this statement. He had not seen or spoken to the Colonel's daughter since that Wednesday two weeks ago when he had driven her back from Salt Lake. He had heard that she was teaching part-time now that school was in session and was using the streetcar station from the fort to get back and forth to her meetings in town. He assumed that since he had gotten so angry with her, she no longer wanted to have him around. And under the circumstances, that was agreeable to him. He felt uncomfortable keeping such an important secret from his commanding officer, and he suspected that eventually the Colonel would learn the truth. Garrett definitely didn't want to be involved in the situation when it happened.

"Garrett? Is there some problem I don't know about? I know my daughter can be a trifle difficult. Is that why you haven't been coming to the house lately?"

He shook his head in response to his commanding officer. "No, sir. Miss Randolph's a fine lady. I've just been busy trying to get these reports assembled for your meeting, and I thought she was more interested in spending her time at those meetings in town." Captain Talbot was very careful not to specify the type of meeting. He didn't want to be a party to this deception, but he didn't want to be the one to reveal the truth to her father either. The lawyer in him decided to be very circumspect.

Colonel Randolph stood up and scratched his head. "Well, Garrett, you never did tell me about your experience riding with Abby. How'd that go?"

"Fine, sir. Although, I confess, I wasn't exactly prepared . . ." Garrett hesitated again, then continued, "Sir, your daughter's a very experienced horsewoman. I could hardly believe my eyes when she got up on Grant without a boost from me. And I had a little trouble keeping up with her once she knew the direction of the trails. I thought we might be out there for a short while before she'd want to return, but truth be told, I was the one who tired first. I'm going to have to get out more often on Pepper if I'm going to be able to keep up with her."

The Colonel laughed heartily and stroked his salt-and-pepper beard while nodding. "Yes, son, she's been riding since she was about three years old. She was still a baby when I took her riding for the first time. While I was away, her grandfather taught her to sit a horse like a man, and she's been at it ever since."

The Colonel grinned a bit, "She told me that she was a little sore the next day, though, because she hasn't had the opportunity to go riding much since she was at college. But, Garrett, she had a good time, and that's important to me. In fact, her eyes lit up when she told me about the day. Perhaps when I'm gone next month you'll invite her out to ride again, after you've had a bit more practice yourself."

Colonel Randolph stood and moved towards the doorway, "Nevertheless, I'll expect you Saturday at 7 P.M. sharp. Major Hempstead and his wife'll be there, and I've invited Captain Randall and Major Johnson along with their wives. I'll expect you in full dress uniform, just so you know." The Colonel nodded toward Garrett to be certain he understood his intent before he exited the office.

Garrett sat for a moment gazing out the smudged window. His memory of Abigail was sharply etched. He could still see her in that riding habit with her thick, copper-colored hair flowing down her back and that mischievous twinkle in her sparkling green eyes. And he could see the shocked look on her face when he chastised her about pulling him into her deception. She had seemed stunned when he dropped her off that afternoon. How could someone be so alluring and so infuriating at the same time?

He shook his head to rid himself of the dreamlike effect her memory had on him, and returned to his desk to finish the work before him. Still, he could feel her presence regularly taunting him. Why couldn't he get the image of that girl out of his mind? She was trouble, nothing but trouble, but maybe she was worth it.

Since the first week of September, Abigail had been busy working with the children at the school four days a week. On Wednesdays, she led them in their reading, spelling, and a little mathematics before sending them home for the day at lunchtime. This schedule freed her to continue her work with the WHA in the afternoon. This arrangement was only until the new schoolmaster arrived. Then she would most probably help out on Tuesdays and Thursdays. At least that was her plan.

This schedule had worked well the past two weeks. Right now, Abigail stood at the back of the gathered crowd alongside of Mrs. Porter listening to Cornelia Paddock expressing concern for Mormon women who had "fallen" into prostitution. Cornelia's pleas and examples had been heart-wrenching to hear, and the crowd that had shown up gave enthusiastic applause to several of her points. Mrs. Porter pointed out from time to time the numbers of people who were drifting toward the crowd to hear the speaker. Abby smiled with gratitude; this had been her idea and it seemed to be working as she had hoped it would.

Then out of the corner of her eye, Abby thought she saw someone standing just a little apart from the crowd. Motioning to Mrs. Porter, Abigail moved in the woman's direction, and in a split second, the woman turned a tear-streamed face towards her. Abby hesitated a moment, but gathering her resolve, she reached into her skirt pocket and pulled out a handkerchief as she approached the obviously heart-broken woman. Perhaps this was to be the moment she made a contribution for this cause.

"Can I help you?" Abby asked extending her handkerchief for the woman to use. She appeared to be somewhat older than Abby, but the mixture of anger and sadness in her eyes betrayed her. Abby's heart was touched by the apparent heartbreak this woman was experiencing.

Accepting the handkerchief, she turned to face Abby, "Are you one of . . . them?" she asked with trembling in her voice. She pointed back to the gathered crowd still listening and applauding to the speaker.

Abigail nodded and answered, "My name is Abigail Randolph. The Women's Housing Association is a group of women dedicated to providing assistance to women who have no place else to go. Are you in such circumstances?"

The woman leaned away from Abby. She seemed suspicious of the motives of the group. She studied Abigail briefly before she turned to walk away. Not wanting to miss the moment, Abby followed her, and when they were both several feet away from the murmuring crowd, she reached out and touched the stranger's sleeve to stop the crying woman.

"What's your name?" Abby asked, thinking that she needed to be a bit more personal with this woman.

The woman dabbed at her puffy eyes, and responded, "Dorothy. Dorothy Broadnax, or at least that's what my name used to be. I don't know if I'm allowed to use that name anymore," she continued wondering aloud.

"Well, Dorothy, my name is Abigail, but my father calls me Abby. So do most of my friends. Why don't we sit down over here on this bench and just talk a bit? I'm new to Salt Lake City. Perhaps you could tell," she continued, smiling at the stranger who reluctantly agreed to sit down with her.

"You don't sound like you're from around here," Dorothy answered with a half choked laugh. For a moment, the woman smiled weakly and dabbed again at her eyes.

Abby grinned, "My accent does kinda give me away, doesn't it?"

Dorothy nodded in response. Suddenly she seemed to relax. She twisted the hanky in her hand, and began, "I guess I'm one of those women that lady is talking about. I was the fourth wife of Matthew Broadnax. I thought that he loved me, so I agreed to marry him eleven years ago."

She continued to dab tears from her face as she spoke, "At first, I was very happy. I was part of a loving family. The other three wives had several children, and even though I didn't have any of my own, I got to be a mother to their children, too. We had a large house, and there was plenty of work to do to keep it running smoothly. Our husband runs one of the most prominent Mormon banks in Salt Lake City. There were lots of business dinners and functions that we attended with him until things changed about five years ago.

"It seemed all of a sudden, having more than one wife became a burden to him, as it did to so many of the men of our community. I really wasn't worried, though, because I thought he loved me. Then his second wife, Rebeccah, died in childbirth last year, and when everyone got to talking about statehood for Utah, he told us that he couldn't keep all of us anymore. He said he would take care of all the children, but he asked his third wife, Hazel, and me to leave."

She turned away briefly. Looking down at the ground, she admitted, "He gave us a little money to tide us over, but it didn't last. Hazel and I tried to find work in town, but other than some clothes washing at the rooming house, we couldn't find much. We finally went to the house on Block 56 to see if we could be housekeepers there. The owner let us in, and gave us a place to stay. But a few girls ran off, and she said we either had to pitch in or leave the house. What else could we do?" she asked sighing heavily.

"Last month, Hazel died. She was heartbroken about leaving her two boys behind. She hadn't been eating since she started, you know. I think she died of shame," Dorothy said with sobs choking her words.

Abby put her arm around the woman to try to comfort her. Dorothy continued to cry on her shoulder. It was as if telling a stranger about her circumstances gave her the release she needed.

Abby responded, "That's terrible, Dorothy. Your husband owes you better than this. He's the one who should be ashamed for putting you and Hazel in this awful predicament." She paused, continuing to comfort the woman before adding, "That's what the WHA is all about, Dorothy. We have rescue homes here in Salt Lake to provide a place for women like yourself who have no other place to go. Would you like me to take you to one? I know we can get you in one tonight."

Dorothy looked at Abigail pondering her choices. Then as if something had suddenly occurred to her, she shook her head, "No, not just yet. But thank you for listening to me. It's been awhile since I had anyone I could talk to about this. Thank you for taking your time to hear me," she answered while returning Abby's handkerchief. A moment later, Dorothy stood up and hurried across the street.

Abby watched and saw a colored man meet up with her, and the two of them turned down Franklin Street and disappeared from sight. Abby closed her eyes and shook her head. She offered a prayer that the woman would be safe and she would return to accept the offer of the WHA. Regretfully, Abby got up from the bench and strolled slowly back to Mrs. Porter as a rousing applause thundered among the trees.

Even though he had arrived fifteen minutes early, Garrett was the last to arrive at Colonel Randolph's dinner party. Corporal Davis opened the door for him explaining that Helen was upstairs helping Miss Randolph with finishing touches. Garrett removed his hat and handed it to the Corporal before stepping into the formal parlor.

Major Hempstead, Major Johnson, and Captain Randall stood in the corner talking raucously with the Colonel while their wives dressed in their formal evening gowns occupied the various chairs and settees in the room. Lieutenant Harris was also present hovering over his lovely young wife who sat and listened intently to some story Mrs. Hempstead was telling to the both of them. Garrett wasn't quite sure where he should be in the room; he and the Colonel were the only bachelors present for dinner. He felt a little awkward, but in the next moment, his unease was forgotten.

"I apologize for being late," Abby said from the staircase. Garrett looked up and was immediately enchanted. Abigail was slowly descending the stairs wearing the most beautiful dress he had ever seen on any woman. The blue satin gown had purple beaded embroidery at the bodice and traveling up from the hem on either side with a train flowing behind her. The square décolleté was balanced by short puffed sleeves under ruffles of beaded satin. She wasn't wearing any jewelry except for a pair of amethyst ear bobs. Her thick auburn hair was arranged in a simple chignon accented with a matching amethyst ornament and a fringe of waves just above her forehead. And she carried an open purple lace fan in her white gloved hand. The effect was stunning, and Garrett could have sworn he heard a collective gasp in the room behind him as Abby glided toward the guests in the parlor. He himself was relieved that he wasn't expected to say anything at this moment. He knew there was no way he could summon up his voice.

Lieutenant Harris's wife was the first to speak up, "Oh, my! Where did you find that exquisite gown?" she asked rushing ahead of the others to greet her hostess.

Abby beamed and answered, "I bought it in New York earlier this year. A friend in college told me that a lady must always have an appropriate evening gown among her wardrobe."

"Well, it is certainly breath-taking, my dear," affirmed Mrs. Hempstead walking over to Abby and taking her hand. "Your mother would indeed be proud."

"As am I, Abby," her father chimed. He was radiant with pride as he gazed at her in admiration. "You do so resemble your mother."

Wrapping her free arm around his, the Colonel proceeded to greet his guests with his daughter at his side. Once everyone had been given a chance to speak to Abby, the Colonel escorted his daughter into the formal dining room and seated her at the end of the table opposite him.

After inviting the rest of his guests to be seated, Colonel Randolph stood behind his chair at the large mahogany table set with fine china for him and his guests. "This is a great occasion for me. Today is my daughter's twenty-second birthday, and this is the first time I have been present to celebrate the day with her. As you know, I haven't had much time at all to spend with her. She grew up without me. Now, at this time in my life, I feel so fortunate to have her companionship. I wanted to share my joy with the people I have come to know as comrades and friends. So I invite you to lift your glasses in salute to my daughter, Abby. May she find the joy and happiness here that she's brought to me by agreeing to move out here." Turning to look directly at her, the Colonel offered, "Happy birthday, Abby."

Everyone followed the Colonel's lead and drank a toast to Abby while she blushed a lovely shade of pink. Several of the guests said "Happy birthday, Miss Randolph." Only Edith Hempstead seemed disturbed by the salute. The Colonel sat and invited the Corporal and his wife to begin serving his guests.

Garrett had been directed to sit at Abigail's right. Directly across from him was Edith Hempstead. Garrett had always thought her to be a stout, old woman. Tonight her dull gray hair tied up loosely on top of her head did nothing to make her seem attractive. Garrett knew she had raised three children, and now boasted of ten grandchildren, but she didn't seem very much like the motherly type. Because of her husband's rank as second in command at the post, she had taken certain privileges, one of which was to know of just about everyone else's business.

Garrett knew she could be intimidating, and he knew it was better not to reveal much about himself to her. Sitting beside Abby and across from this woman made him doubly uneasy. Garrett realized he would have to supervise the conversation to keep Abby from any snares set by Edith Hempstead. And with what little he already knew about Abby, that was a daunting task.

"So, dear, tell me, how do you like Fort Douglas?" Edith asked leveling her gaze on Abby.

Abigail swallowed the spoonful of soup and smiled pleasantly at the older woman. "My visit so far has been just lovely," she replied.

"I must say, I was quite surprised to hear your father suggest that you might be staying with us indefinitely. I thought you were just visiting," Edith stated condescendingly.

"I know it's my father's wish for me to stay. I haven't decided just yet, however. But I do love the country here. The scenery is just breathtaking," Abby answered glancing mischievously toward Captain Talbot.

"Oh, have you been able to see much of the countryside then?" Edith asked looking directly at the captain, perhaps to gauge his reaction.

Garrett leaned in subtly in order to answer the woman's question before Abby had a chance to reveal more information than was necessary for this busy-body, "Well, Mrs. Hempstead, I have taken her riding up on the trails, but I'm sure you already knew.

"And Miss Randolph has learned how to take the streetcar into town to go shopping, haven't you, Abby," he continued looking at the stunned Abigail and winking his warning to her. He hoped his comments would suggest to her that Mrs. Hempstead was not someone she should confide in.

"Why, yes, Mrs. Hempstead, Captain Talbot did take me riding a few weeks ago, and I've now learned my way around well enough to take the streetcar wherever I need to go. I've even located a wonderful dressmaker just off State Street. Perhaps you and I could visit her together sometime?" Abby suggested following Garrett's hint.

The soup bowls had been cleared from the table, and the main course was served. Edith took a sip from her glass and sampled the entrée on her plate. She gave Abby a forced smile before saying, "I hear you've been filling in over at the school with our children. Perhaps I could come and assist you a bit. I do have experience dealing with young ones, you know."

With a bite of food in her mouth, Abby struggled not to choke. Garrett watched as she quickly drank some water and coughed softly.

When she had regained her composure, Abby looked Edith squarely in the eyes.

"I'm sure you have experience dealing with children, Mrs. Hempstead, but as you no doubt know, it is extremely difficult to unteach incorrect information to young children. They are easily confused at this age, so I feel I need to protect them. Since I'm already aware of how you treated the previous teacher, I hope you understand when I say that I do not need, nor do I want your assistance in my classroom."

Garrett resisted the impulse to cheer. Mrs. Hempstead's face registered shock over Abby's reply. He waited for the explosion he expected, but Edith must have realized where she was. She muttered something under her breath before she turned her attention to her plate. For the rest of the meal, she occasionally responded to the lively conversation that was taking place to her left. Garrett, too, concentrated on the meal and listened to remarks made by the others at the table. But all the while, he was aware of a sense of pride welling within him at the small victory he had witnessed: Abby's spunk in confronting Edith. What was it about this girl that made him want to protect her? And not just because her father had asked him to.

When the conversation turned to politics, most of the women sat quietly enjoying their desserts. Captain Randall spoke up in support of the current President, Grover Cleveland, with the other officers nodding their agreement.

Listening to the general discussion, Abigail spoke up. "Back East, some folks call him Uncle Jumbo. He wasn't very popular with the people I knew. While he never spoke against women's suffrage, he never supported us either. But his opposition to temperance won him the support of the Irish in Boston," she offered grinning impishly at the implication her words intended.

Lieutenant Harris turned in her direction surprised that a woman would be knowledgeable about politics. "Why, Miss Randolph, it's nice to have an educated woman at the table."

Turning to face the Colonel, Lt. Harris continued, "I know a few things about President Cleveland. He's the first President to get married while living in the White House, and four years ago, his daughter was the first baby born in the White House," he announced.

"You're only partly right, Lieutenant," responded Abby, obviously unable to keep from correcting him. "He is the first to get married in the White House, but the first baby born in the White House was the grandson of Thomas Jefferson, James Madison Randolph. Our family can trace its ancestry to Thomas Jefferson which is why I happen to know that little tidbit of information."

Lieutenant Harris looked quizzically at Abby. He started to challenge her when the Colonel interceded, "My daughter knows our family history, and she's correct. I know the newspapers all reported that Ruth Cleveland was the first baby born in the White House, but they didn't know all the facts. Let's just say that she was the first baby born to a President while he was in office."

Then standing at his place, the Colonel invited his guests to stand, "Ladies and gentlemen, why don't we adjourn back to the parlor? I have some very fine sherry available for the ladies, and a bottle of Kentucky bourbon for us men." So saying, he beckoned the others to follow him from the table.

Abigail stepped reluctantly into the parlor while the Colonel led the men into his private study. Because he had been at the other end of the table, her father obviously didn't know about her mild confrontation with Mrs. Hempstead. Abby worked to avoid eye contact with Edith who took a seat on the settee and encouraged the other women to join her as though they were her entourage. The major's wife took charge and poured glasses of sherry from the decanter sitting on the table. Mrs. Randall and Mrs. Johnson each sat across from her with the lieutenant's young wife, Kathleen, occupying the large chair. They obediently nodded to Edith's directions.

Abigail remained standing and looked about the room. She was beginning to feel a bit claustrophobic, though there certainly was adequate space available in the large parlor built for entertaining guests. Besides, she had planned something entirely different for after dinner. As the women chattered about recipes and problems with neighbor children, Abby just wanted to fly from the room. She reached for a glass of sherry and swallowed the warm liquid quickly before she excused herself from the company of the women. She eased to her father's study without so much as an explanation to anyone.

Still feeling the warm glow of the sherry coursing down her throat, Abigail quietly approached the group of men who currently stood with their backs to the doorway. Finding Captain Talbot in the group, she quickly slipped her arm in his, and announced to her father, "Excuse me, Father, but Captain Talbot promised to escort me to see the city lights from the hillside."

Captain Talbot frowned and started to protest, but the Colonel smiled and waved his adjutant permission to leave the room.

Abby led him out of the doorway and through the hallway to the back entrance of the house. Captain Talbot walked obediently, closed the door behind them, and asked, "Miss Randolph, where're we going?"

Abby looked up at his face which was somewhat hidden by the evening shadows that enveloped them. "I wanted an opportunity to speak privately with you, Captain, and I thought it best to use the ruse of seeing the lights of the city," she confessed.

She continued to wander away from the side of the house towards the tree lined street and across to a grove of trees overlooking the city. There below them, the lights of the city sparkled and twinkled like glitter. There was a peacefulness seeing the city like this. The Temple was alit, a brilliant beacon drawing attention as it pointed toward Heaven. Abby stood in silent wonder at the spectacle that appeared to lie at her feet.

Garrett walked along just slightly behind her, and when she stopped at the rim, he moved to her side. "It is quite a sight, isn't it," he remarked.

"Yes, it is, Captain. It's a beautiful city, and I'm so glad to be here," she answered. She turned to look up at his face again. There were no shadows hiding his mysterious blue eyes or his clean-shaven jaw line now. Catching him in this light caused her to smile appreciatively. She hadn't really noticed how handsome he looked until this moment. So tall and masculine in his formal dress blues, he had nearly taken her breath away when he sat next to her at the table. Suddenly she felt something she'd never known before, a feeling she wasn't quite sure she could identify just yet. Nevertheless, she was aware that this new feeling had everything to do with being alone with Captain Talbot.

"So why am I here with you?" he asked with just a hint of aggravation in his voice. "Is there some other deception you intend to draw me into?"

Abby smiled nervously, and sighed as she looked away from him. "I wanted a chance to apologize to you, Captain, for my inconsiderate behavior. I didn't take into account that my actions could have repercussions on your job and rank here at Fort Douglas. Though it is inexcusable, nevertheless, I'm asking that you forgive my behavior. Can you?" she asked as she turned and gazed up into his face.

Garrett looked at her. He felt his heart melt just a bit. Her words seemed sincere. The soft glow of the full moon made her face appear like a porcelain cameo. Impulsively, he bent down and gently kissed her soft full lips.

Abby made no effort to move away from him. He lingered just a moment, savoring the taste of her lips, a flavorful sherry. Stepping back a bit, he answered, "Now how could I remain angry with someone as lovely as you?" His fingertips gently cradled her face.

Even in the moonlight, Garrett could tell she was blushing. She hadn't objected to his attention, but her eyes were veiled modestly beneath her dark lashes.

Garrett saw that his words had caught her by surprise. It was at that moment he decided to be honest with her. "I confess. I was upset with you. You did put me in an awkward position with your father who just happens to be the commanding officer of this post and someone whose respect and trust I desire."

He nodded as he continued, "Nevertheless, I believe you when you tell me your actions were not intended to hurt me. But let me say again, your participation with this group could prove dangerous. Regardless of who did what, your father would hold me accountable if anything happened to you. Please promise me you'll be careful," he urged waiting for Abby to agree.

She stood silent for a moment, her eyes appearing to search his face for clues to his attitude. She gently touched his hand as she spoke, "Thank you, Captain. You are indeed a gentleman. Now can I ask just one more favor of you?"

Garrett frowned. He suspected she would ask something else that would get him into trouble with the Colonel.

"Will you take me riding again next week?"

Surprised by her request, Garrett grinned and nodded. "Yes, I think it can be arranged. Now let's return to your father's house before Mrs. Hempstead conjures up even more gossip than she already has."

He turned as if to start toward to the house, but stopped and looked directly at her again. "Happy birthday, Miss Randolph."

Abby nodded her thanks and beamed as she realized her gesture had been successful. She was pleased to have been able to mend the rift between them ever since she had pressured him into taking her to the WHA meeting. He offered his arm, and Abigail wrapped one arm around his while using her other hand to discreetly lift her skirts as they both moved back across the yard. But she was aware of a warm feeling that seemed to spread throughout her as she leaned against this man. Could this just be the effect of drinking sherry so quickly? Or did this have more to do with the warmth of this man's kiss on her lips? She would be pondering the events of this evening for many nights to come.

CHAPTER

Friday morning Abigail knocked softly on her father's bedroom door. He was standing beside his bed folding clothes into his traveling case. He looked up, smiled, and beckoned his daughter to enter. Abby reached methodically to assist him, and the two worked quietly side by side for a few moments with an aching silence between them.

"You looked so beautiful last Saturday night, Abby. Everyone commented on that gown you wore. But, I confess, it is so difficult for me to see you all grown up when I missed most of your childhood," he sighed, "and all of your birthdays until now."

Abby reached over and lifted her hand to touch his shoulder. "I know, Father. It's a little difficult for me, too. I didn't realize it until I came here, but I've always held you in my heart, even when I was confused and disappointed because you were gone. Now that I'm here, I feel very much like a little girl around you instead of a grown woman. Isn't that strange?"

The Colonel stopped his packing and sat on the bed studying her. "I can't get over how much you look like your mother, Abby," he said as he reached to stroke her hair. Then looking down, he frowned slightly before he asked, "Whose picture is in your locket?"

Abigail sighed gently. Her locket had become so much a part of her that she seldom thought of it anymore. She reached up just above her breast to gently pat the antique gold frame. Opening the locket, she held it out for her father to see for himself.

Inside were two tiny pictures facing one another; one was her mother, and the other was her father. "Mother gave this locket to me when I was about nine years old. I was crying one morning about not having my father, I don't remember exactly why, but she came into my bedroom and handed me this locket. It was the one she wore all the time. She told me that with this I would always have both of my parents close to my heart." Abby smiled remembering her mother's kindness and selflessness in comforting her daughter.

Abby noticed the sadness in her father's eyes as he scanned the pictures in the locket. "I missed so much, didn't I, Abby. Oh, sometimes I wish that I could return to those days and make different decisions." Her father looked up at her and asked, "Did she ever tell you how we met?"

Abby shook her head. Her mother had spoken often about Abby's father, but hadn't revealed the details of their courtship and marriage.

"It was after the War. I'd been opposed to the Confederacy and felt I needed to do something to redeem our family's good name. I chose to go to West Point and graduated with my commission the same year my father and grandfather were released from prison. They'd been there since shortly after the surrender. Well, anyway, our family's property had all been confiscated because they had been Confederate officers in Lee's command. With nothing left in Virginia, they decided to move to Kentucky, and I followed them there just before I was to report to my first post. That's where I saw your mother for the first time. Our family had gone to church in town one Sunday, and there she was, the most beautiful red headed woman I had ever seen. I was smitten immediately. We pledged our love in letters while I was away. A year later, when I came home on leave, we were married right there in that little church.

"You know, she was with me early in our marriage, unpacking our belongings and trying to make a home for us on whatever fort I was assigned to. I'd be gone sometimes for days chasing Indians or bandits, but she was always happy to see me come riding through the post gate. She suffered so from the dust and dirt that always seemed to pile up wherever we were. But she never complained. She always said she was just glad to be near me. But after she'd endured three miscarriages, the doctor told us that she had a weak heart and that she'd never be able to carry a baby to term. Then before we both knew it, she was pregnant with you. I told her I would resign my commission and leave, if only she gave me the word. She wouldn't let me do that, Abby. She insisted my life was in the army, she knew I was needed there, and she understood I needed the army for my own peace of mind. She was right, but still, sometimes . . .

"Anyway, that's when I took her home to your grandparents. You know your grandfather was a doctor, so I knew that was the best place for her to be. We had a few wonderful days together thinking about what you would look like, whether you would be a boy or a girl. She really wanted a son, you know, not me. I told her I wanted a pretty girl who looked just like her mother. Then all too soon, I had to leave for Nebraska and more Indian problems. I was away when you were born, and I cried because I couldn't come home to see you or your mother. She planned to join me on the post as soon as you were old enough to travel, but I think she was just trying to make me feel better," he added reaching to caress Abby's face. He smiled, then turned and walked over to look out the window.

"I knew she was in a weakened condition. The stress of moving across the country could have been fatal. I knew she could never travel to where I was, and so I insisted she remain with your grandparents in Kentucky. I came as often as I could to visit with the two of you, and I was always ready to resign my commission, but she wouldn't hear of it. And now I live with the memory of a love I once knew and a daughter I left behind so that I could restore honor to the Randolph name. Just now, hearing myself admit this, I realize how pathetic I must sound," he said with a sigh. He remained with his back to her.

Abby gazed at her father's silhouette. She blinked back a disobedient tear, and then said, "I often thought I was responsible for my mother's death. If I hadn't been born, she probably would have been here with you today."

Her father turned around instantly. "Don't ever think that, Abby. You are not to blame. Your mother wanted so badly to have you, in spite of the doctors' warnings. And once you were born, she was so happy. Her letters were filled with special moments she had with her tiny daughter. She loved you with all her strength."

Impulsively, Abby stepped around the bed to the window where he stood and wrapped her arms around his shoulders. She laid her head on his chest; she could feel his heart beating, and she felt an affection for him she had never admitted before. He had revealed information which had finally explained his absence for all these years. Before this moment, she had been left to draw her own wrong conclusions about why her father was away all the time.

The Colonel returned her embrace hugging her close and pressing his bearded jaw against the top of her head. For a moment she imagined what it would be like to be a little girl in his lap. Then Abby reached up on her tiptoes, and kissed her father on his weathered cheek.

"Well, Father, we're together now, and I find I rather appreciate having a father who can look out for me. I'm not as grown up as I thought I was. Right now, I feel like a little girl who just wants to please her father." Abby strode back over to the unfinished work lying on the bed. She picked up his socks and began to arrange them in his traveling case. Pride spread through her like a warm water bath. How could something so simple bring such unexpected pleasure?

"Now you know I'll be gone about two weeks, Abby. Major Hempstead will be in command while I'm off post," he said matter-of-factly standing beside her to continue his packing. "I've asked Captain Talbot to look after you. I hope you don't mind."

"Not at all, Father. The captain and I are going riding tomorrow, that is, if you let me ride Grant again," she answered. "May I?" she asked in the voice of a little girl.

Colonel Randolph grinned and laughed heartily. "Of course, Abby. You don't need to play to get me to say 'yes.'" He hugged her again, and grinned. "You've had me wrapped around your finger ever since you were born." Then changing the subject, "I met the new headmaster when he arrived day before yesterday. He asked if you would be continuing at the school now that he's here."

Abby nodded, "Yes, I've agreed to come in on every Tuesday and Thursday afternoon. The children have really enjoyed my reading to them since the first week in September, and so Mr. Scott asked me if I would plan to read aloud to them twice a week. Right now I'm reading Tom Sawyer."

"Oh, the book by Mark Twain? I heard he's quite popular back East. Written quite a lot of books, hasn't he?"

"Yes, he has. And with all the books I've brought with me, I'll have something to keep me occupied and perhaps out of trouble, so don't you worry about me while you're gone," she laughed as she reached up to hug her father one more time. Then she left the room for him to finish his packing undisturbed. After he left later in the afternoon, he hadn't been gone more than a few hours when she realized how much she already missed him.

The ride up onto the East Bench of the Wasatch Mountains the next morning was more relaxed now that Abby wasn't trying to impress her riding companion. The crisp morning breezes brought a chill to the air which this last day of September sunshine strained to warm. She was glad she had chosen to wear a heavier coat this time. Passing orchards that had been harvested recently, Abby and Garrett made their way up the hillside to the mountain spring where they had stopped to rest a little over a month ago. Once again, Garrett led Pepper to the grassy bank, and Abby followed with Grant. Then they strolled back over to a spot under a grove of aspen trees and sat down on the blanket that Garrett placed there. After drinking from the canteen, Abby surveyed the natural beauty around her. She wondered if she had ever really felt this good in her life before coming to Utah.

Turning to face Garrett, Abigail asked, "So, Captain, what can you tell me about yourself? I mean, you certainly know a great deal about me, but I know practically nothing about you. I don't think that's fair, do you?"

He smiled. "What do you want to know, Miss Randolph?"

"First of all, Captain, I'm deadly tired of you calling me by my surname. Please call me Abby or Abigail," she demanded gently.

"Well, will you stop calling me Captain? My name is Garrett, and if we're going to be riding out like this very much, you should learn to use my given name."

Abby grinned. "All right, Garrett, tell me about your family."

He closed his eyes and a boyish smile warmed his appearance. "I grew up on a Nebraska farm— very flat country. Nothing at all like this," he waved his hand to display the mountainous area around them. "I've got four brothers and two sisters; I'm the oldest, and I had to watch out for the rest of them all of my life, so I guess giving orders to others like I do here comes naturally."

"It must be wonderful to have so many bothers and sisters. I would have liked at least one to play with," Abby replied.

"Well, at the time, I wasn't always so glad for them. We did get into a scuffle or two through the years growing up. My youngest brother is the baby of the family. You wouldn't know it now because he's bigger than any of us."

"So why did you leave Nebraska? Didn't you want to be a farmer?" Abby asked sincerely interested in his history.

"Naw. It's a lot of work for so little reward. And so much depends on circumstances totally out of your control— sunshine, rain, storms, insects. I saw how it worried my father. I decided by the time I could read that I wanted to do something else with my life. I read stories about soldiers when I was a boy; in fact, my brothers and I used to play like we were soldiers in a battle amongst the cornstalks. My grandfather, we called him Papa Jack, was an officer in the Illinois volunteers during the War. I grew up hearing how it was a man's duty to fight for his country. I guess it was natural for me to sign up after college."

"So where'd you go to college?" Abby inquired watching his face as he spoke of his childhood memories.

"Illinois. I'm not really sure why I got a law degree except maybe I had learned how to argue with my brothers when I was on the farm. There was a recruiter in Springfield who convinced me I should serve my country. I signed up and was given the rank of 1st Lieutenant. And my first post? Fort Robinson in Nebraska. Just like I was back on the farm, in some ways. Then the army needed a lawyer here at Fort Douglas, and I got orders to come here. And that's all there is to tell about me, Miss . . . oh, I'm sorry, Abby," he answered dutifully.

Telling these stories about his family had given his face a softness she hadn't noticed before. His grayish blue eyes sparkled with animation, and the smile on his face brought his shy dimple to life. Talking about his childhood gave him the look of a little farm boy about to get into some mischief. The picture was irresistible to her. She impulsively leaned over and kissed him on the cheek.

Garrett was startled, and reflexively jumped back a little. He turned his face to see a look of amusement in Abby's eyes. Lifting her face with his hand, he slowly breeched the distance between them. When he saw her eyelids slowly close, he knew the invitation had been given. He brushed his lips against hers, and sensing no protest, he lingered long enough to feel the warmth of her breath against his face.

After a moment, he sat back a bit, stroked her ivory face with his thumb, and he kissed her again. This time his passion took over. When her lips parted slightly, he felt himself being lulled into a deep well of desire. He wrapped his arms tightly around her, and they fell gently back onto the blanket. Reaching up to move an errant strand of hair from her face, Garrett ran his fingers along her forehead and down the side of her cheek. He looked into her eyes and noticed the deep green flecks that seemed to dance there. Gazing into those eyes, he felt reality slip away.

Suddenly he was in some fairy story with an enchanted princess. He moved towards her again, pressing his lips against hers with his tongue lingering ever so tantalizingly inside her mouth. He caressed her, running his fingers through her thick wavy hair which had come loose. She lay comfortably and trustingly in his arms making no move to withdraw from his embrace. He found himself drawn to her lips over and over again, each time delving a little deeper. Until finally, overwhelmed with forbidden passion, he pressed his body against hers. He could feel the warmth of her curves. His hand wandered from her back to her waist. Without thinking, his hand gradually edged up toward her breast.

Then almost as if he was called to attention, he stopped. Reality had returned; the enchantment had been broken. Garrett pulled away from her and began breathing heavily through his mouth. He had almost overstepped with the Colonel's daughter. The consequences for that would be far worse than anything he could imagine at this moment. He got up and quickly moved a few steps away, leaving Abby lying on the blanket.

"What is it?" she asked sitting up and straightening herself. She looked around as if searching for something.

Garrett saw her out of the corner of his eye. He stood several feet away from the blanket hoping to regain his composure.

"Did you hear something?" she asked again.

"Maybe, I don't know," he answered trying to cover his real reason for stepping away from her. "It may have been some mule deer; they're often seen up around here. But it could have been a wolf. Maybe we should head back to the post, Abby, now." He moved towards his horse and gently patted Pepper.

Abby stood up and brushed off the dried grass from her split riding skirt. Garrett returned to the blanket, picked it up, rolled it, and put it back on his saddle while Abby retied her hair in place. He returned to her side momentarily, kissed her on the cheek, and led her over to Grant where he boosted her up into the saddle. The pair ambled back to the fort without saying anything more about their romantic interlude.

Abigail sat in the kitchen watching Helen roll out dough for a pie she was planning to make. The rhythmic movements lulled her into a daydream. She could see Garrett's face and feel his touch, the warmth of his kisses, and the sensations which ran through her when he pulled her close. These were definitely new feelings for Abby. While there had been a suitor or two previously in her life, no one had touched her the way Garrett had, and certainly no one had gotten this close until now. So why was she so confused?

"You seem to be somewhere else, Abby," remarked Helen as she picked up the flattened dough and laid it over the pie pan. "Care to share with me?" she asked with a twinkle in her eye. "Didn't you go riding with Garrett yesterday? Did you have a good time?"

"Yes, but," Abby answered still caught up in a dream-like state that she couldn't quite understand.

"Something wrong?" Helen asked as she pressed the dough into the pan.

Abby watched Helen working the dough and wished she had known her when she was a little girl. It would have been nice to have had a sister. Someone to share my thoughts and problems with. Maybe she wouldn't have felt so alone most of her life.

"I'm just a bit confused about men, Helen," she confessed. For reasons she did not understand, she felt close enough to Helen to confide her deepest thoughts.

"You're not alone there, sweetie," Helen said with a laugh. "I'm married to one, and I'm all the time confused about him." She placed the pie pan over to the side, wiped her hands on her apron, and turned to face Abigail.

"You know, I have two younger sisters. I can remember sharing secrets with them. Having you here has reminded me of that," she said as she sat down next to Abby. "Do you need to share a secret with an older sister?"

"Kinda," she answered. She paused considering how best to begin what she herself didn't even understand.

"You know that I went riding with Garrett yesterday?" Abby repeated, trying to find a way to explain her confusion.

"Well, it seems that everything was going well; we rode together up to the hillside where we stopped the last time we went out. He asked me to call him by his first name, and I asked him about his childhood. Helen, you should have seen his face when he talked about his family. It was just as if he was a little boy back on the farm again. He looked so cute."

Abby looked over at Helen, who again nodded as if to say 'Go on'.

"Well, I wasn't thinking about doing it, but I kissed him on the cheek. Then it happened." Abby paused for a moment making sure that Helen was still listening. "He kissed me in a way no other man has ever kissed me before."

Helen nodded again as she moved to fill the pie crust with the freshly sliced apples. In a few moments, she looked up from the pie and asked, "Was that a problem? Did he scare you?"

"No, no, it was just different, and I liked it. I thought that must mean he likes me. Strange, but I want him to like me even though he's a soldier like my father," she answered, frowning just a bit as she contemplated her words. Where had this thought come from?

"So why are you confused? If he kissed you, I think it's a pretty good indication he likes you. From everything I've seen, he does."

"Well, he stopped all of a sudden. I thought he heard someone there or an animal or something, but there wasn't anything there. Then he said we should return to the fort."

Helen frowned, turned away, and walked over to the oven. With her back to Abby, she asked, "Abby, did your mother ever talk to you about how babies are made?"

Abby felt her face grow hot. "Well, yes. I've even seen the birth of foals in the stable back home. And back East, I assisted a midwife once when I was visiting a friend who went into labor. I just don't understand this other stuff. Did I do something wrong?"

Helen turned around and eased back over to the table, sitting beside Abby. She grinned and put her arms around Abby giving her the physical comfort she needed. "No, sweetie, you didn't do anything wrong. Captain Talbot must really like you. My guess is he realized things could get complicated, and he didn't want to take advantage of you. He is, after all, a man, Abby, and men have certain desires which can take over their good judgment. He didn't want to dishonor you. But trust me, he likes you very much, sweetie. Of that you can be certain."

Helen hugged Abby again to reassure her even more. But Abby still puzzled over the way she was feeling and wondered what Garrett was thinking about her. This was all so new, and she wasn't certain that she was happy about these feelings she realized she had for this man. She definitely didn't like feeling so confused. <u>And for a soldier, no less.</u>

"But you don't understand. I made him so mad last month. Is it possible he's still angry with me?"

Helen put her hands on Abby's shoulders and turned her so they could be face to face. "Sweetie, I can guarantee you if he were still angry with you, he wouldn't have gone riding with you, much less kissed you. I've known Captain Talbot for a few years now. He's not made out of the kind of cloth that could hide his true feelings."

Abby sighed. "So what do I do about this, Helen?"

Helen smiled broadly. "Nothing, sweetie. You don't need to do anything. I'm sure he will let you know in his own time." Then changing the subject, "Now let me finish fixing this pie. When I get it in the oven, you can help me clean up this mess so we can get in a few hands of Pan before supper."

CHAPTER

Abigail had only spoken with Dorothy Broadnax that one time two weeks ago. Now the first week of October, she scanned the crowd carefully to see if Dorothy was among the many women present at this park rally. She ambled slowly from group to group and inspected each new participant. She only hoped she would be able to recognize this particular woman again if she actually were there. Abby rehearsed the details she could remember in her mind: a woman in her thirties with brown hair and a small mole on her right cheek bone. But despite searching all around the park, she could see no one matching Dorothy's description.

"You seem to be distracted, my dear," Mrs. Porter said touching Abby on her arm. "Is there anything I can do to help?"

Abby shook her head, "No, m'am. I was just looking for someone I saw here at our last rally." Abby turned away to scan the crowd again.

Mrs. Porter was a very nice woman. She and Abby had talked several times since she had first come to the group's meetings, and the older woman had treated Abby kindly. At the last meeting, Abby had felt a little sad, and Mrs. Porter had made an effort to reassure her. Now

Mrs. Porter moved closer to her. She smiled, took her arm, and gently led Abby to a bench and motioned for her to sit there.

"How's your father, dear? Is everything all right?" she asked with gentle concern in her voice.

Abby nodded, "My father is fine. He's out of town on Army business just now. But I've never felt closer to him in all my life. I'm so glad I agreed to come here to stay with him."

Mrs. Porter squeezed Abby's hand, "How nice, dear. And he must be so proud that you are helping the Women's Housing Association. Does he know these rallies were your idea?"

Abby looked down, "I haven't told him yet, Mrs. Porter. He still thinks I'm coming to the city to meet with suffragettes. He's not thrilled, but he'd be even more upset if he knew the truth. He doesn't want me to have anything to do with the Mormons in town. It could cause trouble for him, and I'm afraid of what he'll think of me when he learns what I've really been doing." Abby knew there was a hint of desperation in her voice. She realized she should tell her father the truth, but how?

Mrs. Porter nodded her head in understanding. "You know, dear, he could find out the truth from someone else which would be far worse for you than if he hears it from you, don't you think?" she offered quietly.

Abby's eyes glassed over filling with tears of regret, "I'm afraid if I tell him, he'll be disappointed in me. In fact, I'm certain his disappointment will be so great he'll send me away for good. After all these years of being without a father, Mrs. Porter, I just couldn't bear losing him all over again," she exclaimed with tears streaming down her face. "It's all such a mess, isn't it? I've made a mess of this whole thing."

"Now, now, my dear. You mustn't think such things. I'm sure your father loves you; he'll understand. He might be disappointed, but I'm sure his love for you will cover everything. Here," she continued, handing Abby a handkerchief to wipe her tears, "don't cry now. When he comes back to town, you tell him the truth so that he hears it from you."

Abby dabbed at her eyes, sniffed, and nodded her agreement. Mrs. Porter stroked Abby's shoulders. Then both of them stood up and walked back to the edge of the crowd to listen to the speaker. Mary Grant Major was addressing the crowd again, and the applause after each point seemed to last longer and longer each time.

Abby, too, stopped to clap, but with renewed determination she continued looking for Dorothy. Then she saw two women standing at the back of the crowd, the way she had first seen Dorothy three weeks ago. Desperate to find her, Abby marched up to the two women and introduced herself. "Good afternoon, ladies. My name is Abigail Randolph. I am a member of the Women's Housing Association, and I am looking for someone named Dorothy Broadnax. Would you happen to know her?"

The two women glared at her. "Who?" one of them asked, sounding almost annoyed.

Undaunted, Abigail pressed on, "Dorothy Broadnax. I believe she works at a house on Franklin Street. I need to get in touch with her. Have either of you seen her?"

"And why would someone like you be interested in anyone who works on Franklin Street?" the other woman asked in mock disdain.

Abigail sighed. Then she decided to continue, "I know you think I'm just some busybody, and frankly, I don't care. If you know Dorothy Broadnax, can you tell me where I might find her? It's really important that I speak with her."

The two women looked at each other. One shrugged her shoulders to indicate a lack of concern; the other woman sneered back at Abigail, then offered, "Well, if you come back a little later, say about 8 o'clock this evening, I can meet you at the corner on Franklin Street and take you to her. A woman like you won't get in the place without some help."

Abigail hesitated, not sure to trust her; but having no other real lead, she nodded her head, "Thank you. I'll meet you at 8 o'clock at the corner of Franklin Street."

Then the two women laughed softly and wandered off across the street. Abby pondered what she would do in Salt Lake City until the meeting took place. Glancing back at the women as they disappeared around a corner, Abby returned to the crowd which was still listening to Mary Grant Major.

Perhaps later tonight she would get the chance to help Dorothy and make a real contribution to the Women's Housing Association. When she confessed everything to her father, perhaps he would see how important this work was; maybe then he wouldn't be as disappointed in her. Maybe, just maybe, she thought.

Sitting in his office looking out the smudged window, Garrett pondered the mixture of feelings which tormented him. His first impression of Abby had been that of a spoiled little girl. She had a pretty face, but a very powerful father, and therefore, his attitude had been one of a subordinate following an order, even though he knew the Colonel intended it to be a favor.

Then after their first riding experience, he had been so resentful of her; she had figured out her father's arrangement with him and was using it to pressure him into deceiving his commanding officer. Garrett had gone along with her only because he didn't want to upset the Colonel; a transfer to Washington was his primary concern at the time. The whole afternoon of driving her to Salt Lake City, waiting for her meeting to end, and driving her back home had been torturous for him. The anger and frustration over being caught up in the situation which she engineered, not to mention his concern the Colonel would demote him or worse if he found out, had simmered in him for hours until it finally found expression when he scolded her severely.

Her naiveté about the danger she might be getting herself into amazed him. He wondered why he had ever agreed to get involved with her at all. She was just a headstrong girl with no real understanding about the way the world worked. He was glad to be rid of her when she decided to use the streetcar to get to town regularly. Good riddance, he'd thought.

Then at the dinner party Saturday two weeks ago, she was absolutely the most beautiful woman he had ever seen in his life. She was a goddess gliding down the stairs and into his heart. He was mesmerized by her beauty and felt so privileged to be sitting next to her.

At the same time, he felt the need to protect her from people at the table who would try to take advantage of her, but he had been delighted to see her stand up to Edith Hempstead. Then later in the evening when she singled him out of the crowd of gentlemen in her father's study, he felt he was in the midst of some dream. In spite of all the anger and aggravation he had felt earlier, now all he could think of was her green eyes and mischievous smile. When she apologized for her actions, he melted like the mountain snows in the springtime. That first impulsive kiss with the Salt Lake City lights in the distance would forever be imprinted in his memory.

And now, after sharing with her about his family and his life, suddenly the connection he felt overwhelmed him. He wanted to hold her, embrace her, kiss her, and more. The more was the problem, because, after all, she was still the Colonel's daughter. How in the world was he going to handle this situation? Colonel Randolph had asked him, as a favor, to befriend his daughter. Would he allow Garrett to court his daughter? And would Abby be agreeable to a new arrangement? So many questions and too few answers.

Questions like this had kept him awake most of the night. He instinctively rubbed his aching head. He would just have to wait until the Colonel returned to get an answer to this dilemma. But how was he going to broach the subject?

"Captain Talbot, sir?" came Roger's voice from the doorway. "May I have a word with you?" he asked standing with a salute in the door frame.

Garrett turned around, saluted back, then beckoned Corporal Davis into the office. "At ease, soldier," he instructed. "What can I do for you?"

"Well, sir, some of the men of the company want to take you out this evening to celebrate your birthday," Corporal Davis offered.

Garrett frowned and looked at the calendar hanging on the wall behind his desk. It was October 4th. Indeed it was his twenty-ninth birthday; he had completely forgotten about it. He looked back at the Corporal who was smiling. "Just what do you and the boys have in mind, Corporal?"

"Well, sir, there's this saloon in town where . . ."

"Now wait a minute, Corporal. You know Colonel Randolph frowns on us going into the town's saloons."

"I know, sir, but this place is special. Old Colonel Connor's nephew owns the place. He serves brews and whiskey half price to soldiers. And there's never any problem in his place; he doesn't put up with any foolishness there, and there're no women allowed.

"Sir, we thought since it's your birthday, well, I could use the Colonel's carriage, and drive you into town, have a few drinks, and get back before 10 o'clock. The rest of the company can take the street car. What do you say, sir? Will it be all right for me to tell the men it's a go?"

Garrett paused and thought about the opportunity. He needed a distraction right now, and maybe sharing a beer with the men in his company would be just the ticket. He nodded his agreement, and the obviously delighted corporal left the room.

Abigail had eaten a light supper at a small café on Main Street after she had wandered in and out of several stores in order to pass the time. From the tall clock in the corner, she could tell it was approaching 8 o'clock. She didn't want to be late and miss the chance to meet up with the woman who said she could take her to Dorothy. She quickly paid the waiter and hurried down 200 South towards Franklin Street.

The early October night was darker and colder than she expected. Though there seemed to be people milling about on the streets, she really didn't see anybody she knew, and she became suddenly uneasy. What if she didn't recognize the woman who came?

The noise from the various saloons was a bit overwhelming. She had never really been out in a city near such places before, certainly not alone; her evening activities had always been social engagements which were controlled and polished and chaperoned. The raucous laughter and loud music coming from these places was repulsive and somewhat frightening to her.

Abby instinctively moved more quickly in order to get away from the noise. She was aware at this moment the decision to meet this stranger alone at this particular place had been an impulsive and foolish idea. She shook off anxious thoughts and continued ahead scouring the people for anyone who looked like the woman she had seen earlier in the day.

She found herself on the corner of 200 South and Franklin. Knowing several of the brothels were located here along this street made her feel even more uncomfortable, but she had to be brave if she was going to help Dorothy escape such a life.

Looking around anxiously and seeing no one matching the description of the woman who had promised to meet her, Abigail slowly crept down the street trying to catch a glimpse of her. Maybe I'm late, and the woman gave up waiting on me, she thought. Abby was desperate to persist even though every instinct told her to leave the dark area at once.

Then from across the street, a woman called to her, "Hey, do-gooder lady! Over here."

Abigail crossed the street hurriedly. "Thank you so much for meeting me. I was beginning to think you weren't coming."

The woman nodded and spoke quickly, "I gotta go in a minute, lady, but I told you I'd meet you here, so here I am. I saw Dorothy. She said she don't need your help. Said her husband's gonna take care of everything like he shoulda in the first place, whatever that means. Anyway, I told you I'd meet you, and I done what I said. Sorry to get you here for nothing, but that's what she said." Then the woman turned and hurried away into the developing mist.

Abigail looked around her and saw she was suddenly enveloped in a dense fog which had settled quietly while she had been listening to the woman. The street was hidden, as were most of the buildings. She edged along slowly trying to find her way. Apparently, most of the people who had been out when the fog dropped, decided to go inside. Lost and anxious for her safety, Abigail found herself totally alone wandering blindly down Franklin Street, the heart of the Red Light district.

"Hey, now here's a fine one," came a voice from behind her. "Wonder which house she belongs to," he added.

Frozen with fear, Abigail stopped in her tracks, pulled her jacket tighter, and instinctively grabbed her locket. Then she turned to face two obviously drunken men who emerged from the fog. Even in the mist and shadows, she could tell they were disheveled. Their clothing reeked of spilled beer and cigar smoke. She scrunched up her nose in disgust.

Nevertheless, Abby decided in an instant to speak up in her defense, "I do not live here, gentlemen. In fact, I am lost. Could you point me in the direction of State Street? I need to catch the streetcar to get home. Do you know how to get there from here?" she asked hoping her trembling voice would not betray her fear.

"Lost, huh? Did you hear that, Al, the lady's lost," he laughed. "Never heard it called that before. In polite society, they call them 'fallen.' Never heard one being called lost before. Some call 'em streetwalkers. Is that what we have here?" he asked moving closer to Abby with each word he spoke.

Abby reflexively backed up to evade him, but found herself in a dead end alleyway with the two men advancing towards her threateningly. Frantic, she called out for help, but they just laughed. "We don't need no help here, honey. I think you can take care of both of us, right here," and the one nearer her reached out to grab her arm.

Abby swung at him hitting him a glancing blow across the bridge of his nose. He paused a moment and broke into a clownish grin. He tore off his own jacket and began loosening his belt.

Abby was horrified at her predicament. She swung again at the intruder hitting him harder this time. His partner laughed and called out, "Hey, Jim, watch out! We've got a live one here!"

The man responded to Abby's attempts to protect herself with a hard slap which crashed across her cheek. She felt dizzy from the blow. She stumbled back against the brick wall hitting her head as she tumbled. Then the man grabbed at her jacket and blouse. They both ripped open with a single motion. In the process, he had lifted her partially to her feet. She put up her arms to try to push him away. She scratched and clawed at him, but even in his state of inebriation, he was quick enough to grab both of her arms and trap her against the wall.

Abby struggled as much as she could. All the while she felt dizzy from having hit her head. Suddenly his mouth was on hers with his beer-soaked beard scratching against her swelling cheekbone. She pulled her face away from his, but cried out again when his hands fumbled to remove her exposed corset. In frustration, he tore repeatedly at her clothing until it hung in shreds from her waist. Crying, she screamed, "Please let me go! I'm not who you think I am."

Suddenly she felt her skirt being lifted as his hands fumbled to undress her more. "Come on, now, honey. Enough's enough. Let's get down to business." He pressed his upper body against hers and pinned her against the wall.

Abby was weak with terror and felt all of her strength leave her body. She felt his wet beard on her neck, and his clumsy hands pulling and trying to expose her breast. Her head ached from being knocked against the wall, and her swollen cheek bone felt on fire. With what she thought would be her last breath, she cried out one more time, "Stop! Let me go!"

"Captain, we could take a short-cut down Franklin Street to get to the carriage," offered Corporal Davis.

"Now, Corporal, you know the Colonel would totally disapprove of us going down the Red Light district," Garrett answered. "We can go the long way around."

"But Captain, we're already late because of this fog. I promised to have you back at the fort by 10 o'clock. It's nearly 9 o'clock now. With this fog around, it's going to be difficult to find our way safely up the hillside. Sir, if we just run down this way, we can be there in no time."

Garrett frowned, but reluctantly agreed. They strode quickly down the street with the fog lifting a bit, when Garrett stopped suddenly. "Did you hear that?" he asked the Corporal.

"What?" he asked, obviously more intent on getting to the carriage.

A voice from the darkened alley just to Garrett's right called out in an accent he recognized immediately. He turned in the direction of the cry. In the rising mist and shadows he could see what appeared to be two or three people. As he moved closer, he heard a man say something like 'hurry up.' Then squinting to see better in the dark and fog, Garrett saw what looked like a man accosting a woman. Taking one more step, he demanded in his officer's voice, "What's going on here?"

One of the men angrily replied, "None of your business, blue belly! Now get!"

"Help me, please," came a familiar voice from the end of the alleyway.

Without pausing to think, Garrett reached and grabbed the man who was forcing himself on Abby. In an instant, Garrett swung the stranger around to face him, and slammed his fist squarely into the man's jaw. He whelped in pain and slumped against the wall in the alley.

The stranger's partner immediately reacted brandishing a weapon, "We saw her first. She's ours. You can have her later," he announced, threatening Garrett with the large blade of a hunting knife.

Garrett grasped the man's unsteady arm, and easily twisted the blade loose with his strong hands. Then he punched the man in the upper belly. The drunk collapsed, coughing and trying to catch his breath.

The other man, by now, was alert enough to realize he needed to fight back. He found a piece of wood lying in the alley and swung it across Garrett's back. The rotten wood broke immediately, raining splinters over Garrett. It was at this moment that Corporal Davis stepped forward and cocked his pistol, "Another move, mister, and I shoot you dead right here where you stand."

Both drunks stopped struggling and didn't move a muscle. Garrett pushed the man nearest him over into the corner of the alley and quickly moved to Abby's side. She had collapsed to the street, her clothing in tatters. He tried to straighten her up, but there didn't appear to be enough fabric left in the top of her dress to cover her. He gasped as he realized her condition. He fought the urge to kill those animals with his bare hands. Instead, he tore off his cape and chivalrously wrapped it around her shoulders gently covering her exposed skin. Then he lifted her in his arms and carried her out of the alley.

"Something I can help you soldiers with?" a policeman asked.

Garrett answered immediately, "These men were accosting this woman. They need to be arrested."

"We don't arrest men for soliciting prostitutes on Franklin Street," the policeman replied matter-of-factly.

"She's no prostitute. She's Colonel Randolph's daughter," Garrett replied angrily. "Arrest them!" he demanded again.

"No, please don't," Abby said weakly. "Father mustn't know. Please, Garrett."

"She doesn't seem to want them arrested, Captain," replied the policeman. "Maybe you should take the lady on home and keep her there out of trouble."

Garrett wanted to argue the point, but his immediate concern was to get Abby home safely. He held her tightly in his arms and edged past the policeman. He hastened to the end of the street with Corporal Davis leading the way. Once they had found the carriage, Garrett handed

Abby to Roger until he climbed up to the seat first, then reached back for Roger to lift Abby up to him. Once she was sitting on his lap, he draped his arm comfortably around her bruised arms while Abby rested her head on his shoulder. She shuddered and trembled, and he tried to calm her with simple shushing sounds.

A thought came to him as they hurried steadily toward the fort. "Be sure to use the back gate, Roger. We don't need to give Edith any more gossip to spread," Garrett said.

Roger nodded, "Yes, sir. I'll get us home without her knowing a thing. Don't you worry."

With the Corporal driving the carriage, Garrett held her protectively in his arms all the way home to Fort Douglas. Tomorrow would be soon enough to talk again about punishing those drunks.

CHAPTER 10

Abigail awoke with a pounding headache. She grabbed her head instinctively, and reacted to the soreness in her arm as she raised it. When she felt a hand softly touch her forehead, she jumped nervously.

"It's okay, sweetie. It's Helen. You're here at home," she said softly.

Abby turned and opened her eyes to see her friend. She sighed, and an errant tear rolled down her cheekbone, the salty tear stinging the open wound there.

"Ouch!" she cried as she brushed the tear away. Then the nightmarish memories of the evening before returned to her consciousness. She remembered the fear and the fog and those drunken evil men. She pulled her covers up to her face and sobbed anew.

"Now, now, there, sweetie. It's all right. You're safe. We're here with you, and nobody is going to hurt you anymore," Helen said softly.

"Oh, Helen, I'm so ashamed!" she cried.

"Ashamed of what, sweetie? You didn't do anything to be ashamed of. You were just in the wrong place, and some bad men tried to hurt you. But you're safe here now. Captain Talbot and Roger got you home, and nobody's going to hurt you."

Abby dropped the covers from her face and looked at Helen who was sitting at her bedside. "Do you know what happened?" Abby asked her. "I was looking for someone who lived in one of those houses because I wanted to help her. Then all of a sudden all this fog was around me, and I couldn't see my way back to the street car. The next thing I knew those men were there, and they thought I was . . ." she paused as Helen shushed her.

"You don't need to explain, sweetie. I know all I need to know. You're all right."

Abby looked down at the patches of blue marks covering her arms. She saw a fresh bandage wrapping a cut just above her wrist. She realized she was wearing a white muslin nightgown, and became puzzled. "How did I get . . ?" she started to ask.

"I bathed you last night when they brought you home. You were covered with dirt and smelled of stale beer. I bandaged that cut, put some witch hazel on the scratches and a cold cloth on the bruise on your cheek. I'm afraid it's quite swollen, but it'll most likely be gone before your father returns next week. However, I don't think we can salvage your blouse or jacket. Maybe I can clean the skirt for you."

"No! I don't want to ever wear it again, or the corset or petticoats. I don't want anything left to remind me. Please," she pleaded.

Helen shushed her again gently and nodded. "Don't worry, sweetie. I'll take care of everything," she said turning to leave the room.

Abby reflexively reached up to her breast bone needing to grasp for security. "Wait! Where's my locket?" Abby asked, panicking once again.

"Your locket? I'm sorry, sweetie, but you didn't have your locket when you got home last night."

She sighed at the thought of losing the one connection she had left of her mother. Then Abby looked up to see Helen easing out the door. "Where are you going?" she cried suddenly terrified to be left alone with this nightmarish memory.

"I'm going to step downstairs to get you something to eat, sweetie."

"I don't want to be alone," she cried.

"You're not alone, sweetie. Roger and Captain Talbot are just downstairs."

"Garrett? He's here?" she asked.

"Wouldn't leave last night. He slept on the sofa in your father's study. Insisted that he couldn't leave until he knew you were all right."

Abby sank back onto her tear soaked pillows. Her arms and shoulders ached, and every movement she made caused her some new pain. She was also aware of a gnawing hunger. She realized she would welcome something to eat, so she nodded to Helen. She lay in her bed with the awful memories of what had happened and what could have happened to her. She felt so foolish. Garrett had warned her, and so had her father. How could she have been so stupid? And now, on top of everything else, the locket her mother had given her was gone. Tears streamed down her face as she thought of the loss. It had been the sole reminder of her mother for the past several years now.

After what seemed to be an interminable period of time, Helen returned with a tray of warmed milk and biscuits. She placed the bed tray in front of Abby and asked, "Do you feel like some company? Captain Talbot is here. He needs to see you're all right. Can he come in, Abby?"

Abby pressed her lips together and frowned slightly. The movement made her head hurt more. Her first instinct was no; she didn't want anyone to see her like this. Then she realized she owed him a debt of gratitude for rescuing her. She should give him at least a personal 'thank you,' so she silently agreed.

Helen opened the door and beckoned for him to enter. He stood in the doorway surveying Abby's injuries. When she looked up at him, shame washed over her. He appeared embarrassed for her, and she couldn't really blame him.

"I brought this all on myself, didn't I, Captain?" she stated humbly. "You warned me about the danger I was getting myself into, and I didn't listen."

Garrett frowned and shook his head, "No, that's not what I'm thinking. I just wish I could have gotten to you sooner. Maybe--"

"You got to me in time, Garrett," she interrupted trying to soothe him. It suddenly occurred to her he didn't appear to be gloating or ashamed of her.

His gray blue eyes were ablaze with anger. "If I ever see those two men again, I'll kill them myself!" he exclaimed and pounded his fist into his other hand. "They should have been arrested, Abby. They're criminals!"

"Garrett, thank you for not having them arrested. I would just die of shame if my father found out," she answered softly.

"Your father would want them punished just like I do," he asserted.

"You may be right, but I don't ever want him to know I deceived him. He would be so disappointed in me, and he'd probably think I got what I deserved," she added guiltily.

"No. He would never think that, Abby. You really don't know him at all, do you?" Garrett carefully stroked her hand. "He loves you, Abby, just like—" He stopped short, then changed the subject. "At any rate, he would never want something like this to happen to you, never."

Tears streamed down her face as the guilt and shame overwhelmed her. Garrett removed the tray from the bed, and sat down at her bedside. Suddenly she collapsed on his shoulder, and he cradled her in his arms. She felt him gently rocking her back and forth, one hand stroking her hair which fell loosely down her back. She realized she had been stupid to think what she had wanted to do was safe. She had wandered into a dangerous situation never imagining what could actually happen to her there. It seemed the tears would never stop. She cried herself to sleep again, but when she woke up, he was gone.

It had been just over a week since the incident in Salt Lake City. The Colonel had returned from his trip just yesterday. Abby had decided to tell her father she had a riding accident to cover the still evident bruise on her cheek. Garrett wasn't totally comfortable with keeping the truth from his commanding officer, but he honored her decision because he knew she was doing this to keep her father from being disappointed in her. Garrett loved her and would keep her confidence even though he felt it was an unnecessary ruse.

When he closed his eyes, he could still see the way she had looked that morning after the assault: her arms scratched and bruised, her eyes puffy from crying, the swollen place on her cheekbone which looked tender and raw from a hard slap. Fiery emotions welled within him as he remembered the result of the evening. He had edged closer to the bed, his hat in his hand, trying with all his might not to cry at the sight of her in pain. He didn't know why, but he had felt responsible. It was all he could do to keep from grabbing her up in his arms.

Now he stood outside of the Colonel's office rehearsing the words he had decided to say. He hoped the result would be what he wanted.

Stepping into the open doorway, Garrett saluted, and waited for the Colonel to invite him inside. "Come in, Garrett," offered the Colonel. "You're just the man I wanted to see first thing this morning." He beckoned his adjutant to sit in the available seat facing his desk.

"Now what's this I hear about a riding accident?" he asked, smiling teasingly. "Must have been some low branch to have fooled her," he continued.

Garrett nodded nervously. Though he wouldn't reveal the truth about Abby's 'accident,' he wasn't going to lie directly. "Whatever she told you, sir, well, that must have been what happened. I only saw the aftermath."

"Pretty nasty bruise, though, wouldn't you say?" he continued.

"Yes, sir. I saw it a few days later, sir. Looks like somebody slapped her hard, but it wasn't me, sir," Garrett offered nervously. He hoped the Colonel was not getting suspicious, and he particularly hoped the Colonel didn't suspect Garrett had done something to hurt his daughter.

"Never entered my mind," the Colonel laughed. "You wanted to see me about something?"

Garrett cleared his throat, his nerves beginning to take over. He was suddenly aware his legs felt a little spongy. "Sir, I wanted to talk to you about our arrangement," he nearly stuttered.

The Colonel looked puzzled. He frowned, and cocked his head just slightly. "Is there a problem, Garrett?"

"Yes, sir, I mean, no, sir. I mean," Garrett fumbled, and reached up to loosen his collar. "Sir, when you asked me to look after your daughter, did you mean if things should change, that you would," he paused, swallowed hard, and continued, "you would allow me the honor of courting your daughter?"

Colonel Randolph frowned again, then smiled at the direction of this conversation. "Are you asking me for permission to court Abby?"

Garrett nodded, almost unable to speak for fear whatever words came out would prove inadequate.

"Have you spoken to my daughter about this?" the Colonel asked.

Garrett shook his head vigorously, "No, sir. I thought it right to speak first to you."

"Do you have any reason to think she would approve of this?" the Colonel asked, looking intently at Garrett to determine what might already be the relationship between the two of them.

"Sir, I don't know for sure. Like I said, I wanted to get your permission first, since you are her father and my commanding officer. You asked me to escort her as a favor to you; now I would like to officially court her with the possibility of . . ." he hesitated, not quite able to form the words.

"Son, are you asking to court my daughter with the intention of marriage?" the Colonel said finishing Garrett's sentence for him.

"Well, yes, sir. That is, if you agree, and if she approves, and oh, sir, this is all so nerve-wracking. This is worse than making an argument in court," he admitted.

Colonel Randolph laughed and stood up to breach the distance between himself and his adjutant. "Well, son, you have my permission. She does, of course, have the last say in the matter. I've learned long ago she wouldn't take orders from me. But I'd be pleased if she gave her consent and if the two of you should decide marriage was appropriate, I'd be delighted to have you as a son-in-law."

The Colonel grabbed Garrett's hand and shook it mightily. Then a thought came to him, "You know, the post Harvest Dance is in two weeks. Perhaps it could be your first official outing. Why don't you come over to the house this evening, and I'll let her know your intentions are honorable. With a little luck, she might agree to this new arrangement," he added patting Garrett on the back as he escorted him out of his office.

The Harvest Dance was an annual event held on the fort the last weekend in October. It was anticipated as much as Christmas and celebrated about as much as the Fourth of July. For weeks all of the women had been planning what they would wear, and the men had polished every brass button on their dress uniforms. Abigail was excited about the opportunity to dance again, though she wasn't quite sure the types of dances that might be available at a military ball. Nevertheless, she and Helen had talked endlessly about the coming event. On the morning of the dance, Abby could hardly contain herself. She felt very much like a young girl again. Now in her bedroom, Abby rechecked her accessories for her ensemble while Helen observed.

"What do you think about this necklace with my dress?" she asked almost giddy with excitement.

Helen looked up and smiled uneasily. Then she frowned and put her head between her knees. "Oh, I just feel awful," she announced.

Abby was alarmed. Helen had been such a rock to her these past three weeks since the incident in Salt Lake. The shared confidences about her feelings for Garrett and that horrible night on Franklin Street had strengthened the bond which had grown between them. They seemed to have grown even closer than sisters. Abby remembered her mother's fragile health, and looked at her friend with grave concern.

Helen had been sick quite often lately. What illness could possibly be troubling her?

"Can I get you something?" Abby asked. "Perhaps some tea?"

"I don't think I want anything just now," Helen offered weakly.

"Here, lie down on my bed," Abby said, gently pushing Helen's shoulder back onto the pillow. "Here, are your feeling any better?"

Helen nodded. She closed her eyes and let her head fall back on the pillow. "I can't remember ever feeling quite like this, Abby. Sorry to ruin your evening."

"Don't you apologize to me, Helen. Not after what you've done for me. I only wish I knew what to do to make you feel better," Abby replied stroking Helen's hair in an effort to comfort her friend. Then she touched Helen's moist forehead—no fever, but she appeared to be warm and damp.

"I'm better now, Abby. I don't know what came over me. I just suddenly felt very dizzy, and my stomach felt queasy. But I feel well enough to help you pick out your jewelry for tonight," she announced reaching for the set of beads Abby had placed on the dresser.

"I think these will do quite nicely," she added. "Captain Talbot will be so glad he asked you to the dance. You will undoubtedly be the most beautiful girl there tonight."

"No, Helen, WE will be the two most beautiful girls at the dance tonight. That lovely yellow brocade we found for you in town will make you the belle of the ball," Abby said hugging her friend. "Honestly, Helen, I don't know what I would have done without you these past months, and especially after what happened to me the night in Salt Lake. Thanks to you, it is beginning to become just like a bad dream. The only thing which makes it real is my lost locket."

Helen flashed a quick smile up at Abby who was standing in front of her mirror staring at the reflection of her gown which she held in front of her. It was light turquoise silk chiffon with darker turquoise ribbons adorning each bouffant short sleeve and one wider ribbon which encircled the tiny waist. Large pink hydrangea blossoms were embroidered eighteen inches up from the hemline with one matching blossom placed at the square bodice neckline. With her hair gathered softly into a bun high on her head, these simple glass beads and matching dangling earrings would be just the right touch, she thought.

"I'm just relieved you have managed to recuperate from that horrible night," Helen answered still looking at Abby who was holding up the dress to the mirror. "And now with Captain Talbot officially courting you, I think you'll be just fine."

Abby pursed her lips and crinkled up her nose. "Just as along as my father never hears about it, I think I'll be fine." She looked at Helen gratefully acknowledging the secret they had all kept for her.

Abby told herself her intention was not to deceive, but to protect her father. She didn't want him to be disappointed in her, not now, not when they were beginning to develop a true father-daughter relationship. And since the near tragedy in town that awful night, Abby had vowed to have no more dealings with the Women's Housing Association. She had come to feel this was a sign of God's will for her, and she was glad to be obedient. God had allowed her to step out on the edge of a precipice to see for herself, but had thankfully sent someone to rescue her from her own foolishness before it was too late. The loss of her mother's locket was disheartening; but thankfully, nothing more precious had been taken from her.

Now her life would take another direction, and perhaps it was God's will for her and Garrett plan a life together. "All things work together for good to those who love the Lord" she said softly to herself. Then Abby frowned as the hint of Helen's predicament began to emerge.

"Helen, you've been sick several mornings this past week, haven't you?"

"Yes, but I've continued to get things done around the house anyway."

"That's not my point. You've only been sick like this in the mornings, right?"

Helen nodded and searched Abby's face for a clue as to her meaning. Suddenly Helen's mouth fell open. "Do you think it's possible?" she asked as she sunk onto a nearby chair.

Abby grinned, "Yes, I think it's quite possible, even likely."

Tears welled up in Helen's eyes as she recognized the meaning of her condition. "It's almost too much to be hoped for," she uttered as tears of optimism and joy fell unhindered down her face.

Abby rushed to her side and hugged her friend. "This is just the best news ever!" Abby gushed with delight. With all they had been through recently, the possibility of something wonderful happening for Helen and Roger was just what they all needed right now. Abby and Helen laughed with each other as the likelihood of Helen's pregnancy became a reality.

Garrett stepped into the cavernous ballroom with Abigail on his arm. He had never felt as important in his life as he did at this moment, with all eyes of the company on him and his lovely companion. There was no doubt she was stunning in her chiffon gown. The combination of the electric lights and candles reflected in the fabric of her dress were like twinkling fireflies. When Colonel Randolph stepped up behind them to enter the room, a round of applause echoed throughout the hall.

They found a spot to both stand and wait for the music to begin. Garrett collected a dance card for Abby and wrote his name in nearly every line. He wanted it to be clear that she was his partner for the night. When the Colonel saw it, he laughed and nodded his appreciation. Garrett felt confident the Colonel approved of his attentions toward his daughter.

Then when he handed the dance card to Abby, she looked and grinned. "But, Garrett, I do intend to dance one or two of these waltzes with my father," she said glancing mischievously at her father to see his reaction.

Her father beamed and nodded. When the music started up for a fashionable two-step, Garrett bowed and led Abby to the floor and began leading her majestically around the room. Suddenly, dancing here with Abby, his world felt so complete.

They had danced to three two-steps and one waltz when Garrett finally felt winded and decided to lead Abby to a chair over near where her father was engaged in conversation with several of the other officers.

Garrett left her side to get some punch for the two of them, but when he returned, Abby was on the floor dancing with her father. Garrett smiled gratefully. He knew the Colonel must be feeling very pleased to be able to dance with his daughter after all these years.

"So it is official now, Captain? You are courting the Colonel's daughter?" asked Mrs. Hempstead who had eased over to where Garrett stood.

He nodded to her as he responded, "Yes, m'am, it's official. Got her father's blessing and all before hand."

The major's wife smirked. "I know he is pleased she will settle down soon. Maybe now she will not make all those weekly trips into town like she used to," she said looking up at Garrett with a squint which made him uncomfortable.

Garrett shrugged. He really didn't want to argue with Mrs. Hempstead, and he knew the least amount of information she got from him would be enough. Still he felt the need to defend Abby.

"M'am, I don't think there's anything I can do to settle her down, as you say, nor do I think I want to try. I'm proud of her just the way she is. But thank you for your good wishes."

"Well, son, I suspect she is willful. You may have to start exerting your influence soon in order to tame her. Otherwise, you will never have a moment's peace," she added, then moved away probably to find some other piece of gossip to deposit.

Garrett shook his head. There were busybodies everywhere, he thought. *I guess it's just lucky for me I know who she is and I can avoid her traps.*

Then suddenly he became alarmed. *Is it possible she knows about the incident in Salt Lake? It would be disastrous for all of us, if she found out.*

"Here you are, Garrett," announced the Colonel. "I'm worn out. I'm too old to be dancing with such a beautiful young woman," he said with his finger on his daughter's chin.

"You're not too old, Father," Abby smiled back. "But, I understand. I'm tired too. It's been quite a while since I went dancing with such fine partners as the two of you."

She gratefully accepted the cup of punch Garrett handed to her. Then she flashed Garrett a look with her sparkling green eyes surrounded by those dark, thick lashes, and he felt absolutely hypnotized.

They finished their punch, and Garrett led her out onto the terrace. He wrapped her shawl carefully around her shoulders so she wouldn't catch a chill in the night air. The stars overhead provided a lovely canopy; a chilly October breeze wrapped around them. Then Garrett turned to face Abby and announced, "Abby, you must know by now the effect you have on me. I'm a lawyer; words are my ammunition, and yet I often can't find anything to express the combination of emotions you inspire in me."

Abby smiled coyly. "Now, Captain, I think you do all right with the words you choose."

"You can be aggravating as all get out, sometimes, Abby, especially when you have some crusade in mind, and at other times, you are demure and graceful. You ride a horse as easily as any man I know, and yet you appear so regal sitting astride the saddle," he continued moving closer to her and placing his hand along the side of her cheek.

The swollen spot on her face was nearly completely healed now; there was only a tiny bruise there to show that anything had happened. He touched the spot gently to remind himself how he had almost lost her. He winced with the instant memory of her in danger, and impulsively, embraced her to shut it out of his mind.

"I couldn't bear it if anything happened to you," he whispered softly in her ear. Then moving back enough to see her face again, he continued, "You know I have asked your father's permission to officially court you. You should know my attentions now have nothing to do with the arrangement your father made with me before you arrived here. I just want you to be sure my intentions are honorable. I envision a life spent with you, Abby, if you will have me. I'm hoping over the next few months, we will make a decision together, and perhaps by spring, you'll agree to be my wife."

Abby beamed lovingly, and they gazed into each other's eyes. She nodded her understanding silently. Then he gently brushed his lips against hers to seal the promise.

Then, once again, desire took him by surprise, and his kiss became warm and intense. Her lips parted to accept his passion, and she reacted by tightening her arms around his neck. They lingered on the veranda in the moonlight luxuriating in the blossoming of their young love with the scent of spruce and pine wafting through the air and the sound of strumming guitars serenading them.

It was a moment filled with promise. Garrett believed the passion blazing between them would last a lifetime.

CHAPTER

11

The first two weeks of November brought with it much colder days sprinkled occasionally with sunshine. Each afternoon that Garrett took Abby strolling along the parade grounds, they noticed more and more leaves had fallen to the ground. Children laughingly gathered up this wealth, making piles to run and jump into. Their running and scampering about amused the pair as they strolled and shared their own childhood experiences. Their love was continuing to blossom even as the season brought an end to growing things.

Abby no longer tried to go into Salt Lake City on her own. Her sense of purpose had changed. Since her disastrous experience that one night, she no longer felt compelled to make a contribution in the lives of strangers. Though she continued to read to the children twice a week, now she focused on her developing relationship with Garrett, as well as her deepening love for her father. Somehow after all this time, it seemed enough to be the Colonel's daughter and to plan a future with a wonderful man. How she had changed since arriving at Fort Douglas.

Shared confidences between Helen and Abby had brought the two women even closer. When Helen had announced she was at least four months pregnant the morning after the Harvest Ball, Abby pitched in more around the house learning how to clean and cook alongside her friend. Only part of her reason was to help her friend. More than anything, she felt she needed the practice of running a household which Helen could teach her. Evening meals regularly included Garrett, and occasionally Abby tried her hand at preparing supper dishes to the delight of everyone. Helen was an excellent teacher in the kitchen.

After the meal, Abby and Roger together made short work of the kitchen detail. Afterwards, Helen could be found knitting in the parlor or playing Pan with Abby, while the three men played their evening game of chess, two playing and the other one watching to play the winner on the next night. With Helen and Roger spending much of their evening together with the Randolphs and Garrett, the five of them were becoming a family. The Colonel's residence was now a comfortable, pleasant place to be. Abby couldn't imagine a life that would be any more enjoyable.

Then one icy-cold morning, just after Reveille, Garrett showed up at the Colonel's front door carrying a lidded basket. When Abby answered the door, he offered it to her without any hint as to the contents. Puzzled, she took the basket from him and ushered him into the house. She carried it into the parlor noticing that whatever was inside seemed to jostle about clumsily. Setting the basket down on the table, she opened the lid, and a fuzzy ball of buff-colored fur crept slowly out of the basket.

"A kitten!" she nearly shrieked. "You've brought me a kitten!"

Garrett smiled; his gift had gotten the expected reception. "He's been hanging around the barracks for about a week. We bachelors have taken turns feeding and playing with him, but the weather is about to get colder, and this little one needs an inside home and someone to care for him regularly.

"Then I remembered that you said you loved playing with the kittens in the barn, and that you had a cat until you went away to Smith. So I hoped that you would like to take care of this little fella," he added reaching over to pet the purring mound of fluff that was now cradled in Abby's arms.

Abby's eyes filled with tears of happiness. "Oh, yes, I would love to take care of another kitty! What's his name?" she asked.

"Name? We never named him. Bachelors, you know, don't hang around long enough to name an animal," he laughed.

She held the kitten up and looked into its little face. She guessed that he was maybe seven or eights week old because his teeth appeared razor sharp. She then stroked his soft fur and put the kitten up close to her neck. He nuzzled there and pressed his paws into the shoulder of her woolen morning dress, purring audibly.

Abby grinned at Garrett and announced, "I'll name him 'Cotton' because he's so soft." Then she carried the kitten and his basket into the kitchen to find him something appropriate to eat.

Garrett watched approvingly; he knew that he would have to share Abby's attention with this little fellow from now on, and that was perfectly all right with him. Just as long as she was safe and happy, that's all that mattered to him.

The Utah sun had been obscured by brief episodes of rain mixed with snow since the beginning of November, but the first significant snowfall of the season arrived the week before Thanksgiving. Helen and Abby hibernated inside the Colonel's quarters, neither woman ready to brave the ankle-deep snow that blanketed the fort. Abby was content to spend time in the kitchen sharing cooking secrets with Helen, and planning preparations for Thanksgiving and Christmas dinners. At other times, the two women would huddle up in Abby's room under the multitude of blankets while Abby read aloud from some of her favorite novels with Cotton curled up asleep at her feet. And Abby was visibly excited about the prospect of Helen's baby which the post doctor thought would be born in March or April. Abby speculated that after the baby was born, she would schedule her wedding to Garrett; she wanted Helen to be her matron of honor, and she knew Helen would never accept if she were still pregnant.

"So, do you want a boy or a girl?" Abby asked as they warmed themselves by the large fireplace in the parlor the day after Thanksgiving.

"I haven't made up my mind just yet. But Roger definitely wants a boy. You know how men are," she laughed gently stroking the still small roundness of her belly. "Roger and I have wanted children for so many years now. I'd just about given up hope that it would ever happen. Now, here I am, looking forward to motherhood come spring. I can't remember being this happy before, except maybe when Roger first asked me to marry him."

Abby smiled her understanding. "Isn't it strange? A year ago I could never have pictured myself being happy sitting in front of a fireplace talking about marriage and motherhood. I was convinced that my life would consist of public involvement and crusades for women's rights. Now the only thing I'm really concerned about is how to make a pleasant home for my family. Look at me, I'm becoming settled, and I like it," she said as she reached down to pet Cotton who had just sidled up to her ankle.

Helen looked seriously at Abby, and suggested, "Perhaps that horrible night in Salt Lake had a positive effect on you, sweetie. You haven't seemed to miss participating in that women's group since then."

Abby shook her head. "I know scripture indicates that all things work together for good. Perhaps that is what has occurred here. I don't presume to know God's will, but I'm relieved that, as bad as it was, my father hasn't learned about that night. That part of my life is a distant memory I don't want to relive. It's a secret I intend to take to my grave."

Abby pulled the compliant kitten onto her lap and stroked his soft fur as she considered her past choices. She could never have predicted the change that had come about in her since Garrett had cradled her in his arms that foggy night. She had been so independent and self-sufficient. She had been determined to fight for women's causes and make a name for herself. Now, all she wanted was to look forward to the life of an officer's wife.

How strange that she should find herself considering living this life after having witnessed first hand the effects that the military life had on her mother. But here she was, and there was no place else she wanted to be. Perhaps knowing some of the details of her parents' choices before she was born had caused her to reconcile her attitude towards being a military wife. Whatever was responsible, she was just glad for the change that had occurred.

Suddenly, a gust of wind poured in through the open front door as Roger entered the house. Calling out for Helen and Abby, he quickly came into the parlor. He was breathing heavily, and gasped trying to catch his breath from running.

He continued to breathe heavily, sucking in large gulps of air. When he was able to catch his breath, he exclaimed, "We've got a problem, ladies. The Police Commissioner from Salt Lake City is here. He asked to see Colonel Randolph about a reported incident in town involving two of his soldiers and his daughter. Miss Randolph, I'm afraid your secret is about to be revealed in just about the most unkind way I can think of!"

Captain Talbot hurried quickly to the Colonel's office after having received a notice to report there immediately from one of the Colonel's staff privates. He wondered what could be so urgent. He had turned in the October reports that he requested last week. Could there be some discrepancy on those documents?

He entered the office with the required salute, and was taken aback at the look of disdain on his commanding officer's face. This reaction couldn't be from last week's reports, he thought to himself. But what could it be?

"Sit down, Captain," he said tersely. Usually the Colonel addressed him by his given name. Garrett realized that something serious was about to be discussed. He quickly complied with the Colonel's command and waited. His left leg began to bounce nervously. He pressed his hands down his thighs to control it.

"I had a visitor this morning, Captain," the Colonel began pacing behind him in the office. Garrett couldn't see the Colonel's face, so he had no clue of what was to happen. "The Police Commissioner came to see me about a report he read. Do you have any idea what that report was about, Captain?" the Colonel asked waiting to see if he could get a reaction.

Garrett's breathing quickened. He wasn't sure what the Colonel knew, so he decided to let him complete the information before adding his own comments. Garrett nodded his head, though, because he knew enough to be honest with his commanding officer.

"He told me about an incident that one of his officers reported in which two of my soldiers broke up an assault on a young woman. The officer at first suspected that the woman was one of the prostitutes that live on that street. But then one of the soldiers told the officer that the woman was the daughter of the colonel. Imagine my surprise to hear of this incident from a stranger, Captain, when my own adjutant was present on the scene and chose not to inform me. When I tried to suggest that there must be some kind of mistake, he handed me this broken locket of Abby's," he continued, motioning to the damaged necklace lying on his desk.

"To say the least, I was embarrassed that no one bothered to tell me about this. And why weren't these two hooligans arrested and charged with assault? If you prevented my daughter from being raped, why didn't you see to it that justice was done to them?" he asked angrily.

"Answer me, Captain! I want to know why my most trusted officer would betray my confidence and deceive me in this manner! What kind of low life would do such a thing? And to think I've given you permission to court her," he demanded furiously.

"Don't blame Garrett, Father," Abby spoke up from the opened doorway tracking in ice and snow as she entered the room. "It was my fault, entirely," Abby confessed shutting the door behind her making their conversation more private. "I was where I shouldn't have been, and I was just fortunate enough that Garrett and Corporal Davis came along when they did."

The Colonel looked intently at his daughter. "And just what were you doing on Franklin Street at night anyway?" he asked, his tone only slightly softened by her presence in the room.

"Father, I was wrong to deceive you. I had been meeting each week with the Women's Housing Association. It's a group of society women in Salt Lake who are trying to help former Mormon wives who are now having to resort to prostitution in order to survive."

The Colonel's eyebrows arched so high that Garrett thought they might actually escape his face. "Why on earth would you want to be involved in such a dangerous venture?"

Abby nodded, "I know. Garrett told me, and in fact, he warned me to stay away from this cause, but I wouldn't listen, Father.

"And don't blame Garrett for not telling you either, because I swore him to secrecy. Neither of us wanted you to be disappointed in me. I'm so sorry, Father," she added, her green eyes glassing over. Suddenly tears streamed uncontrollably down her face.

"I was so embarrassed by my own foolishness. I never wanted you to find out. I was afraid that you'd be humiliated by my actions, and I couldn't bear losing your respect," she sobbed.

The Colonel looked silently at his daughter. Garrett could tell that anger and compassion fought to control his reactions to his daughter's words. Now with tears running down her face, the Colonel seemed to be unable to resist comforting her. He put his arms around her and began patting her back gently while she buried her face into his shoulder. Garrett watched as the Colonel pulled her tightly to his chest and began to cry softly with her. Garrett suspected that the Colonel knew just how close Abby had come to irreparable danger.

Garrett sat motionless at the scene of father and daughter reuniting for the first real moment since she had come to the fort. With this secret now revealed, there was nothing but honest emotion between them. Garrett felt he should leave them alone, but the Colonel saw him edging towards the door, and stopped him.

"Garrett, I can't say that I'm not still a little disappointed that you didn't tell me about this yourself, but I'm grateful to you for rescuing her. I don't even want to imagine what could have happened if you hadn't come along when you did. I appreciate that you're an honorable man, and that you're true to your word. I guess what I'm trying to say is that my daughter is blessed to have someone of your character protecting her." Then Colonel Randolph embraced his daughter again, and let Garrett slip quietly from the room.

CHAPTER

For several days after the revelation of the incident in Salt Lake City, Abigail moved more humbly around her father. It was at least a week before he consented to having supper with her and Garrett again, but after that first night together, gradually things began to return to the normalcy they had experienced.

The Colonel had agreed to a chess match after supper, and later he even let Abby teach him how to play Pan which he won twice. Though she knew he still felt hurt that she had deceived him, Abby hoped her father had essentially forgiven them both, and was now looking forward to their engagement.

Now with Christmas just ten days off, Abby and Helen scoured the downtown shops for appropriate gifts with Roger, trodding behind them carrying their parcels. Abby found a beautiful locket for Helen which she secretly purchased without her friend suspecting a thing. She had also found the perfect pocket watch to give to Garrett. She knew that he had been wanting one since his had been lost two years ago. And now she and Helen were in the local bookstore looking for a gift for her father.

"Do you have a copy of <u>Ben Hur: A Tale of Christ</u>?" Abby asked the clerk. "It's a book written by Brigadier General Lew Wallace," she added trying to help him locate the book for her. "My father is Colonel Randolph, the commanding officer at Fort Douglas. He's heard about this book written by a former general from the Civil War, and he would like to read it. I thought I would surprise him with it for Christmas."

The clerk ran his fingers along the spines of the books until he found the one remaining copy in the store. "Oh, this is just perfect," Abby said. "My father will be so happy to get this."

The clerk quickly wrapped the book for her, and as she was on the way out of the store, her eye was caught by a poster in the window. She stopped in her tracks to read, 'Vote for Matthew Broadnax—A Mayoral Change for Salt Lake City.' Turning back to the clerk, Abby asked, "Is this a Mormon owned business?"

"No, m'am. Why do you ask?" the clerk instantly replied.

"This sign in your window, isn't he a Mormon?" she inquired, knowing the answer.

"Mr. Broadnax? Why, yes, m'am, he is, but Mr. Broadnax has been so helpful to us with financing the improvements. He's a Vice President at the bank, just down the street. Because he's been so kind to us, we agreed to advertise for his campaign. Sure hope he wins, too."

Abby nodded, and strolled out of the store with Helen. Roger was waiting not too patiently outside for them. After agreeing to head back to the fort, Abby glanced back in the direction of the bank. For an instant, she thought she saw someone who looked like Dorothy walking out the door and across the street to a waiting streetcar.

Garrett sat musing over the past several days. This was the best Christmas he could remember since his childhood. He had been part of a family celebrating and feasting, opening gifts, and enjoying the laughter shared with the Colonel, Abby, and Helen and Roger. He couldn't imagine a better time. It had reminded him of his parents, brothers, and sisters, and it made him grateful to be included in this new family.

He caressed the pocket watch that Abby had given to him for Christmas. He could still remember the look on her face when he opened the carefully wrapped gift. He had completely forgotten she knew he had lost his watch, so when he saw the shiny gold timepiece with matching chain, he was totally surprised and pleased. She had selected just what he had envisioned having someday.

And her father had been equally surprised with the book she gave him. Garrett had witnessed another new trait in her character that was ever so attractive, her thoughtfulness. He'd watched as she waited on Helen. He'd seen her cleaning up the supper dishes and bringing everyone coffee. He didn't think it was possible to love her any more than he already did, but each new discovery about her only deepened the feelings he had for her.

He walked over to his dresser and picked up the tiny blue box that held the ring he intended to give her on New Year's Eve. He had debated giving it to her for Christmas, but he had decided that he didn't want the ring to become just another Christmas gift.

Not every man offered a token to his fiancé for their engagement, but he had heard that back East, the more educated men did. Garrett wanted her to know she was special to him, and that he was serious about marrying her.

He opened the box and stared at the sparkling garnet surrounded by tiny diamonds. He had decided upon a garnet because it matched the color of her hair. He hoped she would be pleased with his choice, at least as pleased as he was with the pocket watch.

With New Year's Eve less than a week away, he was still having trouble waiting. Each day seemed an eternity. He fully expected she would say 'Yes' to his proposal. Still the wait was making him feel very tense. He closed the box and replaced it in the top drawer where it would remain. He had no inkling that circumstances were about to turn his life upside down.

Abigail hurried to the Officers' Club trying not to get the edge of her dress and cape too damp from the melting snow. Her father had suggested she offer to assist with the arrangements for the New Year's Eve Party that was being planned by the officers' wives. Since she would be one of them in the near future, her father had said she should get to know these ladies a bit. He felt working together on a project would be the quickest way for her to be accepted.

Even though she had met and talked with most of these women over the past months, this would be the first time Abby had actually worked together with them. She had to admit she felt just a little bit anxious, especially knowing Edith Hempstead was in charge of the event. Just to be sure that everything went well, Abby had practiced biting her tongue several times last night. But she was determined to win all of these women over. It was necessary in order to become a part of the community; she needed to do this for both her father and Garrett.

Coming into the building, Abby sauntered quietly to the room where her father said the women would be working. She noticed some mud on her shoe, so she bent down to wipe it off, when she overheard a woman's voice just on the other side of the door. She moved closer to the door where she could listen without being seen.

"I do not care what anyone else says, the Colonel's daughter is nothing more than a common trollop. You all know how she claims that she was attacked on Franklin Street. Everyone knows that is where streetwalkers and prostitutes do their business. She is just a woman of easy virtue!" Edith Hempstead asserted.

"But Captain Talbot was able to rescue her. Surely you don't believe that he would have done that if he thought she was what you say she is," replied one of the other women there.

"Rescue? More likely he saw an opportunity to take advantage of the situation. Maybe that is the real reason he is pretending to court her now," she added with a sneer.

"I'm sorry, Edith, but I can't believe such a thing about Captain Talbot. He's a decent, honorable man," said Carol Randall.

"Well, at any rate, Captain Talbot is a fool if he thinks that Abigail Randolph is a good catch. Or maybe he just feels sorry for the Colonel because he knows that his daughter would never receive an offer of marriage from anyone else. Poor Garrett. He is caught in a terrible situation. This will certainly end his career," Edith announced.

"Why do you say that, Edith?" Carol asked.

"Well, everyone knows that Colonel Randolph will never be promoted to general because his father and grandfather were officers in the Confederate army during the War. If Garrett marries her, that stigma will follow him, too. And the Colonel's daughter does not follow the rules of proper etiquette, wandering around all sorts of places without a proper chaperone. Did you know that she and Captain Talbot went riding alone together, while her father was out of town? How scandalous! I warned the Colonel, but he would not listen to me.

"And now this latest situation, where she CLAIMS to have been attacked. Well, if that were true, why didn't she want the police to arrest those men? And why on earth would any self-respecting woman be out after nightfall in such a place? I say she just got caught being promiscuous and lied to cover her behavior. At any rate, poor Captain Talbot; he will be the laughingstock of the fort when he marries into that family."

"But I think he genuinely loves her, Edith," Carol protested.

"I seriously doubt that, Carol. My husband told me that Garrett really wants to be assigned to Army Headquarters in Washington. I think he is just trying to please the Colonel so he can get that transfer he wants. I mean, look at the way he helped the Colonel when that little hussy first came here."

"Edith, maybe we shouldn't talk about such things here. Isn't Miss Randolph going to be here to help with the arrangements today?"

"Hmpf! If she shows her face in here, I will tell her a thing or two! We certainly do not want her to be a part of our plans for the party. Why, she will ruin everything. But I do feel sorry for Captain Talbot, I do."

Abby's face was hot with anger and embarrassment. Tears welled up in her eyes as she turned and ran quickly from the club. She couldn't go face those women now, not when they had already formed such an abominable opinion of her. And what Edith Hempstead had said about her father hurt her deeply. Could she be right? Was that true? Was Garrett just trying to get a transfer recommendation? Could marrying her be the end of Garrett's career?

Abby rushed into the house racing right by a startled Helen. Abby muttered something about feeling ill, and wanting to be left alone. When Helen protested, Abby reminded her of her condition; she didn't want to put Helen in jeopardy by exposing her to some illness. Then Abby picked up Cotton, ran upstairs to her room, closed the door behind her, and broke down into uncontrollable sobs. She sank onto her bed still in her visiting dress feeling the weight of the entire world on her aching shoulders. Then she cried herself to sleep with Cotton curling up beside her, offering her the only comfort she would be able to acknowledge on what had become the darkest day of her life.

Garrett sat in his barracks room concerned about Abby. For the past two days, she had been too sick to leave her bedroom when he had called on her. Here it was the thirtieth of December, and she was still reportedly too sick to venture out of her bedroom. He hoped that whatever illness she had was not too serious. Missing the New Year's Eve party was not the issue; he could propose to her privately, just so long as she got well.

He was interrupted from his musings by a soft knock on his door. Opening it widely, he was shocked to see her. "Are you feeling better?" he asked immediately with her still standing in the hallway.

"I know it isn't exactly proper, Garrett, but may I come inside? I need to talk with you privately about something," she said quietly.

He quickly ushered her inside and closed the door. "Is everything all right?" he asked, concerned that her illness might indeed be more serious.

Abby eased to the window and looked out onto the parade grounds. She stood quietly for a few moments, then still with her back to him, she began to explain herself. "I don't quite know how to begin, Garrett. First of all, I haven't been sick, unless you count being overcome with grief and shame an illness," she admitted. "I've come here this morning to tell you I won't be able to accept your marriage proposal. I know this is terribly presumptuous, but I overheard Father telling Helen of your plans to ask me tomorrow night at the New Year's Eve party at the Officers' Club. After much soul searching, I just cannot do that to you."

Garrett was speechless and shocked. As far as he knew, their relationship had been perfect. There had been those bumpy places at first, but now, everything had seemed so completely right for him. "Why?" was the only word he could find to say.

She turned to face him as she answered him. "I'm just so sorry, Garrett. I had no idea the repercussions my behavior would have on you," she said softly, looking away from him. "If I could, I would take it all back, I swear I would. Now it's just too late. My reputation is ruined, and I cannot allow your character to be impugned because of me. I can't do that to someone I love."

"What are you talking about, Abby? How is your reputation ruined?" he asked pleadingly.

"Everyone on post thinks that I am a common trollup. They think that's the reason I was on Franklin Street. I cannot marry you because you would be the laughingstock of the entire fort," she continued with tears welling up in her green eyes. "You would never live down the shame of having a wife who was a woman with easy virtue, as I heard it put earlier this week."

"Who said that?" Garrett asked angrily, now realizing that she was reacting to something she had heard on post.

"It really doesn't matter. The fact of the matter is I didn't want those men arrested, so some people think it is because I wasn't really attacked. They think I lied about it the same way I have lied about other things," she continued tears now streaming unhindered down her face.

"They were right about my lying to my father and about getting you in so much trouble. No one will believe the truth now because I kept it hidden until it was too late. It's all my fault, but there's nothing I can do to change it."

"Who said these things to you?" he demanded.

"They didn't say these things to me. I overheard them saying these things to other people. That's why I know I cannot marry you. I cannot risk your happiness. I won't do that to you!" she cried.

"Abby, who did you overhear?" he asked softly with his hands on her shoulders trying to calm her.

She sighed and answered obediently, "Mrs. Hempstead was talking to the other officers' wives at the Officers' Club day before yesterday. I didn't have the nerve to challenge what she was saying. But she was right. It would be foolish of you to become involved with me. My reputation is ruined because of the hard-headed choices I made."

"I'm not marrying your reputation, Abby, and I don't care what other people think about you. I especially don't care what Edith Hempstead thinks or says about us. I love you, and I want you to be my wife." He reached into the drawer and withdrew the ring box. "See, I even bought a ring to seal the promise," he said showing her the tiny box with the delicate garnet ring inside.

Abby fingered the lovely jeweled item. Then she wiped her tear stained face with her gloved hand, and turned away from Garrett.

"It's not just that, Garrett. She said your career would be destroyed if you married into our family because of my grandfather's support of the Confederacy. I've known for years that my father has felt that he was denied a promotion to general because of his father's and grandfather's involvement. If you were to marry into our family, that stigma would keep you from advancing in your career, as well. I couldn't live with that, Garrett. You deserve so much better than this."

"My career doesn't matter nearly as much as you do to me," he asserted. "So what, if I don't get promoted ever again. My life with you will more than make up for that."

"You say that now, but in time you'll grow to resent me because of the disappointments you'll experience. I would just die if that happened, Garrett. I'd rather end our relationship here and now than to have you grow to hate me and my family."

Garrett became exasperated. "Let's talk with your father about this. I'll bet he can put a stop to her gossip."

"No! Garrett, you mustn't say anything to my father," she said as she turned back around to face him.

"It would just destroy him to know that such things are being said about me and about him. I'd rather die first! No, please, if you love me like you say you do, promise me you won't tell my father about this. I've already hurt him enough by lying to him about the Women's Housing Association and what happened that night in town. I just can't bear to hurt him anymore, and I think this would just kill him!" she cried in desperation.

"Abby, no. We got into this mess because of lies and half-truths. Let's tell him the truth tonight and be done with trying to keep secrets," Garrett asserted.

"Garrett, please. I cannot bear to disappoint my father again. It would just crush him to hear what I heard." She walked away from him and dabbed at the tears streaming down her face.

Then she turned back toward him, sniffed, and began again. "You know that I've spent most of my life yearning for a relationship with him. I can't risk losing what little I have gained these past months. I just can't! Please, try to understand. I love him too much to lose his love," Abby paused, reached to wipe away the freshly flowing tears from her face, then turned away from him to look out the window.

Snow had begun to fall again. The flakes looked almost like large feathers falling gently to the ground. The bitter cold outside seeped unbidden into the room. Garrett shivered reflexively.

Abby continued to stare out the window when she softly added, "Know this, too; I love you, Garrett. I know I'll never find anyone who'll be able to fill the hole which is in my heart at this moment. But I love you too much to saddle you with the humiliation that will certainly come your way if we get married," she added. Abby turned back to face him and took his hands in hers. She gazed up at him with penetrable sadness etched in her eyes.

Garrett looked down at his hands. He gently squeezed her small hands before she pulled away from him. He couldn't believe that just a few short breaths ago he was planning a life with her. Now, all of a sudden, it had vanished like the snow melting below his window. Clutching the small ring box in his hand, he nodded his reluctant agreement with her request, and watched helplessly as she slipped out the door and out of his life forever.

CHAPTER

13

The heavy winter clouds that filled the sky for the first three days of 1896 clearly mirrored the depth of despair in Abby's heart. She spent most of the time in her room rereading her favorite books, but even they brought her no consolation. Her life seemed to have come to a crashing halt, and she had no one to blame but herself. She had made several catastrophic decisions over the past several months which had resulted in misery for so many people in her life, especially Garrett. She knew he was suffering because of her, but there was nothing she could do. She felt she deserved whatever unhappiness that now befell her.

After the initial shock had worn off, her first instinct had been to return to Boston, but her father, who had been totally startled by her breakup with Garrett, had firmly rejected her suggestion to leave Fort Douglas. She needed the support only he could provide, so she had reluctantly agreed to remain, at least until Helen's baby was born. Those were the only bright spots in an otherwise desolate future: a new baby and her relationship with her father. She was really relieved when he had insisted that she remain there with him.

Helen's advancing pregnancy made it necessary for Abby to pitch in more around the house. Working around the house was a welcome distraction. But each time she completed a task, her mind was flooded with the sense of loss that had enveloped her ever since she overheard Mrs. Hempstead's hateful words. She really couldn't argue with the conclusions made about her behavior since she had arrived at Fort Douglas. She had been imprudent in her attempts to make a contribution in the lives of others. In the process, she had been dishonest with the very people she should have trusted with the truth. The result was this disastrous situation she had created herself. She was convinced there was no other recourse for her but to let Garrett go. As terrible as that was, it seemed to be the only appropriate action which would protect both him and her father.

Then late on January 4th, the news came that Utah had been granted statehood. After nearly forty years of disappointment, the citizens of Utah were ecstatic. That first night fireworks blazed against the winter sky until nearly dawn the next morning. Everyone was celebrating. Parties were held in the streets downtown where crowds of people gathered to cheer their local politicians. Bands played, and people danced in the street even with the occasional snow flurries. While Abby could appreciate their excitement, and even feel somewhat gratified that women were going to have the right to vote as guaranteed by the new state Constitution, still she could not join in the merriment. Her sense of personal loss was still too fresh.

Two nights later, Colonel Randolph was invited to be a guest speaker at a public celebration where the formal documents declaring Utah a state would be presented. Afterwards, there would be parties all over the city, as well as another massive fireworks display. Corporal Davis wanted to attend, but Helen was unable to go because she wasn't feeling well. Besides, the icy night air would be a detriment to her health, so Helen decided to stay at home with Abby who still had no desire to go anywhere.

"We can play Pan, Abby," Helen offered, trying to suggest something the two of them could do together. Abby reluctantly nodded, and the two women proceeded to engage in a game they hadn't played since before Christmas.

After the game was set up, and they had played a few tricks, Helen asked, "I know it's none of my business, Abby, but you haven't been the same since you stopped seeing Captain Talbot. I can't believe that your relationship with him is irreparable. Is there anything I can do to help?"

Abby shook her head. "No, there's nothing anybody can do. I've already done enough damage for a lifetime," she admitted as she selected a card from the deck.

"Well, perhaps the Colonel could talk to him and find out what his feelings are," she offered.

"I know what his feelings are. But it doesn't change anything; it just makes it harder to do what has to be done," she continued and laid down her cards. "Are you sure you want to continue playing?"

"I just want to do something, anything, to cheer you up. You've been so unhappy this past week. I've really been worried about you."

Abby looked at the woman who had become her only friend in Utah. "Sorry for worrying you, Helen. You've been such a good friend, but I don't deserve any of your concern. In fact, I don't deserve anyone's concern. I did this to myself by being so dead set on having my way. I got myself into trouble in town, and now everyone thinks I was carousing with drunkards in the Red Light district."

Helen's eyes were wide with disbelief. "What!" she exclaimed. "Who thinks that? Certainly not me or your father. Garrett doesn't think that, does he? How could he? He was there and saw, just like Roger did. Those men attacked you. You have nothing to be ashamed of," Helen continued obviously trying to assuage Abby's unnecessary guilt.

Abby wiped away a stray tear. "Well, if I hadn't lied to my father, and if I had let the police arrest those men, perhaps the rest of the people on the fort would believe that. But they don't. They think I'm a, what is it, 'a trollop.' Marrying Garrett would make him the laughingstock of the post. I can't do that to him. I love him. I can't be responsible for ruining his life and his career," she admitted wiping away a few more tears.

Abby laughed softly, "I thought I had cried so much I wouldn't be able to cry again. Looks like I still have a few tears left."

Helen wrapped her arms around Abby and pressed her head down on her shoulder to comfort the younger woman. "Don't cry now. When we tell your father, he will straighten all this out," she assured.

Abby sat up abruptly. "No! You can't say anything to my father. It would just crush him to know what people are saying. And truly, it's all my own fault. He can't know. Please, please, don't say anything to him. It's enough for me to be heart-broken. I couldn't stand it if he knew what people are saying. I just couldn't take it!"

"But, dear, I know that he would understand, and he could put a stop to this gossip. Please, let me tell him."

"No, Helen. I cannot do that to my father. He's all I have left now. Please. You have to promise me you will keep my confidence. I cannot bear to lose both my father and Garrett. Please!" she begged urgently.

Helen reluctantly agreed with a nod. Then she embraced her again, and gently shushed her as Abby continued to cry softly on Helen's shoulder.

"I know it all looks impossible right now," Helen responded, "but I'm sure in time things will get better. But we don't have to talk about it right now, dear. You just rest here beside me and know that, as your friend, I'm willing to do whatever you need in order to help you, even if it means being silent."

Garrett had been in his barracks room sorting his clothes. Yesterday he had informed Colonel Randolph he would be leaving his commission at the end of the month, not that he had the slightest clue what he would do after he left Fort Douglas. He had been contemplating the possibilities when Lieutenant Chet Morgan had invited him to come along with some other bachelors to the Salt Lake City party in the street. With no other real distractions available to him, Garrett had agreed, hoping a change of scenery would alleviate his sense of hopelessness. But he didn't really expect it would help.

He had never experienced crowds like they found in the city that afternoon. It was more than he could remember at any of their Fourth of July celebrations or even their own Days of '47. The regular businesses were all closed; only saloons and cafes were open to provide for the bustling clientele. He and Lieutenant Morgan witnessed the presentation and saw Colonel Randolph, along with a variety of other dignitaries on the stage, welcoming Utahans into the United States of America. Garrett was proud of the remarks the Colonel made, but he didn't want to stand around too long there. Seeing the Colonel only made his own circumstances more unpleasant. And he didn't want to have to try to explain away the unexplainable again.

Lt. Morgan led him to a spot in a crowded saloon where they could sit for a moment. They ordered some beers to drink which seemed to take an excessively long time to be returned. When Garrett got up to try to find the waiter, through the crowd across the room he saw Corporal Davis talking with a police officer. For a split second, he worried that the Corporal might be in trouble; but then he saw the two men shaking hands. When the police officer turned in his direction, Garrett thought he recognized the man as the officer the two men had seen the night Abby was hurt. He tried to signal to the Corporal that he was there, but in the next instant, Roger and the officer were moving out the door together. Perhaps it was someone else.

Now all of a sudden, with everything Garrett was doing to get her off of his mind, seeing Corporal Davis reminded him of Abby. When the beer finally arrived at his table, he quickly drank the brew and ordered more.

When he wasn't fighting off her memory, he was fighting off the notion he had given up too quickly. Sure, she was headstrong, but what kind of man lets the love of his life just walk out of his life without a fight? Maybe he should have risked telling her father about the lies being told about her on post; but, then, there was the greater risk she would never forgive him if he broke his promise to her. He felt himself trapped in a web, and the more he struggled to get out, the more entrenched he became.

How in the world did he manage to get himself into this mess? Was there even enough alcohol in the world to drown his regrets? He raised the glass and swallowed the frothy brew. I sure hope so, he thought.

"Abby! Abby!" cried Helen standing in the doorway to her bedroom. "Roger didn't come home last night! He's never done that. Not ever," she cried sinking onto Abby's bed. "I'm so scared. What could have happened to him?" she asked with desperation in her voice.

Startled awake, Abby quickly got up and put on her robe. "Where did he go?" she asked, not quite remembering the events of the previous evening.

"To town, last night," she reminded her, "where all those parties and celebrations were taking place. But he hasn't come home. Oh, Abby, I'm so worried!"

"Don't worry, Helen. I'll get my father to go find him," Abby asserted.

"He's already left, Abby. You were still sleeping so I didn't want to wake you. Your father was going to get the captain to go with him into town to try to find Roger. The Colonel said he would probably start at the jail-- Roger probably got arrested for some minor disturbance. He said some folks got quite rowdy last night, even shooting guns in the air along with the fireworks," she replied obviously repeating everything that the Colonel had told her.

"Don't worry. Father will find him and bring him home. We'll just have to wait patiently. Why don't we go downstairs together now?" she said trying to comfort her. "You've got to be careful, Helen, for the baby's sake. Let's get you some tea and sit in Father's study. They'll be back in no time, and Roger will have a reasonable explanation. Just wait and see."

Helen doubled over, grabbing her abdomen. "Oh, what am I going to do?"

Helen fell heavily against the wall of the stairway in obvious agony. Instantly, Abby draped her own robe around Helen's shoulders and wrapped her in her arms. Helen leaned on Abby's shoulder and sobbed heavily while Abby gently rubbed her back. Then, when Helen had regained her composure, they trudged slowly down the stairs and into the study where Abby pressed her friend into the sofa and lifted her feet so she could lean against the side cushion. Then she found a warm blanket near the fireplace and covered Helen with it, tucking it in around her feet.

"I'm going to get dressed as quickly as I can. Then I'll get that tea. You rest here. Don't move. You need to take it easy, for the baby, you know. When I come back, we'll just sit here together until Father brings Roger home."

Garrett had readily agreed to accompany the Colonel back to Salt Lake even though he had a rather serious hangover from all of the alcohol that he had consumed. The ride into town with the icy cold wind blowing about his face helped to revive him some. By the time they stopped at the City and County Building, Garrett was beginning to feel human again.

The two men hurried into the building looking for the magistrate; the police captain saw two men in uniform, and immediately ushered them into a smaller room to wait. They sat there a few moments before the Police Commissioner entered the room and stood opposite from them.

Colonel Randolph stood up and shook hands with him. "I'm sorry to disturb you so early, Commissioner. One of my men didn't return to the fort last night. His wife is frantic, so I thought I would come to get him. I'll pay whatever fine is necessary; and I can assure you he will be disciplined on post as well."

The Commissioner looked grim and shook his head. "I'm afraid there's been a misunderstanding, Colonel. There's no fine for this crime. Your man was found with his gun in the bed of a prostitute this morning."

"That's totally against regulations, Commissioner. My men have been forbidden to use the services of the ladies in the Red Light district. He will be punished for this. I'll take him back now, if you please,"

"No, Colonel, you don't understand. The prostitute was shot, shot with your corporal's gun, and he's being charged with murder."

The Colonel and Captain Talbot looked at one another stunned. "Murder?" asked the Colonel not quite believing his ears. "That can't be possible. I know this man. He's not capable of murder."

"Nevertheless, he was found passed out in her bed, his gun lying on the floor. There's no mistaking that much. He claims he doesn't know what happened, but most criminals profess their innocence. I don't put much stock in that."

Garrett whispered something to Colonel Randolph who nodded in response before he stated, "Well, then, Commissioner, I guess we need to fill out the paperwork to have Corporal Davis transferred to the post stockade until trial." Then the three men exited the small room to the office where the official documents could be handled appropriately.

Abby and Helen were still in the Colonel's study when he returned from town. He took off his heavy cape and brushed dirty slush off his boots. He seemed to be in no hurry to relay the news to Helen, but she heard him come in the door and was on him before he could turn around.

"Where's Roger? What happened?" she asked, her voice betraying her panic at seeing only Colonel Randolph in the doorway.

The Colonel turned to face her, impulsively hugged her, and gently led her back to the study where the raging fire could warm them both. He sat her down on the settee, putting his right arm around her shoulder, as Abby stood next to her.

"Helen, Roger is in a lot of trouble," he began, trying to soften what he knew would be horrific news. "Something happened in town last night, and he's in jail. I filled out the paperwork to have him transferred to our stockade. Hopefully, by this time tomorrow, that's where he will be."

"In jail? In jail? For what, Colonel?" she pleaded, tears streaming down her face.

The Colonel swallowed hard and paused, gathering his words. "He's been charged with murder, Helen."

"What?" she cried, pulling away from him.

"That doesn't necessarily mean that he's guilty. Captain Talbot told me to assure you that Roger is certainly innocent of these charges, and a good attorney should be able to clear him."

"Murder? Murder? Who on earth is Roger accused of murdering?" Helen demanded frantically wringing her hands.

The Colonel sighed. There just wasn't any way to make this easier for her. "Roger was found in the bed of a prostitute who was killed last night. She had been shot, apparently with Roger's gun. They think he did it, though I spoke with him myself, and he says he doesn't remember anything about going to this woman's room last night."

"A prostitute? Roger was with a prostitute?" she exclaimed. "No! No! He wouldn't! I know him! He wouldn't do that to me."

Abby sank down on the settee next to her friend and tried to comfort her. This news was just so unbelievable. This didn't sound at all like the Roger she knew. Abby wrapped her arms around Helen as the woman broke down into uncontrollable sobs. The Colonel nodded at his daughter as he stood and wandered over to the blazing fire.

After several moments, Helen took a deep breath, and looked over at the Colonel. "Captain Talbot will represent him, won't he, sir?" she asked.

Abby stared at her father. He seemed to be struggling to answer her friend. "Ordinarily, yes, Helen. But Captain Talbot's tendered his resignation from the army effective the end of this month. He plans to be gone by the end of January. He won't be here for the trial, I'm afraid. Without any other legal expert on post, I'll have to secure a civilian lawyer for Roger. But don't you worry about this. I'll handle it for you, and Abby and I will stand by you and Roger every step of the way."

Helen's jaw dropped and her eyes grew wider with the realization. Her husband was found with a dead prostitute, charged with murder, and now she would have to rely on a stranger to defend him.

She turned to Abby and, grabbing her shoulders, she pleaded, "Abby, you've got to stop the captain from leaving. He's Roger's only hope! Please, Abby! You've got to persuade Captain Talbot to stay and defend my husband."

CHAPTER

14

Garrett was cleaning out his desk, sorting through the personal items that he wanted to keep. He looked down and saw the pocket watch Abby had given him for Christmas. He picked it up and held it lovingly in the palm of his hand; he'd put it in the drawer just last week because every time he looked at it, he was reminded of her. He was gazing at the face of the clock, when she stepped into his office.

He looked up to see her dressed in a dark blue winter suit dress with matching gloves and hat. She looked very business-like, and yet a softness seemed to radiate from her. Seeing her just now, when he felt so vulnerable to her, made his heart begin to race. He longed to rush to her and embrace her, but instead he took a step back. He just didn't think he could handle any more disappointment.

She closed the door gently behind her and sat in a chair on the other side of his small office. After she had settled there with her hands in her lap, he stepped out from behind his desk and sat opposite her.

"I heard that you plan to resign your commission, Garrett," she said softly. She twisted her hands in her lap, waiting for his reply.

He nodded solemnly. There was no need to explain his reason for wanting to leave.

She pursed her lips, and shook her head, "You can't leave just yet, Garrett. Roger needs you," she said simply.

"I know Roger is in a lot of trouble, Abby. But the Colonel will get him a lawyer from town who'll defend him in court."

"That's not good enough, Garrett. He needs you," her voice only slightly stronger than a moment before.

"I won't be here next month when the trial is scheduled to begin, Abby. I'm leaving in just a few days," he replied, not sure if she could hear the trembling in his voice.

He turned to look away from her. He couldn't talk to her without wanting to embrace her and have her say that she had changed her mind. But she didn't seem to be here for herself. She seemed a little distant and controlled.

"My father will be glad to extend your commission, at least until the trial is over, Garrett. No civilian lawyer can do the job that you can do."

"Abby, I don't really have any criminal court experience. I mean, I know the procedures and such, but I've never tried a murder case before. I don't even think I know how to begin," he added trying desperately not to disappoint her.

"Garrett, you have something no other lawyer has; you know Roger. You know that he couldn't have done this. No one else'll believe in him that way because they don't know him like you do. Please, Garrett, if not for Roger, do it for Helen; and if not for her, then do it for me. Please!" she implored, her voice cracking slightly.

He shook his head. He just couldn't allow himself to give in because it would mean remaining on post without the woman he loved. It was already intolerable enough just knowing that she was just a few steps away from him at this moment, and yet she seemed beyond his reach.

"Oh, Garrett, I know I've hurt you terribly. If I could change the way things happened, you know I would. But this isn't about us. It's about two people we both care about and how their lives are going to be ruined if we don't do something to help them. Garrett, you're the only person who can do this for them. Please, don't let what has happened between us keep you from doing the right thing for them. They need you."

He got up from the chair and moved over to the window. He stared out at the snowflakes which had just begun to drift easily to the ground. Abby was right. He had a duty to Roger who had always been a reliable friend, as well as a good soldier. Even though he longed to put physical miles between himself and Abby, he knew in his soul that he would never forgive himself if he turned his back on his friend. He turned and walked back over to his desk.

Facing her, he said, "I'll need to go into town to get the police report and see it for myself first," he announced matter-of-factly. "Then I'll go see Roger to see if he can give me any insight into what actually happened."

"Oh, thank you, Garrett! Thank you!" she gushed, relief in her voice unmistakable. "Helen will be so glad to know that you've agreed to defend him."

"There's no guarantee that I can get him out of this. They found him in the woman's room with his gun lying on the floor. That's pretty damning evidence. It'll depend on his explanation for how he got there. Believing him is not enough. I will have to find evidence to clear him, and that'll be pretty tough."

"I'll help, Garrett. Just name it, and I'll do whatever you need in order to help Roger and Helen."

He started to take advantage of her offer, but decided against it. He shook his head before he responded, "I'll come by the house later tonight to talk to Helen about the case. I would appreciate it if you would ask your father to extend my commission for awhile so I can prepare to take this case to court."

Abby nodded, then stood and gazed appreciatively at him. She took a few steps so that she was directly in front of him. Her usually bright green eyes seemed to be swimming in pools of tears that would not fall. She covered her mouth briefly, before suddenly reached up to kiss him on the cheek. In the next moment, she turned and eased quietly out of the room.

Moments after she left, he sighed deeply. <u>How in the world am I going to be able to figure this out?</u> He collapsed into his desk chair and covered his face with his hands. Questions swirled around him, reawakening the headache he'd had from the night before. Roger's predicament was critical, and he knew it. But he struggled with his own situation. He knew how he still felt about Abby. Being around her right now would be difficult.

Garrett took a deep breath before entering the stockade where Roger had been moved. He had managed to get a copy of the police report from the guard, and he took it with him to talk to Roger. He needed to get first hand information from the Corporal in order to begin to make sense of the case he had agreed to take. And even then, this was going to be extremely difficult to handle.

Roger was brought into the small interview room wearing heavy shackles on his ankles and wrists. Garrett motioned to the guard to remove the chains, and he reluctantly agreed to do so. Roger sat down at the table across from the captain with his head in his hands as if he was heading to the gallows immediately. Garrett's heart went out to him.

"Captain, I couldn't have done this. You gotta believe me. I couldn't have," he sobbed.

Garrett nodded his understanding. "I know, Roger, I know. That's why I'm here. I'm going to do my best to try to get you out of this mess. But you've got to help me by telling me what happened."

The Corporal nodded, "I don't remember anything. Oh, God, this is some sort of nightmare. It has to be. I couldn't have done that, could I?" he asked, tapping the sides of his head as if to try to shake out a trapped memory in there.

"Relax, Roger," Garrett said. "Stop blaming yourself and help me figure this out? For starters, how'd you end up in that woman's bed?" Garrett asked point blank.

Roger shook his head. "Wish I knew, Captain. Wish I knew."

Garrett frowned. "What do you remember, then?" he asked, puzzled that the Corporal couldn't even conjure up a decent lie about being in the murdered woman's bed.

Roger stood up and began to pace back and forth, his hands holding his head as he swayed to and fro. "I was going into town with some of the company men. I remember being at Connor's saloon, it was really crowded, and the next thing I know I wake up in some dead woman's bed, and I'm arrested for murder," he said. "Captain, I swear I couldn't have done it."

Garrett carefully scanned Roger's face. Unless he had completely lost his mind, Roger was telling him the truth. But how was this possible?

Suddenly Garrett thought about the unusual scene from last night. "Do you remember meeting a policeman at Connor's saloon?" he asked trying to pry his client's memory.

Roger stood still, scratched his head, and slowly nodded, "No, wait, maybe," he said continuing to press his hands against the side of his head. "Yes, I think so. I think he was same one we saw on Franklin Street that night that Miss Randolph got hurt. Yeah, it was him," he answered a bit more confidently.

"I remember now. He came up to me and shook my hand; asked how the Colonel's daughter was doing. Then I think he told me something about a poker game." Roger continued to pace more slowly and frowned as he tried to reconstruct that night's events.

"Yes. It's getting clearer. He told me about a poker game over at Dixon's. I remember now, because I wanted to play a few hands and try to maybe win some extra money for the new baby," he continued as he sat down again in front of the captain.

"I think he went with me over to Dixon's— that part's still kinda hazy. But I think he brought me a drink after I sat down at the card table. But I never drink much when I'm playing cards," he continued, scratching his head as he struggled to put the pieces of the night together.

"When I'm playing poker, I want to keep all my faculties about me. So why does my head feel like I got hit by a train?"

"Do you remember playing cards at all?" Garrett asked, suspiciously.

"No. Not even one hand. And that's really strange. You know how much I love to play and win at poker. There's almost nobody on the fort who doesn't know what a good bluffer I am," he answered obviously proud of his reputation with cards.

Then he continued, more certain than before, "I left Connor's with that policeman. We went to Dixon's saloon, he brought me a drink, and the next thing I know, I'm in the bed with a murdered woman, and the police are arresting me. I swear, Captain, that's how it happened."

Garrett nodded. This story was just too unreal for it to be a lie. Roger's memory, coming back slowly, could only provide a few sketchy details to an event that would be impossible to forget if he had been aware. Was it possible he was so drunk that he committed this horrible crime without any sensibility of his actions? Garrett didn't know for sure. But he did believe Roger. He knew his character. This just didn't fit with what he knew the man was like.

Abby and Helen waited downstairs in the parlor for Garrett's arrival. The Colonel waited in his study, trying to relax by reading the book Abby had given him for Christmas. Abby could see he was having a difficult time keeping his mind on it. She knew he was really worried about Roger and Helen, just like she was.

From time to time, Helen would get up from the settee and pace nervously across the floor while Abby remained seated, though just as concerned. When the captain knocked on the front door, Helen rushed to the foyer, flung the door wide open, and threw her arms around him, thanking him over and over again for agreeing to defend her husband. As they stood in the open doorway, the winter wind rushed in and nearly extinguished the blaze in the hearth.

Captain Talbot finally closed the door and came into the parlor where both the Colonel and Abby stood. He led Helen to a chair, and they all sat down to hear his report.

"Helen, I believe Roger when he says he didn't do this. I believed it even before I spoke with him. Abby was right when she said that I know him. I do, and I know he couldn't have killed this woman," he said pausing to remove his heavy winter jacket. "Proving it'll be difficult, though, I'm afraid, because he has no memory of how he ended up in that woman's bed."

"What're we going to do?" Helen asked obviously frantic at the thought her husband could be convicted of a crime they all knew he did not commit.

"Well, that's the tricky part. I've got to find evidence," he admitted.

"What did the police report say?" asked the Colonel, trying to be of help.

"Not a whole lot. It simply states the suspect, Roger, was found passed out in Dorothy's bed, and his gun was on the floor. The police apparently determined it had been recently fired— one bullet was missing from the chamber. That's about all the information it gives except the address where the prostitute lived, the date, and the time. Oh, and it lists the person who made final arrangements for the body. There's not much to go on in here," he said as he laid the papers on the table in front of him.

Abby sat up straight and frowned, "Did you say Dorothy?" she asked. "Did the report mention a last name?"

Garrett looked at her, curious that she would react to the woman's name. Looking again at the report, he answered, "Yes, her name was Dorothy, but they don't list her surname in the report. That's strange isn't it? I would have thought they would be more thorough than to omit her last name."

"Maybe it's because she was a prostitute," the Colonel offered.

"Dorothy is the name of the woman I was trying to find that night on Franklin Street," Abby said excitedly. "Is it possible this is the same woman I met in the park?"

Garrett's brow was furrowed deeply as he remembered the night Abby had been assaulted. Then he shook his head and shrugged his shoulders. "There's no way to tell."

"The woman I met was named Dorothy Broadnax. She told me her husband was a powerful businessman in Salt Lake City. Surely there's got to be a record that'll let us know if it's the same woman."

"Well, I can ask, but I doubt anyone knows for sure. Sometimes these women only go by one name," he answered shuffling through the papers of the handwritten report.

Then he froze in place. "Oh, my God," he said. "I think you're right. The name of the person who took charge of her final arrangements was Matthew Broadnax."

"Oh, Garrett! That's her husband. Maybe he's the one who killed her, or had her killed."

Garrett shook his head. "What makes you think that? Just because he made her final arrangements doesn't prove he killed her, Abby," he replied seriously. "It could be he just felt guilty for her circumstances."

"Garrett, I know what I'm talking about. He's a powerful man in Salt Lake City; he's a vice president at a local bank; he's even running for mayor. Somehow, he did this."

"But if he was her husband, why was she working on Franklin Street?" the Colonel asked.

"She told me he put her and another wife out of their home after the church no longer sanctioned plural marriages. She ended up there because it was the only way she could support herself. That's the reason I was trying to find her that night, to help her get out of that place," Abby explained excitedly.

"Well, if her husband's responsible for her murder, I'm going to have my hands full trying to prove it," Garrett said emphatically.

"No, we'll have our hands full, because I'm going to help you find a way to put Dorothy's real murderer behind bars. I had wanted so much to help her when she was alive. It's the least I can do for her now that she's gone."

CHAPTER 15

The long ride into town on the street car had brought back memories for Abby. The first time the car lurched to a stop, Garrett had instinctively shielded her with his right arm to keep her from being thrown forward. Even as bundled up as she was, the touch of his arm against hers sent rivers of excitement through her; looking off in the distance, she daydreamed about the day they had last gone horseback riding together, and she felt warm all over. She remembered the feel of his face against hers, the warmth of his kiss, and the sense of safety she felt wrapped in his arms. Being this close to him was going to make the day very difficult for her. But she had to endure for Helen's sake. It was the least she could do for her friend.

On the way into town, Garrett had suggested how she should talk with the secretary at the bank. He wanted Abby to be sure not to tip the woman that they were investigating her boss. They had decided on a ruse, and she had practiced how she would phrase her words carefully so that no one would guess her motive. Arriving at the bank, Abby went in alone, leaving Garrett outside waiting, while she asked one of the clerks to show her to Matthew Broadnax's office. She took a deep breath before she opened the door to enter.

"May I help you?" came the cheery voice from behind the secretary's desk.

Abby nodded, "I hope so. I'm looking for information about my cousin, Dorothy Broadnax. I thought that Mr. Broadnax would be able to help me," she added dabbing her eyes as if she were wiping tears.

"Oh, you poor dear!" the woman offered, getting up from her chair and impulsively placing her arm around Abby's shoulders. "I'm so sorry for your loss. Dorothy was such a sweet lady," she added ushering Abby to a set of chairs in the office.

"Did you know her?" Abby asked as she sat down.

"Well, I met her a few times. She was so nice to me. By her manners and the way she dressed, you would never guess that she was the wife of such a powerful man as Mr. Broadnax," she continued. "He explained to me after that first time she came here they had eleven children, and she often sacrificed dressing well in order to provide instead for the children. I thought that was so good of her."

Abby nodded, realizing the secretary didn't know Dorothy had worked in the Red Light district, and obviously Matthew Broadnax had covered himself with a lie to explain why Dorothy was receiving regular payments from him.

"When was the first time you met her?" Abby asked, sniffing to keep the secretary from realizing this was an interview.

"October, I think. I've only been working here since last summer, you see. I wasn't aware she usually came by to pick up a little extra spending money each month," the girl added matter-of-factly.

"And when was the last time she came in? How did she look then? Oh, my dear, dear cousin," Abby cried softly.

The young secretary patted her on the back gently. "There, there, now. Everything's going to be all right."

She paused briefly, then continued, "I last saw her in December before Christmas. I gave her the envelope of money, and she said she was so glad her husband was taking such good care of her. She wished me 'Merry Christmas' that day. Said she was going shopping for gifts for some of the people she knew. I thought she was very generous to use her money to buy gifts for others," she said nodding her head and smiling. "Such a sweet lady."

"That's just like her, to show concern for others ahead of herself. Well, is her husband here?" Abby asked, knowing the answer.

"Oh, no dear. He's taking some time to be with the children. They've just lost their mother. He said he'd be out for the rest of the week. But I can give you his home address. I'm sure the family would love to see you, dear, especially at a time like this." She went back to her desk and quickly wrote down the address on a card for Abby.

Continuing with the ruse, Abby took the card, sniffed a bit more, and turned to the secretary, "Thank you, so much for your kindness. It was so good of you to tell me about my cousin. It helps me just to know what other people thought of her."

Then Abby glided out of the office and out of the bank. She couldn't wait to tell Garrett that Matthew Broadnax had been regularly giving money to Dorothy. He'd even lied about the reasons, probably to keep people from knowing she was a prostitute. That alone would be a motive for his wanting her dead; she was sure of it.

Garrett stood waiting outside the bank reading the local newspaper. He had scoured the entire paper before he had found at least one article about the crime. The local reporter had not used the Corporal's name or the name of the victim. He did, however, mention that Officer Dandridge had been first on the scene, and had reported that a soldier had killed her.

On the obituary page, Garrett found a brief mention of a funeral for Dorothy Broadnax, listed as the fourth wife of Matthew Broadnax, with eleven children surviving their mother. Abby had told him Dorothy herself was childless, but she had been a mother to all of the other wives' children. It seemed the funeral notice was part of the cover-up to protect Matthew's campaign for mayor. Just another lie.

"Look at this," he said handing Abby the part of the paper with the death notices.

She quickly read the entire notice before she nodded. "He told his secretary that Dorothy was his wife. He explained to the girl Dorothy would come by monthly to pick up a little extra money to buy things for their children. He is such a cad!" she exclaimed bitterly. "If I could just go back to the day when I met her in the park," she sighed and shook her head.

"You cannot fault yourself. You made every effort to help her," Garrett replied, trying in vain to comfort her.

"He kicked her out to fend for herself. She had to resort to working as a prostitute to survive, and now he's even using her death to advance his public image. It just makes me sick," Abby said nearly spitting the words out.

Garrett nodded his head, then ushered her down the street towards a small café. They sat and had some coffee before moving on to their next assignment. Then as they left the café, Garrett wanted to scout out the distance from Connor's to Dixon's. He strolled along the street with Abby on his arm, checking out the two saloons.

They stopped for a moment in front of Connor's where Garrett had last seen Corporal Davis that night. Then he looked up the street for any sign of the place where Roger said he was led to play poker. Looking just to the other side of Franklin Street, Garrett saw a sign with large black letters, "Dixon's Saloon." He pointed at it for Abby to see, and the two of them proceeded down the street to get a closer look.

"It's right here on the corner of the street," Garrett remarked suspiciously. "Awfully convenient to Franklin Street where Dorothy was killed, wouldn't you say?" looking at Abby who nodded her agreement.

"He left Connor's with Officer Dandridge. Came here to Dixon's to play poker, and wound up passed out in Dorothy's bed the next morning. Maybe it's just a coincidence Officer Dandridge is listed as the police officer first on the scene of the crime. But he was working that night. I saw him myself. Whoever did this would have needed help to frame Roger. Who better than a policeman? Maybe that's why he was there first thing in the morning to make sure that Roger was caught in the murdered woman's bed. I don't know how they managed to do this, or why, exactly, but I know that Roger is telling the truth."

Garrett frowned and shook his head as he considered Roger's situation. "I bet there's a connection between Officer Dandridge and Matthew Broadnax. Something has these two men working together, and we need to find out what it is."

He led her down the block to State Street. "I want you to wait here in this bookstore while I go talk with Officer Dandridge. I'll come back for you, and we'll ride back to the fort together."

"Are you sure? Can't I come with you?"

"Abby, please. Do this for me, and for Roger and Helen. Wait here. I won't be too long." Then he turned in the direction of the City and County Building intent on finding the policeman he suspected had participated in framing Roger.

Officer Dandridge entered the room carrying a small notebook and a cup of coffee. With sunlight streaming through the windows of the office, Garrett could see the weathered look on the officer's face for the first time. He was older than Garrett had originally thought, based upon the crow's feet around his eyes and the deep etchings of wrinkles in his leathery face. And the narrow slits that held his eyes did not engender trustworthiness. Perhaps that was just Garrett's biased perspective. Garrett hoped in the next few minutes he could confirm his suspicions about the officer.

"Sorry about the delay, Captain," he offered, "but we had a little problem back at the holding cells that I had to help with." He sat down opposite Garrett, and opened his notebook. "Now, what can I help you with?"

"Thank you for agreeing to meet with me," he said trying to smooth his way into the policeman's good graces. "I just have a few questions, not about the police report, though. I think that was very complete. Thank you."

Officer Dandridge nodded and leaned forward, his arms relaxed on the table in front of him, his notebook open in his left hand.

Garrett scratched his head as if he were puzzled. "This is quite a mess the Corporal is in, isn't it," he remarked smiling. "When was the first time you saw Corporal Davis, Officer?"

He glanced at his notebook before he answered, "It says here, 'At about nine in the morning, one of the girls from Lucy's, that's the house where Dorothy worked, called out to me in the street to ask for help.' At least that's what I got written down here. Actually she was screaming at the top of her lungs for help," he said with a bawdy laugh, "but I didn't want to write all that in my notebook. Anyways, I went in, and found him, Corporal Davis, that is, lying on the bed with the victim."

"Yes, Officer, I read that part. What I wanted to know was when did you first see the Corporal the night of the official presentation, before you found him in her bed the next morning?" Garrett corrected.

"I didn't see him that night."

"Well, I've talked with Corporal Davis, and believe me, he can't remember much, but he remembers meeting up with you. Do you remember?" Garrett asked carefully watching the policeman's reactions.

"No, can't say as I do," he continued, now a little more confidently.

"Well, now that's strange, Officer, because I, too, was there at Connor's that night, and it was really crowded, I know, but I saw you there myself, and what's more, I saw you shake hands with Corporal Davis," he added again watching the officer's reactions.

Officer Dandridge frowned, and though the room was cool, Garrett saw a bead of sweat break out on the policeman's upper lip. "Well, now that you mention Connor's saloon, I was there. But I didn't know that was the same soldier," he added obviously trying to come up with some reasonable explanation for the omission. "Yes, now I remember. I saw him and asked him about the Colonel's daughter 'cause I figured he would know if she was all right. He said she was doin fine, and we shook hands and I left."

Garrett frowned again, realizing that the policeman was having a difficult time getting his story straight. "But the Corporal says you told him about Dixon's and suggested that he come with you. Do you remember that?"

"Dixon's? No, I didn't go to Dixon's saloon. I don't know why the Corporal would say a thing like that."

"But, again, Officer Dandridge, I was there, too, and I saw the two of you leave the building together."

"Well, it's just a coincidence there, Captain. He may have left the same time as me, but we didn't leave together, and I didn't take him down the street to Dixon's to no card game neither. I was on duty."

"How'd you know that he said you offered to take him to a card game?" Garrett asked now that he knew he had caught the man in another lie.

Officer Dandridge squirmed, "Well, 'cause there's always a poker game goin on there, I guess."

Garrett reached across the table to shake the man's hand. "Thank you, again, Officer, for agreeing to meet with me. I know how busy you must be. The Red Light district must keep you hopping like a rabbit," he suggested with a slight laugh.

He'd caught this man in several lies. Now Garrett was actually looking forward to asking some of these same questions with him on the witness stand. He still didn't have enough evidence to clear Roger, but he was definitely onto something.

It had been over an hour since Garrett had left Abby at the bookstore. She'd spent that time browsing the shelves, and had actually found a book or two to purchase and began reading while she waited.

Then she saw the poster in the store window advertising Matthew Broadnax's campaign for mayor, but this one had an illustrated portrait of the man featured in the center. Abby asked the clerk if she could have the poster, feigning an interest in the candidate. That's when she learned she wasn't the first woman to ask for one of the flyers.

She wondered if Dorothy, herself, had asked for one. If she had known her former husband was running for mayor, she might have wanted to use the information to blackmail him. Maybe that's what the other woman had meant when she had told Abby Dorothy didn't need any help because her husband was going to take care of her. If she were demanding more money and threatening to reveal her circumstances to the public if he didn't pay, that could certainly motivate a man like her husband to get rid of her. At least it seemed plausible to Abby. But how could Garrett prove it? It was all just speculation right now.

When Garrett returned, Abby gave him the poster and shared her ideas with him. He nodded, and suggested they needed to hurry to catch the next street car back to the fort. He told her he needed to talk with Corporal Davis, and she was welcomed to come along.

The tone of his voice seemed brisk and business-like. It was hard to believe that earlier in the day there was that same chemistry brewing between them she had felt just a month ago. Now riding back to the fort, he seemed so distant. He focused on the notes he had written and stared repeatedly out the window.

They got to the stockade before 4 P.M. when the guards close it up for the evening. Roger was led into a small interview room, and the guard cautioned that they only had about fifteen minutes available.

Garrett didn't waste any time. "Corporal, I've talked with Officer Dandridge. I caught him in a couple of lies, so I think somehow he's tied up in this mess, but I don't know as yet how. The police report, however, is the most damning piece of evidence against you. It's reported that your gun had been fired. They said it smelled of gunpowder, and of course, the victim had been shot, so they figure your gun did it. What can you tell me about it, Corporal?"

"Well, if it was my gun that killed her, I didn't fire it, and I can prove it," he said. Abby watched as he put both of his hands out for Garrett to inspect. "See? No blisters, no powder burns on my hands."

Garrett frowned, "What are you talking about, Corporal?"

"Sir, my gun misfires regularly. It's not regulation issue, you see. Captain, you know none of the other enlisted men have side arms, just me."

Garrett nodded, but Abby was confused.

"About five years ago I found that gun out on the range out back there," he said pointing in the direction. "The first time I used it, I wasn't wearing my leather riding gloves, and it misfired. Burned like the dickens! Still got a scar; look, see it there?" He showed his right hand to both Garrett and Abby.

"Learned then to never shoot it without my gloves on, sir. Every time I practiced with it on the range, I was careful. Always wore leather gloves. It only took one time for me to learn that lesson. Drunk or sober, I'd never fire it without my gloves," he asserted.

Captain Talbot nodded, "But you could've had your gloves on then, Corporal. It was cold."

"Well, sir, I woke up without them on. I remember I'd taken them off at the table at Dixon's because the rawhide makes it difficult to hold the cards right. No, sir, I didn't have my gloves on when I woke up. Fact is, don't know where they are. Must've left them on the table at Dixon's."

Garrett nodded. Then he and Abby got up to leave when she accidentally dropped the poster on the floor. Roger bent down to pick it up, and stood back confused.

"What's this fella doing here?" he asked. "I saw him that night, too. He was sitting at the card table at Dixon's when I came in," he said. "Didn't get his name, but this is sure the man who sat across from me at the table. What's he doing on this poster?"

Abby was shocked by this revelation. When she regained her composure, she responded, "This is Matthew Broadnax, Roger. He's the husband of the woman who was killed. He's also running for mayor of Salt Lake City."

When Roger was led back to his cell, Abby and Garrett left the stockade and strolled slowly back toward the Colonel's residence. "It's lucky you dropped that poster when you did," Garrett offered. "Now we know that both Officer Dandridge and Matthew Broadnax were present on the scene that night. We've just got to find more evidence to convince a judge Roger didn't do this."

Abby nodded. "According to Roger, whoever fired his gun to shoot Dorothy should have a pretty nasty burn on his hand."

"Well, I shook hands with Officer Dandridge this afternoon. He didn't have any visible wounds on his hands, so he wasn't the one who fired that gun," Garrett replied.

Abby nodded, "Then it could have been her husband."

"Yes, it's possible, but we've still got to prove it." They had reached the front door, and he paused, "Abby, I'm going to go into town tomorrow by myself. I need to go to Lucy's to see the place where they found Roger, and I refuse to take you to such a place. And there's a few other places I will need to go that are not the proper place for a lady. I really appreciate your help today, and I will probably want to talk through what I find out with you later. But tomorrow, I'll have to go by myself," he said softly.

For a moment she thought she saw a flicker of regret in his eyes, like he might have wished the day could have been longer. Then he turned and stepped quickly off the porch and down the street toward his barracks. Abby sighed and walked into her father's house to share the news with Helen who was desperate for any glimmer of hope.

For right now, Abby needed to concentrate on comforting her friend. It was all she could do. Still, later that night, in the privacy of her room, Abby felt a renewed sense of loss. After offering her prayers to God, asking for His guidance in securing Roger's freedom, she cried herself to sleep once again.

CHAPTER

16

The sky was ominously overcast; the dark gray clouds moved threateningly across the valley and up to the bench of the mountains where Fort Douglas lay. The winds jostled the spruce and Douglas fir trees with their warning. It could be a mild snowfall or a blizzard. As Abby gazed out of her bedroom window, there was nothing in the advancing weather to encourage her to leave her bedroom today. Curled up at her feet, Cotton yawned and stretched his agreement; it would be a great day to just stay in bed.

Yesterday had been memorable. If she wasn't totally certain that her relationship with Garrett was over, she could have truly enjoyed the opportunity to work at his side investigating this case. From time to time, she would catch him looking at her, and she wondered what was going through his mind. Did he appreciate the sacrifice she was willing to make in order to protect his reputation and career? Did he really understand the depth of the love she now knew she felt for him? And would this ache in her heart ever really go away? So many questions with so few answers.

Still, seeing his blue eyes beneath those sandy brown eyebrows and the look of intense concentration that had been on his face several times during the day had only reminded her of the treasure she had sacrificed in walking away from his love. Another reason not to get out of bed, she thought.

She pulled her robe tighter around her. She glanced down at the woolen socks her father had given to her last night. Her feet were warm and snug inside those socks. Would her father have cared as much about her if he knew what some people were saying about her? Or would he have insisted that she leave Fort Douglas immediately to avoid the scandal and humiliation of having a daughter with a ruined reputation?

Strange, how less than a year ago, she hadn't really anticipated a life with her father. Now, what on earth would she do if he abandoned her? She couldn't let that happen. Without Garrett, her father's love was all she could hope for. She had to protect it like a delicate porcelain figurine. His love and respect meant everything to her.

She hurriedly wiped away a stray tear when she heard a light tap on her bedroom door. "May I come in?" asked the Colonel who peeked through a slit in the doorway.

After she nodded, he stepped into the room carrying a cup of hot coffee. "I can't do much in the kitchen, but I can brew a serious cup of coffee," he laughed placing the cup on the table near her.

He looked at her, smiled, and reached to put some loose strands of her hair back behind her ears. For a moment he could imagine himself a young father with a beautiful little red headed girl. It was moments like this that made him regret the choices he had made earlier in his life. He had missed so much, and by his choices, had nearly lost all opportunity to be a father to this lovely woman. She had grown up in spite of him. Now he had to do whatever he could to ensure he never lost that spot in her heart he felt he had found. She was all the family he had left in the world, and he was determined to nurture the love growing between them.

"Looks like it might snow today, Father," she offered as she sipped the hot coffee. "Captain Talbot said he was going into town today, but that he didn't want me to come. I think he plans on going to that brothel. He felt it was no place for a lady."

When Abby sighed heavily, her father guessed that she would have liked another excuse to see Captain Talbot today. Then the Colonel nodded his approval of Garrett's decision. "Well, he's right, and I'm glad he doesn't want you to be found in a place like that. Some people wouldn't understand. It could damage your reputation," he said matter-of-factly.

Abby cringed and quickly reached to pet her cat. "Cotton thinks we should just stay in bed today, Father. I tend to agree with him," she laughed half-heartedly and reached for the coffee again. She turned away so her father couldn't see her face.

He took a deep breath. Having decided to broach the subject of her relationship with Garrett, her father cleared his throat. "Abby, I've noticed something these past several days, and I need to ask you something," he said sitting on the side of her bed methodically stroking a purring Cotton.

His voice communicated that this would be a serious topic of conversation. Abby slipped out of her bed and pulled her robe tightly around her. Then she moved toward the window where the first flakes of snow had begun to gather.

"What happened between you and Garrett? Just now you referred to him as 'Captain Talbot' when just a few weeks ago, the two of you were on a first name basis. I was pretty sure from the tone of his affections that he had intended to propose to you by now. But now, all of a sudden, he's asking to resign his commission, and you, you don't even want to leave your bedroom. As your father, I want to intervene, but I don't know what happened, so I don't even know where to begin to help."

Abby remained standing at the window with her back to her father. Outside the window, snowflakes looked like butterflies dancing in the wind. They appeared to twist and dart around before making their way to the ground where they lay silent. Gradually the snowflakes increased in size and gathered strength in numbers. She stood watching the snowfall as the wet ground below began to turn to white, covering the mud with each new layer.

Her father's voice penetrated the distance between them, but she couldn't bring herself to reveal the truth. At the same time, she couldn't lie to him anymore. She struggled for an explanation that he would accept. Still staring out the window, she softly began, "Father, I know you want to help, but there's really nothing you or anyone can do now. Captain Talbot and I have accepted the fact that we are not right for one another. He deserves so much more."

She paused only long enough to wipe away another tear that had struggled to find its way down her cheek. "I'm just not the right woman for him. I'm too stubborn and spoiled, I think. I have all these ideas about things I should be doing like marching for voting rights and maybe teaching at a women's college. Like I said, he deserves so much more than to be saddled with a woman like me."

The Colonel frowned. There was definitely more to this situation, but he knew better than to pry further right now. He could tell how delicate his daughter was at this moment, and he didn't want to risk alienating her. It was enough for him to suspect that she was in love with his adjutant, and he had no doubt that Captain Talbot was hopelessly in love with her.

He would have to tiptoe around the issue with his daughter a while longer, but when the time was right, the Colonel would breach this subject with Garrett and get the answers he needed. His daughter was too precious for him to just sit by and watch her waste away like this. Not while he still had breath in his body.

All the way into town, Garrett thought about Abby. Just yesterday he had sat next to her on the streetcar reaching out to protect her when the car came to a stop. He had welcomed her comments about the case just so that he would have a reason to hear her voice. Yet the memory of that voice haunted him all night in his sleep. Her deep green eyes and that bright copper hair, her porcelain skin, and a barely visible sprinkle of freckles lying across the bridge of her nose— he had memorized every detail over the past few months. He had gotten caught up in the whirlwind that was Abigail Randolph, and his heart was in ruins.

"Difficult case, isn't it, sir," interrupted the voice of his companion on today's trip into town.

Garrett nodded back at Lieutenant Morgan. "Yes, it is. Nothing really makes much sense except that somehow someone put Roger into the woman's bed, probably after she was killed. And from the information Roger gave me about his sidearm yesterday, whoever he is, he probably has a burn on his hand," Garrett answered. It was good to have someone to assist him in viewing the crime scene and talking with witnesses today. He was just sorry it definitely could not be Abby.

Shaking off the reverie, he turned his thoughts to Roger's situation. There was little doubt in his mind that Abby was right, and Dorothy's husband had something to do with her death, even if he didn't shoot her himself. But how to prove it was still a mystery. Having gathered bits and pieces from different witnesses to the crime, Garrett struggled to put together the events leading up to the unfortunate woman's murder.

There was a light icy mist falling in downtown Salt Lake as Garrett and Lieutenant Morgan sauntered to the brothel on Franklin Street. Garrett showed him how Dixon's and Lucy's seemed to be next door to one another even though the buildings faced in separate directions. They agreed that the location probably wasn't just a coincidence.

Knocking on the door of Lucy's, Garrett and the Lieutenant were invited into what appeared to be a cigar store for men. Once inside, they were ushered to a stairway near the counter which led up to a different store for men. Walking up, Garrett suddenly found himself in a world that he had no real desire to participate in. He'd heard about such places, but for him, there was no allure. He really felt no interest in spending time with a woman for money, though he knew plenty of men willing to do so.

Several women beckoned to them, but Garrett asked instead to see Lucy, trying to make their intentions clear. When the madam showed up in her open dressing gown, Lieutenant Morgan smirked, while

Garrett cleared his throat and stated his reason for being there. She laughed, tied her robe to hide her provocative undergarments, and led them to the end of the hallway where Dorothy's room was located.

Opening the door, she announced, "Well, here it is, Captain. The scene of the crime, so I'm told. I wanted to clean the place up right away, but the Police Commissioner told me I had to wait until you had a chance to view it, as he put it. I'm glad you men came so quick. I'll get the place cleaned up tomorrow. Rosie's had her eye on this room for awhile now," she said matter-of-factly.

He glanced around the small room. The dark red wallpaper was starting to peel in several places. The brass bed was the prominent feature of the room, as one would expect. There was a small pine dresser with a cracked mirror and a beat up chifforobe on the opposite wall. The Lieutenant stopped and inspected the bed. He pointed to what looked like blood on one of the brass poles at the head of the bed and a small pool of blood on the pillow. He remarked that the blood stain in the center of the bed didn't seem to be very large, especially for a gunshot wound, but Garrett dismissed that notion because it seemed a rather grotesque thought.

"I tell you this seems very odd, Captain. You said she was shot in the chest. There should be a larger blood stain than is here."

"Well, I will be sure to ask the coroner about it," Garrett replied.

Then Garrett noticed the window looking out onto the back alley. He moved to it and scanned the area just down the stairs. "There's a door down there," he said pointing. "Does that lead into Dixon's?" he asked.

When Lucy nodded, Garrett noticed a back door from Dorothy's room which opened onto a set of steps leading down to the alley. He opened the door and glanced down into the vacant alley. He caught a glimpse of a man there below him, but the man darted off like a thief before Garrett could even get out the words to try to stop him.

"That's primarily the reason Rosie's all hot about having this room—them backstairs are convenient to sneak out clients who don't want other folks to know their business," Lucy stated.

"Who's that man down there?" he asked, pointing towards the fleeing shape.

"Oh, him. Nobody pays him no mind. Name's Joe Little. He's a colored man that Dorothy befriended, though God only knows why. He sleeps in the shed under the stairs there. She gave him money every once in awhile, and shared food with him when she went to the market. He hung around down there in the alley hoping to get someone's sympathy, I guess. With times like they are, I guess it's really hard for a colored man to find a job."

Garrett looked first at Lieutenant Morgan, then back at her, and probed further, "Is he there most of the time?"

"I don't really keep a record, Captain," she answered haughtily. Then she softened her tone and replied, "Probably. He doesn't seem to have many options, you know. And Dorothy was nice to him. I even think I heard her mention he was going to go with her to San Francisco when she got enough money saved."

Garrett frowned, thinking carefully about the information she had just offered. "She was planning to leave?"

"Oh, my yes! She always said she was just doin this to get by until she got the money she needed to get out of town. I think she said something about a cousin who had a dress shop out in California. Think she planned on being a partner with her, or something like that."

Garrett started to leave, then stopped suddenly and turned back to ask, "Didn't anybody hear the gunshot or anything out of the ordinary that night?"

She shrugged. "We were all out enjoying the celebration, Captain. There was a lot going on, you know. Fireworks and folks firing their pistols in the air. No one was here but poor Dorothy. I'm sure no one woulda heard anything over all the racket in the streets."

Garrett nodded and thanked his hostess. She had indeed provided him with more pieces to the puzzle, though as yet, he didn't know quite what to make of this information. There seemed to be as many questions as answers.

"This case just keeps getting more and more complicated," Garrett remarked to Lieutenant Morgan as they left the brothel. "We're going to need to find this man, Joe Little, to see what, if anything, he knows about the murder. I bet he knows something that could help us."

"That may be, but who's going to take the word of a colored?"

"One problem at a time, Chet," Garrett said. "Let's find him first. Then we'll figure out how to use whatever information he has."

After leaving Lucy's, the two men roamed around to the back alley, but there was no sign of Joe Little anywhere. The icy drizzle had begun to turn to tiny snowflakes, so they turned back around and hurried by Dixon's on their way back to the streetcar. The place was empty. Not even the bartender was inside, so Garrett decided to come back and visit there another day. When he turned around to retrace his steps, he nearly ran headlong into Officer Dandridge.

"Hear you men went to see the crime scene," the policeman stated. "Kinda open and shut, I'd say, wouldn't you?" he asked, nodding at Lieutenant Morgan.

Garrett smiled weakly at the man. He already knew enough not to trust anything the officer said. He nodded his head, and replied, "Yeah, I guess you could say that."

Garrett moved toward the doorway, but the stocky policeman didn't give way for him to walk by. Garrett looked at him again, and decided he might distract the man with a question, "What do you know about a colored man named Joe Little?"

Officer Dandridge stepped back a bit, and laughed loudly. "Oh, you really are desperate for another suspect, aren't you?"

Garrett nodded, then added, "Maybe he's the one who killed her?"

Officer Dandridge scowled. "Aw, he ain't nothing but an old drunk, Captain. He might be able to tell you what kind of liquor is being served, but he don't know nothing about what happened at Lucy's that night." He shook his head and ambled off in the opposite direction laughing under his breath.

"That does it," Garrett announced to the Lieutenant. "We'll have to come back and find Joe Little. I'm sure he knows something about what happened that night. I just hope he knows enough to stay clear of Officer Dandridge until we can find him."

The soft snow fell silently outside gradually inching its way up to the bottom step of the porch. Abby had finally been persuaded to get dressed and join her father downstairs. Now she stood at one of the parlor windows watching the flakes again, like graceful fairies, gently drift to the ground. She was mesmerized by the peaceful sight. In so many ways she needed that frozen precipitation to insulate her heart just as it did the ground below. Maybe then she wouldn't be agonizing over Garrett.

Her father sat quietly reading a book and looking up regularly to watch his daughter. The way she held onto the heavy brocade drapes reminded him of the thousands of times he himself had stared out of windows wishing he could see his wife and daughter coming up the walkway. A lonely, empty feeling crept over him. Five years ago now, and it still feels like yesterday. He reached for the picture of his wife and gently stroked her image.

He glanced back up at his daughter still staring out the window. She seemed so unhappy these days, and he didn't quite know what to do about it. But at least he had been able to convince her to come downstairs. And mercifully for all of them in the house, she had made a late breakfast for them to eat, even pressing Helen to eat something. With both women feeling miserable, the Colonel really had his hands full.

The sudden loud crackling in the fireplace caught his attention, and he stood up to add more firewood, when there was a knock at the front door. Abby turned around from where she had stood guard, her heart pounding with anticipation.

When her father invited Garrett into the house, her heart nearly leaped from her chest with excitement. And yet, she had to force herself to act restrained, interested only in the news he had learned about the case. She couldn't let on to him or to anyone in the room how wretched she felt for having made the decision to end their courtship.

"Sorry for the mess," he said as snow melted around his feet inside the doorway.

"Don't worry about that," the Colonel urged. "Just come in here by the fire and warm yourself. We are all anxious to know what you were able to learn this afternoon."

Garrett nodded stretching out his hands in front of the fire to enjoy the heat. Abby came back into the room ushering in Helen who had taken refuge in her bedroom. The two women sat down with the Colonel and waited to hear the news Garrett brought.

"Well, we got to see inside the . . room where," he started then cleared his throat. He suddenly felt very uncomfortable talking about such places in front of the two women in the room.

Helen, possibly sensing the reason for his unease, spoke up, "Please, Captain, we all know where you went today. Don't be concerned for our ears. We know that Roger was found in a brothel, in the bed of a prostitute. Don't mince words on our account," she said gesturing to include Abby in her explanation.

"Yes, of course. Anyway, I found out some interesting details today which I needed to share with all three of you. Maybe together we can make some sense of these puzzle pieces."

He sat down opposite the three of them and began describing the alley and the back entrance to Dixon's. "I think that explains how nobody saw Roger or anyone else go upstairs to Dorothy's room that night. Whoever killed her used those back stairs, then they got Roger up those stairs without anyone suspecting a thing. They would have had to drug Roger in order to get him up there, though. That could explain why he has no memory of anything after sitting at a card table in Dixon's."

Abby and Helen nodded silently. Abby glanced over at Helen who seemed dazed, having been awakened from a nap.

"The Lieutenant and I went over to Dixon's earlier, but there was no one there. We ran into Officer Dandridge, though, which was a little strange. We went back around 3 o'clock and talked with the bartender. He didn't really have any decent information to help us. I asked if he saw Officer Dandridge or Roger there that night. All he could say was that Dandridge is a regular customer, couldn't say for sure if he was there that night, and there was a card game in the back room, but there always is. And no, he couldn't say if he saw Roger there either. I don't think there's any use in continuing to follow that lead. It's a dead end."

Helen appeared ready to cry. Abby scooted closer to her and put her arm around Helen's shoulder to comfort her.

"Oh, I almost forgot. Lucy told me that Dorothy was planning to go to San Francisco when she got enough money together. There was apparently a cousin there who owned a dress shop which Dorothy thought she could buy into with enough money."

"Maybe it's why she was going to Matthew's office each month," added Abby. "She was saving money to leave Salt Lake. But why wouldn't her husband be glad for her to leave? That would effectively solve his problem, wouldn't it?"

"Money's really tight right now, Abby," offered the Colonel. "Maybe this man was finding it difficult to get enough money together for her. Or maybe she kept changing the amount she needed."

"And, don't forget, he's trying to run for mayor. That would take some of his funds to run a campaign," Garrett added.

"And didn't you say he has eleven children?" the Colonel asked. "It must be expensive trying to provide for such a large family, don't you think?"

Garrett nodded. "Colonel, I still need to interview the husband. So far, he's been unavailable, and it's critical that I meet him face to face before the trial begins. The prosecutor has tentatively set the trial to begin February 3rd, but with this snow, I know I'm going to need more time. This weather is going to make it difficult for me to interview all the potential witnesses before the trial date. Could I get you to call in a favor and get me at least three more weeks?"

"Of course, Garrett. The assigned judge is a good friend of mine. I know that we can work out something. Do you need more than three weeks?"

Garrett glanced at Helen whose face registered terror. "No, sir, I think just three weeks'll be enough for me to properly mount a defense. If the weather will cooperate, I'll go back into town to meet Matthew Broadnax next week. And thank you for assigning 2nd Lieutenant Morgan to the case. He's proving to be quite an asset. It was really good to have a second pair of eyes to view the crime scene today. He noticed a few things which were curious. Thank you again, sir. Well, I guess I better be getting back to the barracks."

Abby looked up as he stood to leave. "Oh, why don't you stay for dinner, Captain? I'm sure that we can rustle up something." Abby took Helen by the hand. Helen nodded her agreement.

Garrett acquiesed weakly. Then realizing how seriously tired he was from the day's events, he collapsed in the chair by the fire and nodded off while the women left the room to prepare the evening meal. For a moment, in his reverie, he was able to forget that he and Abby were no longer a couple.

CHAPTER

17

The weather hadn't cooperated. Eight inches of snow fell and effectively shut down all avenues of transportation into the city for another week. Helen and Abby had been able to navigate their way to the stockade to visit Roger daily, though they often had to wade through mounds of white fluffy powder.

The Colonel and Garrett regularly discussed the case along with other business, but Garrett felt anxious about interviewing Matthew Broadnax. Every day that went by was another day that a burn wound could heal and possibly disappear, and with it, any real hope of proving Roger's innocence.

Finally, the snow had melted enough to clear passage into Salt Lake City, though because the roads from the fort were not yet paved, it meant traversing through slushy mud and puddles. Nevertheless, Garrett was anxious to complete his investigation of the crime, so he enlisted Abby's help and borrowed the Colonel's buggy for the trip into town.

The melting snow had created new ruts on the muddy roads that led into the city. The buggy jerked and lurched clumsily through the mud, but Garrett's patience with the horse made the trip possible in spite of the odds. The two of them arrived at the bank a little over an hour after they began their trip into town which was about twice the time it usually took.

Entering the bank, the two "detectives" immediately fell into their roles Garrett had chosen for this particular interview. Abby was to be his "meek little secretary" with the main purpose of watching their suspect while Garrett asked the questions. She would use the shorthand she had learned while in college to write down what she observed.

Garrett, on the other hand, would try to ingratiate himself with the man in order to squeeze information from him. In this manner, he hoped they would be able to get information from the man Abby suspected had killed Dorothy. But it was still quite a gamble.

They entered Matthew's office together, and Garrett extended his hand to greet the middle aged man who stood behind his massive desk. "Good morning, Mr. Broadnax. Thank you for agreeing to meet with me," Garrett offered after initial introductions had been made.

He vigorously shook the man's right hand looking for any sign of a burn wound, but there was none. Somewhat disappointed, Garrett sat in the chair offered by the businessman. "I know that you are a very busy man, what with the bank business and your mayoral campaign."

Matthew Broadnax nodded and smiled his appreciation. He was a tall, thin man with a neatly groomed short beard, dark narrow eyes, and eyebrows that appeared to connect across his face. He sat down behind his desk and offered pleasantries, "Yes, well, with the weather like it's been, I find that I have the time to devote to answering your questions about Dorothy."

When everyone was seated comfortably, Mr. Broadnax leaned forward to speak. "Such a shame and a waste. You know that I was trying to put some money together to help her leave town, but she was killed before I could make those arrangements," he added with a tone of sadness in his voice.

"How generous of you to offer to help her," Garrett said, hoping to feed the man's self-righteous attitude. "It's too bad that things transpired as they did. However, we both know she was in a dangerous occupation. It certainly wasn't your fault. A religious man like you must've been shocked to learn she was working on Franklin Street."

Mr. Broadnax nodded and frowned. "I'd no idea about that until this past October," he volunteered, one hand on the desk and the other hand in a jacket pocket.

"She came to see me, and I was appalled. When she and Hazel left my home over a year ago, I'd given them what I considered to be adequate funds for them to provide for themselves and hoped they'd find work as seamstresses or laundresses. It never occurred to me that they'd choose to live on Franklin Street in the midst of the Red Light district," he uttered softly, leaning closer to Garrett so as to not be overheard outside of his office.

Garrett continued by nodding his agreement. Then turning to Abby, he replied, "Some women just are not satisfied with menial work. I'm so fortunate Miss Randolph here is not opposed to taking notes for me." He could see from the look she returned to him that she did not appreciate the patronizing tone, but they both understood its purpose. She demurely bowed her head and continued to watch their suspect as she wrote down the summary of the conversation.

"Well, I for one think that you went above and beyond for Dorothy. I understand she came to your office several times for a hand out. That must've been embarrassing to you."

Matthew Broadnax cleared his throat, obviously uncomfortable that Garrett knew of his arrangement. He reached and stroked his neatly groomed beard. "Only somewhat. I made arrangements for her to pick up an envelope of cash once a month from my secretary so that I didn't have to see her myself. And I had to keep the arrangement rather quiet since with my campaign, I couldn't afford for the whole town to know she was working at Lucy's."

Garrett responded agreeably, but continued to ingratiate himself with the man. "On the other hand, some people might be quite impressed with your generosity towards such a woman. They might see that as a character trait worthy of a potential mayor," Garrett said.

Then changing the subject ever so slightly, Garrett asked, "Were you invited to speak at the presentation of statehood the night she was killed? I know that our commanding officer was there, and I expect that with your prominence in the community, you were there also."

"Why, yes, I was. I gave a short speech earlier at one of my campaign rallies," he responded.

Admitting he was downtown that night was just the first step. Garrett needed to get further details, so he probed, "And where were these rallies?"

"Over on State Street," he answered oblivious to Garrett's true purpose.

"Forgive me, I'm still a novice here in town. Where is that in relation to where Dorothy worked?"

"Just one block away, but it's worlds away when you consider the kind of business done on State Street," Matthew added laughing. "Yeah, I think the rally was over at around 8 o'clock that night. There was quite a crowd of folks there for me to meet. I spent some time shaking hands, you know, for my campaign."

"So where'd you go after the rally?" Garrett asked.

Matthew Broadnax squinted just a bit. He seemed uncomfortable with the question. He stared down at his desk rather than at Garrett. "I'm not quite sure where I went after the rally. The streets were extremely crowded, you know, because of the celebrations all over the city. I think I walked around a bit meeting folks on the streets, shaking hands with whomever I could find to speak to. A politician's life's like that, you know."

Garrett nodded. Then he asked his next question without looking up so that Matthew would not suspect Garrett's true purpose. "I think I've written it down here somewhere, oh, yes, here it is, you were reported to be at Dixon's saloon later in the night. Is that correct?"

He frowned and leaned back in his overstuffed chair. "Who told you that?" he asked, his voice betraying anxiety.

"Oh, let me see, yes, here it is, Officer Dandridge was there at Dixon's and he must've been the one to report you were there also," Garrett answered nonchalantly.

Matthew hesitated, not quite sure what to believe. Then he cleared his throat, "Well, if Dandridge said I was at Dixon's, then maybe I was. I honestly don't remember, though. Like I said, it was very crowded everywhere that night. And I was in and out of several establishments trying to encourage citizens to vote for me. I could've been there, I just don't recollect when or for how long."

"Oh, so you know Officer Dandridge well then," Garrett continued, pretending to just be carrying on a polite conversation with the man.

"Well? Yes, I guess so. He's not a Mormon, but he's a regular patron here at the bank, and he and his family live in my ward," he responded, and pulled at his collar.

Recognizing that he had gotten about all the information he would be able to from the man, Garrett closed his notebook, and stood to thank him for his time.

Then he asked, "I do hope that you'll be willing to testify in court, Mr. Broadnax. It would certainly help our case if you could speak to Dorothy's character; and I don't think it would hurt your campaign one bit for people to learn about your generosity towards this fallen woman," he added hoping to encourage the man to be present in court.

"I'm not sure how much help I can give your client, Captain, but I'm certainly willing to testify to the few things I know. And, as you say, if it'll enhance my campaign for mayor, I'm more than willing to participate."

Garrett nodded, and again reached across the desk to shake the man's hand. Then he and Abby hurried out of the office and out of the bank. Garrett shook his head ruefully, "It doesn't appear that he fired Roger's gun. I looked several times, but he didn't have any sign of a burn on his hand."

"Maybe he was wearing gloves that night. It was cold," Abby offered.

"Well, if he was, there would be no wound to incriminate him."

Abby sighed, visibly frustrated by their experience with Matthew Broadnax. "Ooh, I'm so angry, I could just spit nails," she exclaimed. "He had something to do with poor Dorothy's death, I just know it. Why else would he hide who she was from his own secretary?"

Garrett shook his head. "I know there's something out there that'll prove Roger's innocence, but for right now, we're just speculating. We need evidence. Somehow, someway, we've got to find someone who can help us get Roger out of this mess."

After they left the bank, Garrett led her to the City and County Building where he checked on the court date. That was the first time he met his opponent on the case. Jacob Moore, the prosecutor assigned to the case, had even less experience than Garrett did in a courtroom. He admitted to Garrett he had never tried a case before a jury. Then, speaking in a hushed tone, he admitted that because the victim was a prostitute, no one seemed in any particular hurry to charge into the halls of justice.

But Garrett knew Roger was eager to clear his name, and Helen was desperate to have her husband out of the stockade, so he urged the prosecutor to agree on the last Monday in February, which was just about three weeks away. Mr. Moore reluctantly agreed to take this date to the judge, and they shook hands cordially. As he and Abby stepped out of the building, Garrett hoped he had done the right thing, pressing for a court date in February. If Roger was going to have any hope of acquittal, Garrett and Lieutenant Morgan would have to locate this crucial piece of the puzzle, Joe Little. And they had very little time left to do that.

Garrett decided he would discuss with Abby their messy relationship on the ride back to the fort. He had been contemplating for the past two weeks how he might be able to change her mind, and he was intent upon doing so. He felt he had given in to her demands too easily. At the time, he had been stunned. Now he meant to mount his own defense to win her back. If necessary, he was prepared to enlist her father's help to achieve his purpose. He pulled the reins and guided their carriage to the side of the road. To accomplish this purpose, he would need to look at her which he couldn't do safely while driving up to Fort Douglas.

"Abby, I've been thinking more and more about what happened in December, and I can't allow you to end our relationship because of lies and rumors. I think the way we feel about one another can triumph over any obstacle."

Abby wrapped her arms closer to her body and turned her face away from him to stare out the window of the carriage. She couldn't afford for him to suspect that her resolve was wavering. "Captain, I'm sorry, but I disagree. My reputation is ruined, and yours will be, too, if we were to marry. And for me, the worst of it would be the embarrassment and shame my father would have to endure. I cannot allow anything to destroy the relationship I now have with him. If these rumors become public, which they would if we were to announce our engagement, it'd absolutely destroy his respect for me."

He'd heard this argument before, and he was prepared for it. But he chose to listen to the rest of her concerns before bringing up his counter argument.

"I hurt him terribly by not telling him about that horrible night. He'd be crushed to know people actually think I was there because I wanted a wild adventure, of sorts. And he'd also find out what some of these people think about our family heritage. The humiliation would just destroy him. I have to protect him from knowing what people are saying about him and about me. And your career'd be destroyed by association. I just can't live with the thought that I'd be responsible for ruining your life as well as disappointing my father more than I already have."

Garrett heard her convoluted reasoning, and began to apply his own argument, "You said you are concerned about my reputation and my career. That's no longer an issue, Abby. I will be leaving the fort as soon as this case is over. We could leave together, and build a life somewhere else, if you wish."

"No!" she cried. "Captain, I cannot leave now. I've waited all my life to have a father. I can't leave him to run off with you. I could never forgive myself."

Tears began to flow unrestrained. Her life was in such turmoil. Her personal heartbreak was tempered only with the consolation that she still had her father's love. She couldn't bear the thought of losing her father after so many years of secretly yearning for his love. Not like this.

Garrett began to experience the same frustration that had been eating at him for several weeks now. If he remained at the fort, there would be no way to avoid knowing she was there, too, but unavailable to him. If he left, her memory would haunt him, for how long, he couldn't be sure.

He felt trapped in a web of lies and deceit; and yet, she was refusing to defend herself against those who were spreading the rumors, nor would she allow anyone else to defend her. It didn't make sense to him, but he was growing tired of trying to make sense of this woman who seemed to be more like a child than an adult. Angrily, he asked her, "Then why are you willing to work alongside me? I know that you love me."

Abby shook her head. She, too, felt confused about the myriad emotions racing through her. Then, determined to turn his attentions away from her, she hatefully spat out, "No, I don't," she retorted. "Captain, the only reason I'm doing this is to help Helen. She's the one who begged me to get you to defend Roger. I would've never bothered you again, except for my loyalty to her. When the trial's over, I'll never disturb you again."

There was no way to counter her decision. Frustrated, embarrassed, and angry, he snapped the reins to urge the horse forward at a little faster pace, even along this muddy road. The best thing to do was to end the torture of sitting beside the woman he loved.

CHAPTER

Garrett sat quietly at the table in the Officer's Club waiting for his commanding officer. He had received a handwritten invitation for lunch to discuss the progress of the Corporal's case suggesting that he would prefer to have their discussion in a more informal setting. Lately, whenever they discussed the case at the residence, Helen was getting more and more stressed. Garrett knew the Colonel was very protective of both women living in his home. It made sense for two men to talk about Roger out of their earshot. Though Garrett didn't have much of anything new to report about the case, he had decided perhaps he should let him know about Joe Little. There was at least the hope that the colored man he had seen in the alley could provide more information about the night of the murder. In fact, he was the only real lead Garrett had left to follow.

But Garrett prayed the subject would not turn to Abby. He wasn't sure how he would be able to respond to his commanding officer and the father of the woman he loved. It was already difficult just being around her and her father. Talking about it would definitely make things worse, if that were possible.

When Garrett saw him enter the room, he stood to attention with a salute. Then when his commanding officer issued his 'at ease' command, Garrett said, "Congratulations on your promotion, sir; it's long overdue. Have you told Abby, yet?"

"I plan to tell her right after our lunch, Captain." They shook hands, and General Randolph nodded his thanks. Then the two men sat down to share a meal together.

"I'm glad you had the time to meet me today, Garrett," the General announced sitting in the seat opposite him. Their meals arrived shortly after he sat down, and, between bites, he went right to the business of inquiring about the case. Garrett explained the progress so far, how both he and Abby had gone to interview Matthew Broadnax and how they had developed a theory of the crime, though as yet, they had no concrete evidence to support it.

He told the General about their search for someone named Joe Little who may have been a witness to the crime. Since the trial would begin week after next, Garrett was really hoping that this potential witness would be the answer he was looking for. After each point Garrett made, the General nodded approvingly, and so Garrett felt maybe their lunch would end without any further inquiry about his relationship with Abigail. Relieved, he placed his napkin on the table, and prepared to leave the Officers' Club.

But then suddenly, Abby's father decided to breach the subject.

"I'm not going to waste any more of your time with chit-chat, son. I need to know why the two of you decided against an engagement."

Garrett knew his reaction to the question was written all over his face.

"Sir, you will have to ask your daughter. She's the one who decided that it would be best if we didn't get married. I've tried to change her mind, but she's determined she doesn't want to marry me."

"If that's the case, why's my daughter so broken-hearted?" the General asked quietly in order not to be overheard by others in the room. He leaned across the table closer to Garrett and almost whispered, "If this is what she wanted, why does she mope around the house like a lost puppy on those days when she's not going to be around you?"

Garrett felt his jaw drop. He was almost as stunned by this revelation as he had been the night Abby had come to his barracks to end their courtship. "Sir, I wasn't aware of that. I've been working alongside her these past few weeks, but she's given me no clue she's changed her mind about our relationship. In fact, she insisted yesterday she's not in love with me."

The General sat back in his chair and frowned. "Well, can you at least tell me the reason the two of you ended your courtship so abruptly. I mean, really, Captain, one minute you're planning to give my daughter a ring, and the next thing I know, she's up in her room crying, and you're asking to resign your commission. That just doesn't make any sense to me."

"Sir, I really should let her tell you. I promised her I'd keep the reason for her decision confidential."

The General could feel his blood pressure beginning to rise. His daughter was hurting, and he was determined to know the reason immediately. "Captain, I demand that you tell me yourself, and I don't want to have to wait another second, do you hear!" he said, crashing his fist onto the table.

All of the other officers had scurried quickly out of the room after eating because they saw the General was in what appeared to be an argument with Captain Talbot, and they didn't want to be the next target. The room was empty now except for the two of them.

Garrett leaned back a little in his chair. He bowed his head, and after he considered what he might say, he obediently complied with the General's command, "Yes, sir, I'll tell you everything, but I don't think you're going to like what I have to say," he said, pausing slightly.

"Abby overheard Major Hempstead's wife talking to several of the officers' wives about her and me. To say the least, Mrs. Hempstead was uncomplimentary about Abby. She told the other women that Abby was a wild woman of easy virtue who got exactly what she deserved by messing around in the Red Light district the night she was attacked. Edith further stated that I was either a fool to consider a union with Abby or that I had taken pity on her because no other man would ever offer a marriage proposal to a woman of such low repute. She concluded her remarks by saying if I were to go through with marrying Abby, whatever my reason, it'd be the end of my career. Abby heard all those lies, and a few more, and decided our engagement was off."

The General's face was hot with the blood that had sped up into his temples. He could barely contain the rage boiling just below the surface. Then he squinted, and asked, "What few more, Garrett? I want to hear it all," he commanded impatiently.

Garrett sighed. "Mrs. Hempstead said that marrying Abby would end my career because of the stigma associated with your father's and grandfather's support of the Confederacy during the Civil War. She said you'd never be promoted to general, and that I'd suffer the same disgrace by association. Abby was afraid I'd be the laughingstock of the fort if I married her, so she called off the engagement. And she swore me to secrecy because she didn't want you to suffer any more humiliation because of her. She's adamant that having your love and respect means more to her than our happiness together, sir."

The General took a deep breath and pursed his lips as he considered all he had just heard. He nodded repeatedly as if he was replaying Garrett's words in his head. His daughter's happiness was of utmost importance to him. It had always been so, even though she was thousands of miles away. A course of action decided upon, he looked Garrett straight in the eye, "Son, do you love my daughter?" he asked quietly.

"Yes, sir," Garrett answered without hesitation.

"And this is the only reason the two of you are not planning a wedding at this moment?" he asked, just to be sure.

"Yes, sir," Garrett answered again.

"Then come with me," the General ordered, standing up from the table. He had seen Major Hempstead's wife holding court in another room of the Officers' Club as he had come into the building looking for Garrett. There was no time like the present to correct this situation. Finding her quickly, General Randolph stood directly at her left to address her and the other women in her group with Garrett standing just in sight of the impending confrontation. Under the circumstances, Garrett didn't want to be too close to the action.

"Mrs. Hempstead, I hear you've been spreading more of your venomous lies around the post. I've known for quite awhile now how vicious and evil your tongue could be, but until now, I've chosen not to correct it. I considered your indecent character to be your husband's problem, though I cannot imagine anyone on earth envying him." The General stopped for just a moment to allow the impact of his words to have their effect.

It was working. Mrs. Hempstead was seething with anger and embarrassment at this public chastisement. "Well, I never!" she stated angrily, turning to stare up at him.

"That's part of the problem. Nobody's ever taken the time to put you in your place," he replied glaring daggers into her eyes.

Mrs. Hempstead reflexively leaned back from the General, as if she thought he might strike her at any moment. Under the circumstances, Garrett couldn't be certain that he wouldn't.

"Good! I've got your attention then," he continued. "My daughter, Abby, was on a mission to help an unfortunate soul when she was accosted by two drunken bastards who nearly robbed her of her virtue. How dare you intimate that she deserved such treatment! How could any woman of any level of compassion suggest that a young girl should deserve to be raped!" He scowled aggressively at the object of his daughter's grief.

"And how dare you suggest that Captain Talbot would be a fool or worse for marrying my daughter! He is a fine officer who happens to be in love with my lovely daughter. How dare you try to interfere with their happiness by spreading these vicious lies about her!"

His fists were clenched, and he nearly bit off every word as he spoke. Mrs. Hempstead continued to lean back, almost paralyzed by fear of what might happen next. The rest of the women at the table sat frozen in their seats in total shock at this public display. They obviously thought that any minute this confrontation might become physical.

The General's breath was hot and quick; then, suddenly, he turned to Mrs. Randall who was sitting across the table. "Mrs. Randall, have you been any part of this hateful treatment of my daughter?" he asked more softly.

"No, sir," came the startled response.

"Good. Then you won't mind planning my daughter's engagement party for this Friday night."

"Sir, you want that to be at the Valentine Ball?" she asked hesitantly.

He paused to consider this idea for a moment. Yes, Valentine's Day was tomorrow, and the Valentine Ball was set for Friday. A perfect setting for a surprise engagement party, he thought. "Yes. Just make certain the decorations and refreshments are plenty, and EVERYONE on the post knows the true purpose of the evening will be to reunite my daughter with the love of her life."

Then turning back to Mrs. Hempstead, the General continued, "I will expect Major Hempstead to be present, of course, because he's second in command. You, however, will NOT be invited. You'll make some excuse to your husband why you cannot come, or I'll tell him myself, whichever you prefer, but you'll not be there to in any way interfere with my daughter's special evening, am I clear?" he asserted, waiting for her answered nod.

He turned to leave the room, but then did an about face, "And just so you know, Edith, my promotion to brigadier general came through yesterday morning. I intend to have the ceremony pinning on my two stars tomorrow afternoon.

"So let's get this much straight. If I hear of you spreading anymore of the vicious, hateful lies that you have spouted over the years, I'll kick your fat fanny off this post, and send your husband down to Arizona to guard the Indian reservations! And I'll make sure he knows that you're the reason for his transfer! Is that clear?"

Then the General turned, put on his hat, and marched quickly from the room with Garrett at his side. For the first time since just after Christmas, Garrett had hope of a life with Abby again. Friday evening was just a few days away, but it seemed like a lifetime to him. Now if he could only resolve the Corporal's case as completely.

Abby and Helen were sitting in the parlor when her father entered at the end of the day. Helen was showing Abby how to knit, and she had just about learned the basics. Her father came into the room and sat opposite the two women.

"I talked with Captain Talbot today about the case. He thinks he's got a good chance of proving that Roger didn't do this. He told me Abby's been helping him a little," he winked at his daughter and grinned. "He's going into town tomorrow to try to locate a key witness who may be able to tell us how Roger fell into this mess."

Helen sighed. Tears welled up in her eyes as she responded, "I'm so grateful to all of you for helping us through this crisis. I feel so much better knowing Captain Talbot is defending Roger, and to have the two of you believing in him helps me tremendously," she said wiping away free-flowing tears. Helen stood by the settee, nodded her head to signal her appreciation, and left the room for her own private quarters.

After Helen shut her door, he sat down by his daughter. "Abby, I appreciate your willingness to help Roger and Helen the way you have. I know it wasn't easy for you to ask Garrett to stay and take on the case for Helen. That just proves to me how considerate a friend you can be." He stood up and took a few steps until he was standing in front of her.

"Now I have two favors to ask of you, and I'm not really going to allow you to turn me down. First, there's a little ceremony scheduled for tomorrow that I need you to attend."

She started to protest, but he shook his head. "I'm going to have my stars pinned on, and I want you to be there with me," he announced quietly.

Abby's eyes grew wide with excitement. "Your stars, Father! You got your promotion?" she screeched with delight. "It's really true?" she asked.

The General nodded and smiled again. "Some people said it would never happen, didn't they, Abby." He gently pulled her to her feet facing him and looked into her eyes in an attempt to signal he knew what she had overheard.

"I'll be there, Father. It'd be an honor for me," she replied as she impulsively wrapped her arms about his neck and hugged him tightly.

Then stepping back she asked, "And what is the second favor?"

He nodded, and replied, "I want you to pick out the prettiest frock in your wardrobe and attend the Valentine's Dance with me on Friday night."

The smile on Abby's face disappeared in an instant. Instead a look of frozen fear replaced her easy spirit. "Oh, Father, I can't do that. I can't be around . . . I don't want . . . I'd only embarrass you if I were to attend the dance with you, Father," she finally found something to say to try to explain why she felt she couldn't walk into a room with the other officers' wives. It would just be too unbearable.

The General nodded his understanding, and admitted, "Yes, I know that would be a bit difficult given the lies and rumors that Mrs. Hempstead has spread about you."

Abby's mouth fell open. "You know?" she asked, horrified her father knew the depth of her humiliation.

"Yes, Abby, I know, and I've put an end to it all. If you'd come to me right then, I could've saved you and Garrett so much heartache. If you'd only trusted me with the truth," he said quietly.

Tears welled up again in her eyes. The shame and embarrassment, as well as the sense of loss, had all conspired to destroy her happiness. Now there was at least some relief that her father knew, and from the tone of his voice, it hadn't caused him to stop loving her. She felt confused. She had been so sure he would disown her if this had ever been revealed.

"I didn't want you to know because I was afraid you'd be disappointed in me again. You had just about gotten over the whole mess on Franklin

Street. I was afraid you'd be ashamed that I was your daughter," she cried softly.

He put his arm around his daughter and drew her close to his side, her head leaning against his shoulder. "You should know that there's nothing you can do or say which would make me stop loving you. You are my daughter, my flesh and blood. And point of fact, these lies and rumors were not of your making. Mrs. Hempstead has long been a thorn in my side ever since she and her husband moved in here. I'm sure she eyed living here in the commanding officer's quarters, but that's another story."

Then he turned his daughter's face towards his and looked intently into her green eyes. "Abby, when you love someone, truth is your ally. Regardless of the information, whether it's happy news or difficult news, it's always better to be honest than to try to protect someone by concealing information from them. Even the Bible tells us we should speak the truth in love. You must learn to trust that the people you love deserve the truth, whatever it may be. Do you understand?"

Abby nodded her response and hugged her father again, relieved once again she hadn't lost his love, the love she had sought her whole life to know.

"So, you'll pick out your best dancing gown, and escort me to the dance Friday?" he continued.

"Father, are you sure? Mrs. Hempstead . . ."

He interrupted her with his explanation, "She won't be present at the event, Abby. I've seen to that. Nor will anyone there make any mention of these horrible tales she's been spreading. Everyone knows what a gossip she is, and they also know most of what she says is fabricated to make her sound more important than she is. No, Abby, there's no excuse for you not to attend which I'll accept. In fact, if I have to, I'll issue an official order for you to be there," he said as he winked and smiled at her.

She recognized that no amount of protest would change his mind, so she nodded her head and laid it again on his shoulder. It was so good to feel accepted by him, to feel loved.

"Oh, and one other thing," he added reaching into his pocket and withdrawing her locket. "Roger insisted on fixing this for you, as a thank you for your help."

Abby looked with astonishment at the repaired necklace. "Father? How?"

"The Police Commissioner had returned it to me the day he informed me of the incident. I didn't tell you about it, well, because I wasn't certain that it could be repaired. Roger took it and has worked on it while locked up. He gave it to me this afternoon to give to you," he said reaching to secure the locket around her neck. "There. That's better."

Tears trickled down her cheeks as she reached to touch her beloved locket. For a moment she felt her mother's presence in the room. She could imagine her smiling her appreciation for the repaired relationship between father and daughter. After over twenty years of not knowing, Abby was now certain that her father truly loved her, and it was a glorious feeling.

Garrett, along with 2nd Lieutenant Morgan, had searched several of the back alleys just off Franklin Street, and they were just about to give up, when they finally found the man they knew to be Joe Little standing on the back corner asking for change from the passersby. Garrett offered him a dime, and asked him if he would like to trade his dime for lunch and a little information. Joe frowned, obviously skeptical that the offer was real, but sauntered easily with Garrett and the Lieutenant to a nearby café for coffee and fried chicken.

After the man had eaten his fill, Garrett asked, "So Mr. Little, did you know Dorothy Broadnax very well?"

Joe frowned again. "You two ain't no police, is you?" he asked suspiciously.

"No, Mr. Little. My name is Captain Talbot, and this is 2nd Lieutenant Chester Morgan. I'm the lawyer representing Corporal Davis who was accused of killing Miss Broadnax, and Lieutenant Morgan is assisting me," Garrett answered respectfully.

"Long as you ain't no police. Can't trust 'em, you know. They's as crooked as they get around here," he uttered quietly so no one could overhear him.

Garrett nodded his head and asked his question again, "Did you know Dorothy Broadnax?"

"Yes, sir, I did. She was a decent woman, all in all. She'd see me and give me some money now and then so's I could get somethin' to eat. You know, I used t'work in the mines, until they had to cut back. I wound up having to beg for change on the streets. She always treated me with respect, like you is, sir. I's appreciate that, I do," he added swallowing his last bite of chicken and wiping his hands on his ragged coat.

"Were you outside her window the night she died?" Garrett asked, looking first at the Lieutenant, then back to his witness hoping to get an affirmative response.

Joe nodded his head as he drank another swig of coffee. "I was. I sleeps in that lean-to shed under the steps most of the time 'cause nobody will bother me, and Miss Dorothy'd see to it that I had a bit to eat. She was good t'me.

"Sure was strange goin's on that night, though. I was told that all of Lucy's girls was gonna be out celebratin with everyone else, so I was surprised to see that police fella comin down the back steps. I was hidin in the shed, but I could see through a crack who it was. It was that Offica Dandridge who always runs me off when I tries to get money in the streets. I didn't see no light in Dorothy's window, and I didn't see Miss Dorothy neither. It got real quiet like back there, except for the noise of the parties out in the streets. I thought I'd take a little snooze, but it was cold. Weren't nobody around, so I thought I'd head up them stairs to get another blanket that Miss Dorothy always let me have. That's when that police fella and some other buzniss fella came carrying some soldier lookin fella up the steps. Them two kept on bickerin all the way up there. I got t'thinking that it didn't make no sense to take 'im up there 'im bein passed out like he was." Joe laughed and winked at Garrett. "Know what I mean?"

Garrett was visibly startled, as was Lieutenant Morgan. Not only had Joe been there that night, he could describe actually how the murder took place and how Roger had been set up for it. Joe Little was the answer to Roger's mess. Officer Dandridge and some other man were involved in Dorothy's murder. One of the two of them had actually killed her. Then he and Officer Dandridge had carried a drugged Roger up the stairs and left him to be found with the body the next morning. It didn't matter who had fired the pistol. With Joe's testimony, everything would be solved.

"So what happened next?" the Lieutenant asked.

"Well, I started to leave the alley, and then I heard a loud noise and saw a spark up at Dorothy's window. Then I heard a man scream, which was awful strange to me. Wasn't sure it was a gun 'cause of all the fireworks that was going off at the same time. Then I saw them same two come down the stairs without the soldier fella. And I heard that bizness fella cussin all the way down the steps."

"Will you testify to that in court next week?" Garrett asked excitedly.

Joe Little shook his head vigorously. "No, sir, I won't. Won't do no good anyways. Nobody's gonna believe an old colored man like me," he added matter-of-factly.

"Why do you say that, Mr. Little? We believe you; why wouldn't anybody else believe you?"

"Cause that's what that police fella said when that bizness fella asked him what to do 'bout me. They saw me there in the alley, and the bizness fella wanted the Offica Dandridge to get rid of me right then. But police fella said ain't nobody gonna believe anything that I says anyway, so's they let me be," replied Joe as he finished stuffing the last of the muffins in his pockets.

Then Joe Little shrugged his shoulders. "If I'd let on for one minute that I knew he was her husband that woulda been the end of me."

Garrett's jaw dropped in amazement. But Lieutenant Morgan quickly followed up with a question of his own, "How do you know it was her husband?"

"Cause she showed me his picture on that poster she had. He wants to be mayor, don't he? She said that's why he would be willin to pay her to get out of town. She was goin to take me with her 'cause she said I was the only one somebody in the world that cared if she lived or died. Still nobody's gonna believe what I has to say in a courtroom."

"You know, Captain, the man's probably right," replied the Lieutenant. "No judge will allow a colored to testify against a white man, especially someone as prominent at Matthew Broadnax is."

Garrett frowned. The information was here in this man, a perfectly credible witness at the scene of the murder. How was he going to use that information if the witness couldn't testify?

He thought a minute, and gradually the kernel of an idea began to surface. He nodded to himself, then said, "Tell you what, Mr. Little, if you will just come to the courthouse two weeks from now, I promise I'll not call you to testify. I just need you to be there. But I also can guarantee that your being there will bring justice to Dorothy's murderer. You do want to see him brought to justice, don't you?" he asked.

"Why, yes, sir, I do. Dorothy was good to me. Helpin' put her killer in jail is the least I can do."

"Good. Then you be there at the courthouse in two weeks. Don't forget, now. And when court is over that day, we'll bring you back here for more fried chicken and muffins."

Joe nodded, shook their hands, and wandered out of the café. Abby had been right all along. Matthew Broadnax was involved in his wife's murder. Garrett realized he had the information he needed to free Roger, but it would require a great deal of skill and luck in a courtroom. As the two of them rode the street car back to the fort, Garrett shared with Chet his idea. But they both agreed, they'd have to spin this out very carefully, or it would never work.

CHAPTER

19

Helen brushed Abby's waist-length hair vigorously until it shone like polished copper. She then twisted the mass of waves onto the back of Abby's head and secured them tightly with several combs and pins. She finished off Abby's coiffure with several curled tendrils along the right side of the nape of her slender neck and several smaller curls that settled playfully just above the cheekbones of her face. Helen smiled at the result; staring back from the mirror was the reflection of an angel.

Abby gazed into the mirror and admired Helen's handiwork. She noticed that her green eyes reflected the mixture of excitement and sadness that she felt. Abby now felt secure in her father's love; she realized that there was virtually nothing she could do that could destroy the affection and concern he had expressed for her. After so many years secretly yearning for the physical companionship of a father, Abby now rejoiced that she at last felt complete.

But her heart ached for Garrett. She had been cruel to him, and she felt there were no words which would erase the pain she had caused him. Tonight she would be proud to be on her father's arm at the Valentine's

Ball, but she knew this pride came at the price of her first love. It was a bittersweet realization.

"Helen, why don't you come with us?" Abby asked again having been turned down twice before. "You can still fit into one of the gowns we altered for you in December."

"Now, Abby, I have other plans this evening," she announced happily. "Your father has arranged for me to spend a belated Valentine's with Roger at the stockade. He even arranged for a special dinner for us there, and Sgt. Major McCormick will escort me there and back home safe again. I cannot remember feeling as excited about dinner with my husband in many years." She positively radiated a glow of pleasure.

"You go on to the Ball with your father. I'm sure you'll have a wonderful evening. I'm sure Captain Talbot will be there."

Abby shook her head, "No, I don't think so. I hurt him terribly the last time we came back from town; he tried to argue with me about my decision to end everything. I was afraid so I lied and told him I didn't love him. I told him the only reason I was working with him was because you asked me to. I'm sure he'll never forgive the way I spoke to him. Even if he does decide to attend, I'm certain that I'd be the very last person he'd choose to speak to."

Helen sighed, "I'm so sorry, Abby. I truly thought the two of you were destined to be together. Perhaps when a little time has passed, you can try to apologize."

Abby nodded, "Perhaps."

Helen moved behind her and cinched her corset one more time. Then she steadied her while Abby stepped into the gown. After Helen buttoned the bodice in back, she adjusted the shoulder straps for Abby and flounced the sleeves to enhance the effect. Abby reached to her dressing table and selected a triple strand of tiny pearls that had belonged to her grandmother. She fastened them around her neck, and attached the matching earrings. For her final touch, she slid on her white evening gloves and put on a pearl bangle bracelet on her right wrist. Her black lace fan completed her ensemble for the evening.

Abby gazed wistfully into her large oval mirror at the gown she had chosen for tonight. It was deep blue satin brocaded with delicate green leaves that danced across the fabric. The bodice was slightly square, gently dipping ever-so-slightly at the center which helped to accentuate the tightly cinched waist of the dress. The bouffant sleeves were draped with frills of lace and chiffon, and the shoulder straps were accented with white lace and satin fabric designed roses. The fully gored skirt was cut to enable dancing, and yet would definitely rustle regally as she glided across the dance floor. If she got the chance to dance, maybe with her father.

"I still think this is the most beautiful dress I've ever seen," Helen said. "You have so many lovely dresses, but this one is by far my favorite of all."

Abby nodded and fought to keep an errant tear from falling. "Yes, it's my favorite, too. I had thought I would wear it in December for the New Year's Ball at the Officers' Club. But . . ." she turned away and gazed out the window and left her thought incomplete.

Abby took one final look at her reflection. Staring back was the picture of a lovely young woman with sad green eyes. She took a deep breath, then started down the stairs to join her father. After a few well-chosen words of admiration, he placed her fur cape upon her shoulders and escorted her proudly out of the house.

Between the electric chandeliers and the candlelight sconces, the ballroom in the Officers' Club was ablaze with light when the General entered the doorway with Abigail on his arm. The Sergeant called attention to the hall, and all the company immediately saluted the commanding officer. General Thomas Jefferson Randolph returned the salute, and the company was then called 'at ease'. He stood in the entryway for a few moments with his lovely daughter at his side, her copper-colored hair glistening in the amber glow of the room. After the desired effect, he led his daughter down the three stairs into the ballroom to greet his waiting officers and their wives.

The officers and their wives gathered around the General and his daughter. Mrs. Randall was the first to extend her gloved hand welcoming Abby. "You look absolutely lovely, my dear," she commented. "And that gown is breath-taking," she gushed.

Abby blushed modestly and softly uttered her 'thank you' in response. She felt a bit nervous wondering how many of the women there had heard the awful rumors which Major Hempstead's wife had spread, but as the minutes elapsed with several of the women chatting pleasantly with her and with no mention of those lies, Abby began to relax. The women gathered about her, complimenting her and one another for their selection of gowns for the evening. For a moment, Abby thought she could be at one of the many parties she had attended in college back East. It seemed that women everywhere paid attention to what other women chose to wear to social occasions.

She glanced furtively around the room, but she didn't see Garrett anywhere. Her heart sank. On the one hand, if he were there, she might feel worse knowing he wouldn't be interested in talking with her. On the other hand, in the crowded hall without him, she felt lonely. If only she hadn't tried so hard to discourage his attention. But that was her own fault.

The music started up, and couples began to make their way to the dance floor. Abby stood quietly watching as several of the officers' wives and their husbands walked gracefully away from her. Then her father was at her side, and with a simple, "My dear" he led her to the floor to waltz with the others.

Abby's emotions soared as she was swayed and whirled around the room holding ever so securely onto her father's shoulders. The rhythmic swish of the ladies' gowns and the gleam of the men's polished boots added to the ambience of the moment. The music, the motion, and the sense of belonging all combined to give Abby an ecstatic rush. Then when the music stopped, and the gathered couples stood still, she took a deep breath and sighed. Looking up into her father's eyes, she saw a man who truly adored her, and her returning gaze communicated her appreciation. For a moment, she was a little girl again.

"Sir, may I have your permission to cut in?" came a familiar voice from behind her. She instantly turned to see Captain Talbot standing on the dance floor in his full dress blue uniform, the gold braid insignia and the polished brass buttons reflecting the sparkling light of the room. In the instant she saw him, she caught her breath. She felt frozen to the floor, unable to move or speak. She heard her father's reply and mechanically moved to accept the captain's lead.

Suddenly aware that she hadn't breathed in a few moments, Abby gulped several times until she felt she could breathe normally again. She heard the music begin, and she felt herself moving with him, but as yet she could not find the strength to speak a word. Instead she responded willingly to his lead and swayed gracefully to the music until it swelled to a crescendo.

"Abigail Randolph, in all my life, I've never met a more exasperating woman. You're smart and charming one minute, and the next you are stubborn and pig-headed. From the first time we met, you've baffled me beyond belief. And yet I confess, there hasn't been a moment from that time till now that I could get you completely out of my mind," Garrett said to a startled Abby.

Her knees felt a little weak, so she held onto him more tightly to keep from falling as he waltzed her quickly around the floor. She was grateful that both the movement and the music made it difficult for her to reply. She was at a loss for words.

The music stopped, and Abby stood still with her left arm on his right shoulder and her right gloved hand trembling in his hand. She felt that her feet were frozen in place to the floor. From the corner of her eye, she could see other couples leaving the dance floor, and suddenly she felt very exposed. Then, without any warning, Abby watched as Captain Talbot bent down on one knee, still gently holding onto her right hand.

"Miss Randolph, it seems that everyone in the room knows how I feel about you, and they've conspired to help me get your undivided attention," he said loudly enough so that all of the guests in the room could easily hear him.

"Since you've arrived here at Fort Douglas, I've found myself unable to think of anything without also thinking of you. I've tried, with your insistence, to put you out of my mind and heart, but I've found that to be an impossible task. So in front of your father and all of these witnesses, I'm going to ask you, just this one time, will you do me the honor of becoming my wife and partner in life?"

Then he reached into his pocket and withdrew a small box. He opened it, and presented Abby with the ring he had planned to give her six weeks ago.

Abby remained shocked in place, unable to speak or even to breathe. Her eyes were filling with unspent tears. Then she looked at the lovely token he offered to her— a reddish-orange garnet surrounded by a double row of diamonds.

She glanced from the ring back to the handsome face of the man she felt she didn't deserve. His gray-blue eyes glowed with anticipation, but she couldn't find the words to answer him. She pursed her lips and unrestrained tears trickled down her cheeks. She instinctively brought her right hand up to her face and took a deep breath, then nodded her assent.

"Miss Randolph, I'm afraid I'm going to need to hear your response," he replied.

Abby took a deep breath, blushed modestly, and answered, "Yes, Captain Talbot, I'll marry you."

He grinned and breathed deeply while Abby removed the glove from her left hand. When he slid the ring over her finger, the room exploded in applause and cheers. Garrett stood up to greet his bride-to-be holding both of her hands in his. Then he pulled her closer and gently kissed her. When she responded, he wrapped her tightly in his arms and kissed her with a passion that had been restrained for well over a month. When the music started up again, he led her back to her father's side and accepted the congratulations of the waiting officers and their wives.

"Well, it's about time," General Randolph laughed. "It sure took you two enough time to see what I've known since the day you arrived here at Fort Douglas."

He hugged his daughter tightly before he turned to shake Garrett's hand. "Now, I don't want to hear about any long engagement. You two've been separated long enough."

"No, sir, I don't intend to allow her to have the time to change her mind," Garrett replied. "As soon as this trial is over, we'll work on the arrangements."

She beamed and blushed, still feeling a little like she might just be dreaming this night. Most of the other couples had now returned to the dance floor leaving her to catch her breath alongside her father and her fiancé. The words began to echo in her consciousness, and she was stunned.

Earlier tonight she had felt that she had lost Garrett forever; now, here she stood in this dream-like state, slowly coming to the realization that she had accepted his marriage proposal in front of the entire company. Then it dawned on her— everyone had applauded. There was no laughter or cat-calls, only the polite response of an assembled crowd which apparently approved of the choice Garrett had made.

He wasn't the laughingstock of the post as Mrs. Hempstead had implied, and she was going to be Captain Garret Jackson Talbot's wife. And once the trial was over, the two of them would be planning their wedding. Her father had expressed his opinion that there should be no long engagement. She wouldn't have to wait long before she would be married to the man of her dreams. She caught her breath for fear she might wake up and this beautiful night would vaporize.

"I can't believe this," she expressed, finally able to formulate words.

Garrett smiled and nodded. "I know, it seems a little strange to me, too, especially after you were so explicit about your feelings. To tell the truth, Abby, if your father hadn't told me how you were acting at home,

I never would've guessed that you'd agree to marry me tonight." He touched her face with his hand moving a stray curl from near her eye. Then he gazed lovingly into her eyes, "Abby, I think I could drown in your eyes. What a wonderful fate."

They spent the rest of the evening dancing and receiving congratulations from the guests at the Ball. Abby laughed and danced until she had to admit she was exhausted. During one of the breaks from the dance floor, Mrs. Randall volunteered to help Abby with the wedding plans, and several of the other officers' wives were giddy with excitement over the coming nuptials. They all wanted to help with the plans and pre-wedding parties. For the first time since she had arrived at Fort Douglas, Abby truly felt that she was an accepted member of the community there.

Martha Jennings took Abby's hands in hers, congratulating her again. "I'm so happy for you, my dear; everyone is. But I have a confession to make.

"Remember when you asked me if I'd ever voted since I've lived here? Well, I couldn't say so in Edith Hempstead's hearing because I knew she'd disapprove, but I did once. It was such a thrilling experience for me. I just wanted you to know. And what you were trying to do to help those women in town, well, we are all so proud of you, risking your own safety to help someone." She patted Abby on the shoulder and smiled approvingly as several of the officers' wives began milling around the General's daughter.

Abby felt tears well up in her eyes, tears of happiness. She was suddenly aware of how blessed she was: she had her father, Garrett, Helen, and now all of these women friends. Helen's baby would be born in the house later this spring, a wedding would be celebrated, and soon she would have a family of her own to nurture. There was much to look forward to once the trial was complete. She only hoped Garrett's efforts in the courtroom would gain Roger his freedom, and perhaps, identify the real murderer.

CHAPTER

Ten days later as Abigail and her father rode up to the new City and County Building, the edifice seemed to emerge out of the ground like an immense sandstone monument. The reddish gray sandstone structure was designed in the Romanesque Revival style with giant round turrets and squared towers. The central squared clock tower had four faces so that the time could be read from any of the four entrances to the building. Above each entrance were pressed metal statues as well as intricate leaf friezes carved into the stone.

The steps leading up to the east entrance were polished pink granite, and at the top of the steps were massive pink granite columns, three to a side. The door itself was more than fifteen feet tall carved oak wood with glass insets; attention to detail included the carved brass faceplates at the doorknobs and at the hinge plates. Just approaching the building and gazing upon the artwork presented there brought Abby to a sense of awe she had never felt before.

"Father, look at this place," Abby exclaimed as she entered through the double doors on her father's arm. She was amazed at the grandeur displayed in a single building. Marble steps lined by carved polished oak banisters were supported by elaborately carved black ironwork.

At the top of the steps, Abby could see the massive brass chandelier which lit the center archway opening into the four entrances. In the center archway, cream-colored geometric shape outlines emerged from the flat red painted wall surface. Even with people streaming in to attend the court session this morning, Abby could see that the floor was inset with multi-colored mosaic tiles. The entire building seemed to be an intricate work of art.

The walls along the hallway to the courtroom were marble about three feet up to an oaken chair railing, and above the railing, the walls were a dark reddish brown below a bright cream-colored carved ceiling. The hallway was brightly lit by the wall sconces and three large chandeliers. The doorframe above the courtroom was fifteen feet high with a glass inset above the doors and twin frosted glass insets in the oaken doors themselves; shiny brass doorknobs reflected the light from the chandeliers.

The entire experience of coming into this building and into this courtroom overwhelmed Abby with reverence. Several times she had placed her gloved hand up to her mouth as she took in the beauty of the premises. She gazed up at her father and saw the intensity of concern etched on his face. The awe of the building was suddenly replaced with a realization of the seriousness of the situation. She knew that the next few days were critical for all the people she had grown to love. And it would all be played out here in the City and County Building in Salt Lake City, Utah. She took a seat next to her father and waited as the stage was set for Corporal Davis's trial.

"All rise." called the bailiff from the front of the courtroom. Immediately, a hush fell across the room as the judge entered and took his seat behind the enormous desk.

Captain Talbot, Lieutenant Morgan, and Corporal Davis stood together behind a table; an oaken railing separated Helen from her husband. General Randolph sat between Helen and his daughter in an effort to bring what comfort he could to the Corporal's wife. The prosecutor, Jacob Moore, stood at a table adjacent to the defense table alongside his assistant. When the bailiff called for the assemblage to be seated, everyone sat except for the prosecutor who proceeded to address the judge.

"The prosecution is ready to begin, your Honor."

The judge nodded and turned in the direction of the defense table.

Captain Talbot stood and immediately responded, "We're ready, too, Your Honor." He shuffled through some papers before he announced, "Your Honor, if it please the court, the defense does not wish a jury trial. We are more than convinced justice will be served by relying on your judgment in this matter."

"I object, your Honor," came the response from the prosecution's table. "We are prepared to impanel a jury at this time."

The startled judge at first frowned. Then a look of pure amusement came over his face. "Sir, you cannot object to the defense's request for a non-jury trial. That is his right as the defendant. Now, let's move along with opening statements and witnesses."

"But, your Honor, the prosecution was prepared to deal with jury selection today," replied the befuddled attorney. "We will need some time."

"Fiddlesticks," the judge nearly shouted. "Either make your opening statement now, or call your first witness."

Garrett sat down at the defense table. The first battle was his; the judge saw the apparent inexperience in the prosecution which could work in Roger's favor. Asking for a non-jury trial was no accident. The General knew Judge Wyatt Monroe very well. His reputation for fairness and honesty made him a target of less scrupulous jurists and politicians. Garrett knew that they would receive fair treatment at his hands. And it would be less risky than relying on a jury made up of entirely Mormon citizens.

"Well, Your Honor," began the prosecutor strutting from behind the table, "on the night of January 6th of this year, a woman was shot to death in her own residence. The defendant, Roger Davis, was found passed out in her bed the next morning, and his gun was found lying on the floor next to the bed.

"One can only conclude the obvious. That on the night in question, Corporal Roger Davis did with malice of forethought enter the chamber of Dorothy Broadnax and shoot her to death before passing out in her bed. The state will prove beyond any doubt that this indeed was exactly what happened, and that the defendant, Corporal Davis, is guilty of murder." He returned to the prosecutor's table and sat down.

Captain Talbot stood, nodded in the direction of the prosecution to show respect for the opposition, then stated, "Your Honor, the prosecution has indeed given an accurate account of the crime. Certainly, someone entered Mrs. Broadnax's chamber that night, and certainly someone fired my client's gun killing her. However, the defense will prove that my client was not the one who shot Mrs. Broadnax. In fact, the defense will show that my client, Corporal Roger Davis, is also a victim in this crime. We will show that someone else actually killed Mrs. Broadnax and put Corporal Davis in her bed to take the blame."

The room exploded with excitement as everyone began to mutter and share their disbelief. The judge pounded his gavel repeatedly calling for order, and again the room was covered with a reverent hush.

Captain Talbot uttered, "Thank you, Your Honor," and returned to his seat. The drama had begun.

Abby watched the scene with amazement. Here was the man she loved at work. He seemed so self-assured and confident as he spoke on behalf of Roger in the courtroom. She felt a sense of pride she didn't know she could feel. When he sat down at the table in front of her, she had to restrain the impulse to cheer.

"Call your first witness, Mr. Moore," the judge ordered, and the prosecutor obediently called for the coroner, Dr. Gibson, to come to the stand. The bailiff placed a Bible in front of the witness and recited the oath to tell the truth. Jacob Moore stood up and approached the witness stand to begin his questioning.

The testimony was expected— Dorothy Broadnax was dead on the scene that morning from an apparent gun shot. The doctor had examined her body in her room after the defendant had been taken into custody. Her cause of death was ruled homicide from gun shot. Then the prosecutor turned the witness over to Garrett.

Abby looked at Garrett sitting at the defense table and saw Lt. Morgan slide a small piece of paper in front of him. Garrett stood, picked up the paper, nodded to Lieutenant Morgan, then stepped toward the witness stand. "Dr. Gibson, did you notice a lot of blood in the room where Mrs. Broadnax was found?" he asked folding the paper up and slipping it into his pocket.

The witness frowned and answered, "Why, no, I didn't."

"Have you examined victims of gun shot before?" Garrett went on.

"Yes, I have, many times."

"Is there usually evidence of a lot of blood when someone has been shot?"

"Yes, indeed there is. Once I examined a miner who had been shot; there was so much blood it was difficult to get to the body without stepping into the pool that surrounded him. Why do you ask?"

"Well, I examined the scene of the crime after Mrs. Broadnax's body had been removed from the room, and both my assistant and I were puzzled by the very small amount of blood found on her bed. Did you find that odd?"

"I didn't think of it at the time, Captain, but now that you mention it, that was odd," Dr. Gibson added, frowning as he reflected on the event.

"Doctor, what would cause there not to be much bleeding from a gun shot?" Garrett asked hoping to elicit from the doctor that the cause of death might not be from Roger's gun.

"Well, I can't really say. But now that I think about it, that small amount of blood was certainly strange."

Since the doctor wasn't going to say the words, Garrett asked a different question. "Were there any other marks on the victim's body, Doctor?"

The witness frowned and seemed to be trying to remember how Dorothy's body looked that day. Then he referred to his notebook and replied, "I remember there were some bruises on her, like she might have been in a fight or something."

"Bruises, Doctor? Where in particular?"

"On her face and some on her arms," the doctor answered nodding.

"Bruises like she had been in a fight. Could those bruises have been from a struggle of some sort?"

"I suppose they could have. I really can't say. But there was definitely a gunshot in her chest."

"But there wasn't much bleeding, was there, Doctor? Is it possible she died in some sort of struggle with her attacker when she got those bruises, and she was shot after she was already dead?" Garrett had to just come right out and say the words.

"Objection!" exclaimed the prosecutor, realizing the direction of the questioning.

Judge Monroe looked at the prosecutor and back at the witness. He seemed interested in what the doctor might answer to this question. He shook his head and replied, "Objection overruled. The witness may answer the question."

Dr. Gibson scratched his head and pondered for a moment before responding, "Well, I suppose it's possible, Captain. But why would someone want to shoot her if she were already dead?"

"Good question, Doctor, and one I hope we all have the answer to before this trial is over. No further questions," Garrett said as he walked back to the defense table.

Then the prosecutor stood again and called the next witness, Lucy Powell. She swayed into the courtroom and took her seat on the witness stand, adjusting her skirt and petticoats as she sat down. The prosecutor asked her to give her full name and business which she ran on Franklin

Street. Lucy didn't even blush when she obediently responded that she was the proprietor of a gentlemen's establishment.

Abby giggled to herself as she watched the woman. This was probably the first time she had received such attention in public. Suddenly she had celebrity status. Just as with the doctor, Lucy's testimony was expected. She found Dorothy's body and Roger passed out in Dorothy's bed; she called for the police, and she led Officer Dandridge into the room. She was present when the police discovered the gun on the floor of the room and arrested Corporal Davis for the murder. Then the prosecutor returned to his seat, and Garrett stood to question Lucy.

"Good morning, m'am," he said as he approached the witness stand. "How are you doing today, Mrs. Powell?" Even though he knew she wasn't married, he gave her the title he knew would please her in this audience.

Lucy smiled broadly at the obvious respect. "Fine, Captain. Just fine. Thank you for askin'," she replied.

Garrett nodded and continued with his questioning. "Mrs. Powell, I went to Mrs. Broadnax's room shortly after the murder. Could you tell the Judge about her room for me?"

"Why, of course, Captain. I'd be ever so happy to tell 'm." Lucy turned towards the Judge and batted her eyes before she began, "Well, your Honor, Dorothy had the room at the top of the stairs that all my girls wished they could have. You see, her room had a back door. She used it so some of her clients could be more discreet in the use of her services," she said winking at the judge.

Judge Monroe's eyes widened with embarrassment as the woman obviously flirted with him in open court. But rather than call attention to the situation, he instead cleared his throat repeatedly and motioned for Garrett to continue his questioning.

"Would Corporal Davis be one of those kinds of clients, Mrs. Powell?" Garrett asked.

"Goodness, no, Captain. Those back stairs were reserved for her high payin' clients, those men of the community who could afford privacy, if you know what I mean?" she answered shaking her head saucily.

Garrett grinned in response. "Well, Mrs. Powell, had you ever seen Corporal Davis in your establishment before that morning?" he asked.

"No, never. We don't get many soldiers at Lucy's because the General over there has kinda ordered them to stay away. Guess he doesn't want the kind of trouble that goes with my line of work, if you know what I mean." The courtroom audience laughed loudly in response to Lucy's remarks. But one stern look from the judge and all was quiet again.

"You've never seen Corporal Davis there before that morning?" Garrett asked again to emphasize her response.

"Like I said, we don't get soldiers much, and I didn't see him the night before and any other night for that matter. The first time I ever saw him was that mornin' when I walked into her room and found him passed out in her bed and poor Dorothy next to him."

"Then you can't say for sure that he was in her room before she was killed, can you?" Garrett continued.

"No, I can't, Captain. I can only speak to what I know. He was there that mornin' in her bed and she was dead."

"Thank you, Mrs. Powell. You've been a most charming witness."

Lucy grinned broadly as she stepped down from the witness stand. Abby watched as Garrett returned to the defense table. When their eyes met, he winked at her. She was sure that he had gotten the information he needed the judge to hear from the witness.

The prosecutor stood again to address the Judge. "Your Honor, my next witness is not present in the court. May we have a recess to notify him?"

Judge Monroe looked at his pocket watch. "Mr. Moore, it's just a little past noon. Why don't we break for lunch and resume tomorrow morning at 9 A. M. sharp. You can have the rest of your witnesses present by then, can't you?" he asked.

The prosecutor nodded, and Judge Monroe pounded his gavel on the desk. The bailiff called for the assemblage to rise as he left the courtroom, then those gathered in the room began to exit.

Abby watched as Garrett and Lieutenant Morgan spoke with one another. Then her father ushered her and Helen from the courtroom and down the hall to a conference room where Garrett and Lt. Morgan had brought Roger. Helen embraced Roger emotionally, and the rest of them stood watch. After the guards led Roger back to the stockade, Abby left the room with her father. Garrett and the Lieutenant could plan their next move. Abby knew that so far, everything had gone as they had hoped it would; tomorrow, Officer Dandridge would take the stand, and Garrett would have his first real challenge to face in the trial.

CHAPTER

21

A bleak icy wind had pressed in on them as Abby rode in from Fort Douglas with her father and Helen. She drew closer to Helen in order to get warmer under the riding blankets her father had spread across them before they had left that morning. She shivered as she wondered if the weather wasn't a signal of the day's events in the courtroom. She shook her head as if to chase these frightening thoughts away.

But stepping into the massive court building overwhelmed her with a sense of dread. She felt a chill run down her back. She tried to shake off the feeling when she sat down in the courtroom. She hoped for Roger's sake that she was just imagining the worst. She said a quick prayer in an effort to calm herself. It wasn't good to entertain these negative feelings.

As was promised the day before, the prosecutor called Officer Dandridge to the stand, and as expected, he recounted the events of the morning when Roger had been found in the murdered prostitute's bed. When the prosecutor turned the witness over to Garrett, Abby took a deep breath. She felt that this man was tied up in the plan to implicate Roger. If that were true, he was probably expecting something in return for his involvement. He would not be an easy witness to discredit this morning. Garrett had his work cut out for him.

"Good morning, Officer," Garrett said. "I just have a few questions for you. It shouldn't take too much of your time." Garrett strolled out from behind the defense table and approached the witness stand.

"That morning wasn't the first time you had seen Corporal Davis, was it?" He purposefully posed the question so that the policeman would know he knew the correct answer to it.

"No, I saw him the night before, as we discussed," he answered obediently. "I believe I saw him at Connor's; it was very crowded there, as it was just about everywhere that night. There was so much celebrating going on. My job was just crowd control."

"And where did you see him later that same evening?" Garrett asked leading his witness.

"At Dixon's, I think," Officer Dandridge replied. "I think he was there playing cards."

"Did you see anyone else there that you knew?"

"Yeah, there were plenty of people there I knew. See them just about every night," he answered laughing.

"How about Matthew Broadnax? Do you remember seeing him there?"

Officer Dandridge frowned, "No, I don't recollect seeing him there."

Garrett frowned, too, "Well, that's strange, because he admitted to seeing you there."

Officer Dandridge's face reddened noticeably. "Oh, well, I guess, now that you mention it, he was there, too, at a card table, I think. That's probably why I didn't remember right off."

"So, let me get this correct. You were in Dixon's and you saw my client and Matthew Broadnax, among others, playing cards. Is that correct, Officer?" Garrett asked.

"Yeah, that's correct."

"Officer, are you aware that a back door at Dixon's opens onto an alley that is shared with the back entrance to Lucy's?" Garrett asked, leading the witness to state facts into evidence.

"Why, yes, I guess so. Most anybody knows that, Captain," he answered cockily.

"Well, not just anybody. I daresay the judge was unaware of it until you confirmed that information for him," Garrett answered nodding his approval.

Officer Dandridge hesitated. He was obviously not pleased that Garrett had led him to reveal information to the judge. His forehead seemed totally scrunched together like wadded up paper.

"Oh, and Officer Dandridge, with your years of experience in police work, could you answer a question posed earlier by one of the witnesses? Dr. Gibson wondered why anyone would shoot a person who was already dead. Can you respond to that?" Garrett asked.

"I don't know. Maybe to be sure they was dead, I guess."

Moving towards the witness, Garrett then asked what he intended to be his final question of this witness.

"Officer Dandridge, what reason might Corporal Davis have for murdering a woman he'd never met before?"

Officer Dandridge scowled at Garrett. Abby imagined she could see steam rising from his head. He squinted and glared first at Garrett, then at her. She could feel his eyes blazing with the formation of an answer.

"I guess you'll have to ask Corporal Davis. But since you've asked me, I guess it has to do with that little lady there," he responded, extending his right arm to point at Abby.

Everyone, including Garrett, followed the direction of that index finger, and Abby turned beet red with embarrassment.

"You know, I heard it was Dorothy Broadnax that Miss Randolph was looking for the night those men assaulted her on Franklin Street. I guess Corporal Davis got drunk and decided to avenge the lady's honor by killing the woman who was responsible for the General's daughter nearly getting raped last fall."

The room burst into buzzing, muttering voices as those present began to debate the issue. Abby felt hot from being made a spectacle all over again. And to have her trauma connected so easily to Corporal Davis's dilemma was even more shameful. Now the entire courtroom knew that she had been attacked on Franklin Street; but even more damaging than that, was the witness had provided a credible motive for Roger killing Dorothy, and Garrett had elicited this information with his question.

Like unringing a bell, it was impossible to take back. With just a few words, Garrett had helped the prosecution's case against Roger. Garrett dismissed the witness, and turned to see Abby sitting by her father. She looked up helplessly at Garrett as tears streamed uncontrollably down her face. She sniffed and quickly left the room with her father behind her, as the prosecutor announced that their case was complete.

The judge called for a brief recess before calling witnesses for the defense. Garrett shook his head repeatedly as he sat at the defense table. How could he have been so careless as to ask a question when he didn't know how the witness would answer it? And from a key witness, no less. How in the world was he going to be able to salvage this case?

Lieutenant Morgan patted him on the back, and spoke softly, "Sorry about that, Captain. It's just too bad he felt obliged to bring up Miss Randolph's misadventure. But we have other witnesses, and some really important evidence that we've not yet revealed in court. There's still a good chance that you'll be able to turn Matthew Broadnax's testimony against the two of them."

Garrett shook his head again. "Damn! I wish I'd never asked that question. What was I thinking?" Then turning to look behind him, he asked, "Where's Abby? Is she all right?"

Lieutenant Morgan nodded, "She'll be fine. She's the General's daughter; she's made of tougher stuff, just like her father. We need to focus on our next move, Captain. Who do you want to call first?"

Garrett sighed. Chet was right; there were more important issues at hand than Abby's embarrassment. Roger's life depended on what he did from this moment on. He needed to focus on this case and try to comfort Abby later.

"I think we might as well start with Roger," Garrett answered turning his attention to the order of witnesses.

"What about recalling Lucy Powell, Captain? You can ask her about Dorothy's plans to go to San Francisco and about Joe Little."

"Yes, that sounds like a plan."

The bailiff called for everyone to stand as Judge Monroe reentered the courtroom. Garrett called Roger to the stand to have him recount the events of the night Dorothy was killed— meeting Officer Dandridge, leaving Connor's to go to Dixon's to play cards, seeing Matthew Broadnax at the card table, as well as Officer Dandridge in the room, then waking up the next morning not knowing how he had gotten there. Garrett intentionally left out the information about the gun misfiring; he hoped he could introduce that information when Matthew Broadnax was on the stand. Jacob Moore tried in vain to shake Roger's story. When he had asked his last question, he shrugged his shoulders and sat down confidently.

Then Garrett recalled Lucy Powell to the stand. After being reminded that she was still under oath, Garrett approached the witness stand to ask a few more questions. "Now, Mrs. Powell, you told us yesterday that you'd never seen Corporal Davis in your establishment before that morning. Is that still your testimony?"

"Yes, of course it is," she said obviously offended that her veracity was being questioned.

"Has Officer Dandridge been in your establishment before?" he asked.

"Now, Captain, it's not polite to ask about my clients," she answered with a kittenish voice.

The judge turned toward her with a frown. "Mrs. Powell, has Officer Dandridge been a customer in your establishment?" he asked.

Lucy turned toward the judge, pursed her lips, and nodded.

"I believe we need to hear the response for the record, Mrs. Powell," Garrett stated.

"Oh, all right, yes, he has," she answered grudgingly.

"Many times?" Garrett asked following up on an idea.

"Yes."

"So he might know about the back door leading up to Dorothy's room?"

"Why, of course. All my most regular clients knew about that. Many of them used it to avoid anybody knowing their business, though Officer Dandridge didn't seem to care if folks saw him comin' and goin' from the house," she replied.

Garrett nodded. He had opened the door to evidence that Officer Dandridge knew his way around the brothel and the back entrance. Now he was ready to change the direction of her testimony some. "Thank you, Mrs. Powell. Now, can you tell the court who Joe Little is?"

"He's just a harmless drunk who hangs around the back alley some," she answered with an annoyed frown. "He was friends with Dorothy. She was nice t'him. Gave him money from time to time."

"You say he was in the back alley some. Was he ever a problem for Dorothy?" he asked.

"Heavens, no," Lucy Powell exclaimed, pausing before offering the rest of her information. "Fact is, Dorothy talked about takin' him to San Francisco when she got 'nough money together."

"San Francisco? Why? Was she planning to leave?" he asked, glad that he didn't have to bring up the money issue himself.

"Yeah, she was. Told me she had a cousin there with a dress shop where she could be a partner when she got 'nough money to buy herself in."

"Do you have any idea where she was getting this money, Mrs. Powell?"

"From her former husband, Matthew Broadnax, of course. She was plain as day 'bout that. All of us knew she expected he would provide her the money to get out of town so he wouldn't be embarrassed for folks to learn what'd happened to her when he put her out."

There it was; Matthew Broadnax's motive for killing Dorothy, and it was stated in open court without his having to encourage the witness.

Once again the room exploded with whispering voices at the evidence revealed. The judge pounded his gavel, and the room hushed obediently. Garrett thanked Mrs. Powell for her cooperation, and when the prosecutor had no questions, she stepped down from the witness stand. Good.

"Gentlemen, if you are in agreement, let's recess today until tomorrow morning," announced the judge. Garrett breathed a sigh of relief and nodded. Jacob Moore shrugged his shoulders. When the judge left the courtroom, the majority of people exited as well. Garrett looked at Lieutenant Morgan and nodded.

"I think we have set the stage. Let's have Broadnax on the stand first thing tomorrow; and it's critical that Joe Little is present when I question her husband. I need him to be here so that Broadnax knows that I know the truth. Got to make him think that I would put Mr. Little on the stand, even though we both agree that we can't ask that of him. No, Roger's only hope is for me to get Broadnax to break on the witness stand."

When Garrett entered the General's residence later that evening, he could tell that Abby had spent most of the afternoon crying. Her eyes were red and puffy, and her nose appeared tender. He rushed to her side and wrapped his arms around her. For a few moments, the two of them rocked back and forth together, Abby crying quietly with Garrett gently stroking her back. Finally, he drew back and wiped the tears from her face with his handkerchief. Then he led her over to the settee where they both sat. Garrett put his arm around her shoulder and gently pulled her to his side.

"I'm so sorry, Abby. I regretted asking that question just a soon as the words left my mouth. I knew better than to ask a question like that. The one thing my law professor stressed in class was to never ask a question if you aren't sure of the expected response."

"It's all my fault, Garrett," she protested as she pulled back from him enough to look at his face. "If I hadn't been so pig-headed, none of this would have happened. We wouldn't all be tangled up in this mess now. And Roger and Helen wouldn't be separated at this special time in their lives. It's all my fault! I should never have come here. I've created nothing but havoc."

"No you haven't," he answered. "None of this was your doing, Abby. That bastard killed his wife to try to preserve his chances for election, that's the truth, plain and simple."

Abby sniffed again and looked up at him. "But you were right. I should have listened to you. It was so reckless of me to get involved with that situation."

"Now, Abby, I don't want to have to keep repeating myself," he said and smiled as he continued to wipe the traces of tears from her face. "You have a magnificently large heart. You wanted to help strangers who were not in a position to help themselves. You are brave and strong, and I love you for that.

"None of us could have predicted how all of this would play out last fall. We had no way of knowing the lengths to which this man would go in order to cover his crime. Now, go wash your beautiful face, and let's get ready for supper," he said as he stood up and gently lifted her from the settee so she could follow his directions. She nodded and responded by walking obediently to the washroom.

General Randolph, who had been watching the interchange between his daughter and her fiancé, stepped from the corner. "After what I just saw, there's no doubt in my mind that you do truly love her, Garrett. All the way home I tried in vain to persuade her everything would be all right. She kept insisting she had ruined all of our lives by coming here, and I couldn't convince her otherwise. But in just a few moments, you were able to reach that spot inside of her no one else can touch," he announced reaching to shake his adjutant's hand. "I'm so very proud that you'll be my son-in-law."

"Thank you, sir. I apologize for the mess I made of things today in court. But Lieutenant Morgan got me back on track after you and Abby left; I think we've salvaged the case. Tomorrow will be the critical stage. I've got to lead Broadnax very carefully in order to get him to break on the stand. And it's absolutely crucial that Joe Little be present in the courtroom in order for my plan to work. This is the most dangerous assignment I can ever remember, sir, and I hope I'm up to the task."

"You are, Garrett, I'm certain of it. Your plan will work, it's got to work," replied the General. "I have faith in your courtroom skills, son. And with God's help, we will all be having supper with Roger right here in this house tomorrow night."

CHAPTER

Abby took a deep breath before walking up the steps into the City and County Building. The scene of her humiliation just yesterday was quite intimidating, but Helen and Roger needed her support. So she clung tightly to her father's arm as he led both women into the building and down the hall towards the courtroom.

"Miss Randolph?" came a voice from behind them.

Abby turned to face the person calling her name while her father stood close behind her with Helen still on his arm. "Yes?" Abby replied.

"Do you remember me?" Rachel Porter asked. "At the Methodist Church? The Women's Housing Association?"

Abby smiled, somewhat embarrassed. She hadn't seen or spoken with anyone from that organization since that horrible incident on Franklin Street last fall. "Of course, I remember you," she finally answered. Then she stepped closer and took the woman's hand. She felt a tear start to roll down her cheek, then she impulsively hugged the woman who had offered her counsel so many months ago. Mrs. Porter had been right, Abby thought. How much trouble might have been avoided if she had only followed this gentle woman's advice back then.

"We've been following the trial, you know," Rachel said. Then she stepped back and was joined by two other women that were only somewhat familiar to Abby.

"I know you don't remember me," offered the one standing to Rachel's right. "But I remember you. You saved my life."

Abby frowned and shook her head. There must be some mistake.

"I met you in the park. You asked my friend and me about Dorothy. I told you to meet me later on Franklin Street, remember?"

Abby's eyes began to fill with tears. This was the woman who had told her that Dorothy didn't need her help.

"I never really thought you'd show up, you know. It was a dangerous place for a lady. So when I saw you there that night, well I couldn't believe that someone like you'd risk her life to help someone like us," she said gesturing to the other woman standing beside Rachel.

"Anyways, when we heard the next morning what had happened to you, well, I guess I felt guilty 'cause you wouldn't have been there if I hadn't told you to come. But then it made me think that all of you was serious about helping women like me. That afternoon, Alice and me packed up our few belongings and walked over to the Methodist Church. We told them a red-headed lady said we'd get help here, and right away, Mrs. Porter took us to the rescue house. We were so grateful that we got five other working girls rescued by Christmas. And it's all because of you, Miss Randolph. You saved my life, and six other women, too."

Abby felt chills cover her arms as her eyes filled with tears. Whatever humiliation or embarrassment she had endured no longer mattered at all.

"God can make something good come out of something bad, my dear, just like the Bible says," Rachel stated. "You didn't know it at the time, and often in life, we never see it for ourselves, but here is living proof that your example brought hope and salvation to others."

Abby smiled and hugged both of the women whom she had met briefly in a park almost six months ago. The three of them stood crying softly and smiling through their tears of relief.

"Miss Randolph, I wanted to contact you myself earlier last fall, to see if you were all right and to let you know that your efforts had produced seven saved women. But I didn't know if you had told your father about your involvement with WHA. I didn't want to risk creating more difficulty for you at the time. And when Dorothy Broadnax was killed, well, we were all in shock. But we're all relieved to see that you are doing well and your father is by your side still," she said nodding to Abby's father who had moved directly behind his daughter. "Perhaps you'll be willing to rejoin our organization after all this mess is cleared up."

"There's no doubt that she will want to continue her work with you fine Christian women," her father said, reaching to shake Mrs. Porter's hand. "I'm very proud of my daughter. And I want to thank you for giving her this encouragement this morning."

Abby was astonished that her father would make such a suggestion. But standing there before her was living proof she could be useful in helping save the lives of other women. She hadn't done anything all that special. She had simply extended herself to reach one person. And now that one person was dead, the victim of a horrible crime, and Roger and Helen's lives were in jeopardy as well. God had intervened before; they needed His help once again. As they all strode into the courtroom and took their seats, Abby prayed that God would direct Garrett as he interviewed Matthew Broadnax on the stand. They needed a miracle. She just prayed God would provide another one today.

With the bailiff calling for order in the court, Garrett took a deep breath. So much depended upon his carefully phrasing his questions in order to elicit the correct response from the witness; and this particular witness would make or break the case for him and for Roger. He knew he had to proceed slowly and cunningly. He had to make Matthew Broadnax believe that Garrett was sympathetic to his situation in order to trick him into revealing his true nature. This much was critical.

Standing behind the defense table, Garrett called for his key witness, Matthew Broadnax, to take the stand. The banker and candidate for mayor lumbered across the room, one hand in his jacket pocket and the other waving to potential voters. But Garrett was distracted. He looked across at the sea of white faces that surrounded him, and panic began to replace his sense of confidence.

Garrett quickly shot a look to Lieutenant Morgan. Instantly, the Lieutenant left the room, and the General followed him without uttering a sound. Garrett had to rely on his assistant and his commanding officer to locate Joe Little. In the meantime, he had to gently lead this witness to reveal enough about the case to convince the judge there was more evidence here. He just hoped that he could work slowly enough in order to give Joe Little time to arrive.

"Good morning, Mr. Broadnax. I appreciate your taking time out of your schedule to appear here today. I hope it wasn't too much of an inconvenience for you. I know how busy you must be between your responsibilities at the bank and your mayoral campaign," Garrett began.

The witness nodded nervously just as Garrett began his initial questioning. "Could you tell the court about your relationship to the victim, Mr. Broadnax?"

Matthew Broadnax cleared his throat and nodded. "Dorothy was my wife for about eleven years."

"For the record, Mr. Broadnax, will you tell the court about your religious affiliation?"

"I'm proud to say, I am Mormon," he answered with an air of confidence.

"And, as a Mormon, you previously had more than one wife, isn't that true?"

"Yes, just as most of the saints that are in this valley. We followed the directives of Brigham Young. It was sanctioned by our church."

"Yes, we know, Mr. Broadnax. You are not on trial here for polygamy, sir, and nothing you say here about your multiple marriages will be used against you; trust me on that," Garrett assured.

Looking around behind him, Garrett saw Jacob Moore and others in the courtroom nodding their heads in agreement.

"How long have you been a married man, Mr. Broadnax?" Garrett continued, still painfully aware that Joe Little was not present in the room.

"Eighteen years, Captain, prior to the Woodruff Manifesto, of course. I had four wives. And I'm proud to say I have eleven fine children," he added smiling for the audience.

"Eleven children?" Garrett repeated. "That must keep you very busy trying to provide for so many mouths."

"It's my family, Captain. I'm not complaining. I've got six strapping boys, two of whom are heading off to college this fall; and I have five daughters. I'm proud of all my children, Captain."

"Of course, you should be, Mr. Broadnax. It's every man's dream to have such a family. Congratulations, sir," Garrett continued facing the crowd of onlookers. He saw quite a few men and women in the courtroom who were nodding their heads in agreement. Good.

Garrett nodded in response, and asked, "So when did your marriage situation change, Mr. Broadnax?"

"Well, that happened right after my second wife, Josephine, died in childbirth."

"Oh, I'm so sorry for your loss. Could you tell the court what happened after that?"

"Well, I was overcome with grief, and there was so much controversy about the change of policy within the church toward multiple marriages. With Josephine passing, I felt that maybe it was the right time to end my other marriages."

"How did you manage to do that?"

"Well, Captain, if you must know, like I said, I was overcome with grief, and so I talked with Dorothy and Hazel who were my last two wives, and suggested that they might find happiness outside of our marriage."

"How did they respond to your suggestion, Mr. Broadnax?"

"Your honor, I fail to see the importance of this man's marriages to this case," interrupted an impatient Jacob Moore.

Garrett immediately looked Judge Monroe in the eyes. "Your honor, I'm laying out the history of this man's relationship to the victim in order to show how the situation influenced the death of Dorothy Broadnax. Just a few more questions, your honor, and I promise, you will see the connection," Garrett urged.

Judge Monroe frowned, but then nodded, "All right, Captain, but make it just a few more questions, or I will have to call a halt to this line of questioning."

"Thank you, your honor," Garrett nodded respectfully in response, and returned to the witness, "Mr. Broadnax, how did Hazel and Dorothy respond to your suggestion?

"Well, at first, they were terribly hurt. They cried and begged me not to put them out. Hazel, especially worried about her boys, but I promised they would be taken care of. She begged me not to make her go. But finally, both she and Dorothy understood that this decision was for the best for all of us. I gave them some money so that they could find a place in town. The day they left, I thought they'd be fine."

"You expected that these two women would manage, didn't you. So, Mr. Broadnax, when did you learn the truth of Hazel's and Dorothy's situation?"

Matthew Broadnax shook his head, and Garrett could see there was evidence of genuine remorse for the decision he had made. The witness cleared his throat and replied, "Last fall, Captain. That's the first I knew about it."

"What did you find out, if you don't mind sharing this evidence with the court?"

Matthew Broadnax sighed heavily. "Dorothy told me Hazel had died." He choked up and wiped unspent tears from his eyes. "She said Hazel had just stopped eating until she starved herself to death."

"That's terrible. I'm so sorry, sir. That must have come as quite a shock to you. You had given them money to live on, and now all of a sudden you find out that one of your former wives had taken her own life in this manner. Such terrible news must have stunned you," Garrett added trying to sound sympathetic.

"Yes, it was. I couldn't believe it."

"You had expected that they would find some sort of work to support themselves because you trusted their ability, didn't you?"

"Yes. I thought they could find work as laundresses or even housekeepers. It never occurred to me that they would . . ."

"That they would resort to working as prostitutes?" Garrett finished the thought for the witness. Matthew Broadnax nodded and again wiped away tears from his eyes. Garrett knew he would have to be very careful not to alienate the judge with so sympathetic a witness.

"What a terrible discovery. What did you do to try to correct the problem, Mr. Broadnax?"

"When Dorothy told me what had happened, I was stunned. Then she asked me to help her out so she could leave Salt Lake and go to San Francisco to live with her cousin there. I knew I couldn't let anything more happen to her, so I arranged to give her money each month."

"And what were the arrangements, sir?"

"Well, I told her to come by and my secretary would give her whatever I could spare at the time. I hoped that in time, she would have enough to leave town like she wanted."

"But you're a prominent businessman, Mr. Broadnax. She must have known how difficult a position she was putting you in. How did you handle the embarrassment?"

"Well, I confess, I was embarrassed, and since I was running for mayor, I knew I had to do whatever it took to try to help her. And I almost succeeded, Captain. But now she's dead, and there's nothing more I can do to help her."

The witness broke down in sobs on the stand. Garrett reached over to pat the man on the shoulder in an effort to comfort him publicly.

He wanted the judge and those sitting in the courtroom to see him behaving in this manner. Matthew Broadnax needed to feel safe in order for Garrett to be able to break his story on the stand.

"Your honor, may we take an early recess for lunch so that my witness can have some time to regain his composure before continuing this afternoon?" Garrett asked hoping that in the interim, Joe Little would be found.

The judge looked at his pocket watch and nodded his head. "Court will be in recess until 1 o'clock this afternoon. We will continue with this witness at that time."

The bailiff called for everyone to rise, Judge Monroe left the courtroom, and Garrett returned to the defense table. He glanced at Roger, then turned to Abby. "Helen, why don't you and Roger have lunch together in the conference room? Abby and I will head to the café. Let's hope that Morgan and the General can bring our key witness here when court resumes this afternoon. Otherwise, I don't know if I can break his story."

Abby had lunch with Garrett at a local café on State Street near the City and County Building. All during their shared meal, Garrett spoke repeatedly about the need for Joe Little to be present in the courtroom after lunch. She knew how important it was for Roger that Garrett be able to break Matthew Broadnax on the stand. She said a brief prayer asking God to help her father find this witness in time.

But here, now that they had returned to the courtroom, neither the Lieutenant nor her father had returned, and there was no sign of Joe Little in the courtroom. Abby shook her head and pursed her lips. How was Garrett going to make this happen?

The court was called to order, and the judge instructed Captain Talbot to continue with his questioning of the witness, Matthew Broadnax, who the judge reminded was still under oath. Abby watched nervously as Garrett obediently rose from the defense table and approached the witness stand. She saw him inhale deeply before he addressed the witness again.

She closed her eyes and prayed for a miracle. Garrett needed Joe Little in the courtroom, and Roger needed this to happen in order to prove his innocence. Her father had to find this witness, and he needed to find him immediately.

"So, Mr. Broadnax, let me summarize my understanding of your testimony so far. You are a Mormon, and as such, in obedience to church doctrine, you took four wives. Is that correct?" Garrett asked, hoping to stall a bit.

"Yes."

"But there came a time when the church no longer sanctioned plural marriages, and so at some point after that, upon the death of one of your wives, you suggested to Dorothy and Hazel they should leave your household. Is that a fair statement?"

"Yes."

"And, you fully expected these two women were resourceful enough to find employment and support themselves, is that correct?"

"Yes, I did," Matthew Broadnax answered nodding his head in agreement.

"So when you learned about the tragic death of Hazel and about Dorothy's line of work, you were shocked, were you not?"

"Yes. Yes, indeed, I was," he answered nodding again.

"You offered to help Dorothy out of a sense of responsibility for her well being, didn't you?" Garrett asked hoping to lead his witness further.

"Yes, of course, I did. She needed my help to be able to leave town, and I wanted to help her achieve that goal."

"She came to your office at least once a month, didn't she?" Garrett asked, knowing the answer.

"Yes. I made an arrangement so she could pick up some money from my secretary each month."

"But you have eleven children to provide for, don't you, Mr. Broadnax, and Dorothy kept wanting more and more money, didn't she."

"Yes, you're right."

"You had responsibilities for those children, and she was making things difficult for you, wasn't she?"

"You're right. I tried to help her, honestly I did, but she didn't seem to care that I had to provide for my children first," he answered with a tone of desperation in his voice.

"You are an important businessman and a prominent member of the community, and she was making things difficult for you. You had to protect your reputation in order to be successful in your campaign for mayor, didn't you?"

The witness nodded without uttering a sound, and Garrett continued, "And she kept pressuring you for more money. Here times are tight for all of us right now, but she didn't seem to care about the lengths you had to go to in order to meet her demands, did she, Mr. Broadnax?"

"No, she didn't, Captain. She kept wanting more and I tried, but especially around Christmas, it was difficult because I wanted to give a little something special for each of the children. She didn't seem to care; she just demanded I get her more money," Broadnax admitted.

"She didn't care, did she? She kept demanding more and threatening to reveal her status to the public, didn't she?" Garrett continued.

Abby could see that Matthew Broadnax nodded in response. He was like an insect that was struggling to get out of the web that had been spun around him, and perhaps not even realizing where this testimony was heading. But she felt that Garrett was on the verge of getting the man to admit that Dorothy was blackmailing him.

"So you had to come up with a different arrangement. She wasn't going to be satisfied, and you weren't going to be able to continue to help her out with money like she wanted. So you had to do something else, didn't you?" Garrett asserted.

"Yes, I mean, no, I mean, what are you suggesting?" the witness replied desperately.

"You had to find some other way to resolve this situation, didn't you, Mr. Broadnax? You couldn't let her ruin your chances of becoming mayor, could you?"

"What are you suggesting, Captain?" he asked, his eyes wide with terror.

Abby saw Judge Monroe leaning toward the witness, obviously keenly interested in the direction of the testimony. She knew from the expression on the judge's face that he understood where all this was leading.

Then Garrett looked back at Abby, apparently glancing around to see if Joe Little had arrived. He turned again toward the witness and continued his pressure.

"Mr. Broadnax, what if I told you that there was a witness in that darkened alley that night who saw everything?"

Low murmuring rose from the court audience. Garrett paused to let the intent of this information sink in. He wanted the judge and the witness both to consider his words carefully.

Then after glancing once again at the judge and back to the witness, Garrett continued, "What if he saw two men carry a drunken soldier up those back stairs to Dorothy's room? And what if those two men had previously drugged that soldier so he was completely unaware of what was happening? This would explain why Corporal Davis has no memory of going up those stairs, wouldn't it?" he asked confidently. "What would you say to that, Mr. Broadnax?"

Matthew Broadnax frowned and leaned back in his chair. A look of disdain, followed by amusement covered his face. His eyebrows were so arched they almost jumped off of his forehead, Abby thought.

"Mr. Broadnax, you haven't answered my question, sir. What would you say to that?" Garrett asked again.

Jacob Moore stood as if to object, but was interrupted when the witness began to speak.

"I'd say that was a pretty amusing story, Captain, almost like the fairy tales I've read to my children at home," he answered cockily.

But then all of a sudden his jaw dropped open, and the color drained from his face.

Abby turned to look behind her and saw her father and Lieutenant Morgan ease into the room with a colored man between them. She watched as her father ushered the stranger in a suit that smelled brand new past Helen and her. The colored man sat down on the front row just behind the defense table, and her father moved on the other side of him. At the same time, Lieutenant Morgan slipped silently into a seat beside Roger.

Abby looked back at the witness who seemed frozen in place. Garrett, too, had turned to see his key witness enter the courtroom, and nodded his approval. Then he stepped back to the witness on the stand and stood directly in front of Matthew Broadnax.

"Would you like to repeat your response to that question now, Mr. Broadnax?" Garrett asked.

Matthew Broadnax hesitated, obviously stunned by the arrival of Joe Little in the courtroom. Then he repeated, "I'd say that was a good story."

"Well, what if that same witness knew one of those two men because he was a regular, so to speak? And what if that witness recognized the other man because his face was on posters all over town?" Garrett announced.

Abby watched as the judge leaned forward again frowning intently.

"You can't take anything that old drunk says seriously! He's likely to make up any story for attention," Matthew blurted out pointing at Joe Little.

"Who are you talking about, Mr. Broadnax?" Garrett asked feigning innocence.

"That old drunk, Joe, that hangs out behind Lucy's," he answered not realizing he had just stepped into the trap that Garrett had previously sprung for him.

Garrett turned in the direction of Matthew's pointing finger. "Do you mean that colored gentleman sitting on the front row over there?"

"Yeah, that's him. He's just some old drunk who sleeps in the alleyway there behind Lucy's," he answered nodding his head.

"But how would you know that, Mr. Broadnax? Have you been in that back alleyway before?"

The witness was suddenly befuddled; he reached into his breast pocket to pull out his handkerchief and wiped his forehead. He glanced around the room to try to gain support from someone there. But the audience seemed to be more interested in what he had to say next. He shook his head. "I don't know what you mean, Captain. Can I please have a glass of water?"

"Why, certainly, Mr. Broadnax," Garrett answered.

Garrett turned and met Lt. Morgan halfway to the defense table bringing a glass of water for the witness. He quickly handed it to Matthew Broadnax, and watched as he gulped down the liquid. Then giving the witness a moment to swallow, Garrett repeated the question, "Mr. Broadnax, did you see Mr. Little there that night? Is that why you know he was there?"

"Yes, I mean, no. I mean, he's always there, I hear," he answered.

"What do you mean, Mr. Broadnax? Did you see him there or not!"

"I told you, he's always there, so I just assumed you meant him," Matthew Broadnax answered trying to regain his composure.

"But how would you know unless someone had reason to tell you? Who told you about Joe Little, Mr. Broadnax?"

The witness shook his head and said nothing in response. Abby saw that he was obviously confused; the judge appeared to recognize his confusion, too, and continued to lean forward.

Garrett continued, "Let's retrace your testimony. You were at Dixon's that night, weren't you, Mr. Broadnax? We've heard Officer Dandridge testify that you were playing cards at the table with Corporal Davis. Is that right?"

Matthew Broadnax frowned. He apparently wasn't aware that Officer Dandridge had said he was there in Dixon's that night. He glanced around the room nervously. Then his voice cracked as he answered, "Yes, I was there."

"So did you see Joe Little in the back alley that night?" Garrett continued pressing the witness to respond.

Matthew Broadnax frowned and seemed to bite his lip. His face began to redden intensely. Then all of a sudden he stood up and pointed as he shouted, "It was Officer Dandridge! He's the one who killed Dorothy!"

"You lying son-of-a-bitch!" shouted Officer Dandridge sitting right behind Abby. She turned instantly and watched as the policeman shot up from his seat like a jack-in-the-box. "You damn fool! All you had to do was keep your mouth shut!"

"He's the one! He killed her!" Matthew insisted.

"You lying coward! She was your problem, not mine," replied Officer Dandridge.

The room exploded with gasps of disbelief. Judge Monroe repeatedly pounded his gavel and ordered the room to be silent. But the shock of the information revealed on the stand caused the bystanders in the courtroom to utter their amazement and ignore his demand for silence. It took several minutes before the crowd responded appropriately.

Abby watched as people in the crowd turned to one another in shock and disbelief. Their voices buzzed like horseflies. The truth was finally out. Now everyone knew that Roger hadn't killed Dorothy Broadnax. Garrett had carefully led this witness to reveal the truth.

CHAPTER

23

"Captain Talbot, I think you have reason to request a dismissal now," announced the judge.

"Yes, I know, sir, but I think I can clear this whole mess up with just a few more questions of this witness. Do I have your permission to continue?" Garrett asked respectfully.

The judge nodded as Garrett walked over to the evidence table and picked up Roger's gun.

"You know, Mr. Broadnax, Corporal Davis told me an interesting story about how he happened to have this particular gun. You probably don't know this, but most enlisted men do not have sidearms. But about five years ago, the Corporal found this gun lying out in the grass at the edge of the fort. He picked it up, examined it carefully, and seeing that it was still loaded, tried to fire the gun. But the gun misfired, and he got a terrible burn on his hand. He showed me that he still has a small scar from that first time. He told me that from that time on, he learned to never fire that gun without wearing his leather gloves for protection."

Garrett watched as the color drained again from the witness's face. "You know what that means, don't you, Mr. Broadnax? It means that anyone who tried to fire this gun would have a burn on his hand, too."

"Well, there's no burn on my hand," Matthew announced proudly displaying his right hand for the judge and Garrett. "See?"

Garrett nodded, "Yes, I know that your right hand is just fine, Mr. Broadnax. I remember commenting on that when we shook hands the first time we met."

"Yeah, you're right. So it couldn't be me, could it," he asserted.

Garrett paused and looked intently at the witness. Something didn't seem to fit. Joe Little had indicated that a man had screamed after the spark had appeared in the window, and he also had said that Matthew Broadnax had cussed repeatedly as he and Officer Dandridge had run down those back stairs. Here was that same man clearly waving his right hand in the air for everyone to see, while at the same time keeping his other hand covered in his coat pocket. Garrett continued to watch and saw what could have been a white bandage on that hand. All of a sudden, he knew the answer. It hadn't occurred to him until just this moment.

"Yes, your right hand has no evidence of a burn on it. But I also happen to know that unlike the majority of folks in this room, you are left-handed. Aren't you?" Garrett said, praying that his guess was correct.

Matthew Broadnax sat back and continued to hold his left hand close to his body in an effort to conceal it from peering eyes.

"Is that true?" asked the judge. "Let me see your left hand, Mr. Broadnax," demanded Judge Monroe.

The witness shook his head vehemently. Then the judge motioned for the bailiff to approach the witness stand. A look of panic covered Matthew Broadnax's face as he realized that his deception was about to be publicly revealed.

Then all of a sudden he stood up and declared, "Yes, I fired that gun, but only because Dandridge insisted on it. I sent him to scare her into leaving right away. She was threatening to tell everyone that I had thrown her out of our home and that she was forced to earn a living as a prostitute. I couldn't let that happen. He was just supposed to scare her, I swear, that's all I asked him to do. But she wouldn't back down, and he lost his temper. They fought, and he killed her. I only shot her to make it look like that corporal had killed her. I swear!"

Again the room exploded in shock. Disbelief was etched on the faces of those spectators in the courtroom. Several voices called for the witness to be hanged. Again the judge pounded his gavel on the desk and called for order.

Garrett waited until a hush finally returned to the court before approaching the judge's desk and asking, "Your honor, the defense asks for a dismissal of all charges against Corporal Roger Davis for the murder of Dorothy Broadnax."

"The State joins in that motion, your honor," declared Jacob Moore standing just behind Garrett.

"So ordered," replied the judge. "Bailiff, take Mr. Broadnax into custody, arrest Officer Dandridge, too."

But then a shriek came from behind him. Garrett turned to see Officer Dandridge pulling Abby out of her seat with his left forearm pressed around her throat. He waved a gun around in his right hand, using Abby as a shield against anyone who might shoot at him.

"Anyone comes near me, and I'll kill her!" he announced angrily. He edged back towards the double doors which exited into the hallway. "Don't anybody move, or I swear, I'll kill her and anyone else who gets in my way."

The spectators in the courtroom were frozen with astonishment. Officer Dandridge continued to drag an uncooperative Abby with him. She struggled against his forearm which prevented her from even screaming. No one else seemed to move.

Helen screamed, "Garrett, do something!"

Instinctively, Garrett rushed towards the woman he loved. In an instant, he jumped the rail that separated the onlookers from the court. He saw no one but Abby. She was in danger, and he had to do whatever he could to rescue her. He would give his life for her if he had to.

As he approached the man who was holding Abby hostage, Garrett thought he saw some sort of movement just to his right. But he continued to focus on Abby's face, and the terror registered there.

"Don't worry, Abby. He won't hurt you," Garrett assured Abby in order to keep her calm in the midst of this new terror. He continued to advance toward the pair slowly and deliberately. Nothing would deter him.

With Abby struggling each step of the way, Officer Dandridge continued to pull her out of the courtroom and down the hallway to the west exit of the building. Garrett followed, as Abby continued to cough and choke as she tried to free herself from her captor's grasp. He moved his arm down from her throat and pulled her tightly against him holding her shoulder.

"Garrett! Please! Stay back! He'll kill you!" she cried, finally able to speak.

"Smart woman, Captain," Officer Dandridge agreed. "Better do what she says, and both of you will live another day."

"Let her go, Dandridge," Garrett demanded. "You don't need her. Look you can take me instead."

"Already got a hostage, thank you, Captain. She'll do just fine for now. Better stay back, or I'll have to shoot you just to get away safely."

"Can't do that, Dandridge. I'm not about to walk away and let you take Abby away from these grounds."

"Suit yourself, Captain. At this range, I don't think I'll miss. Sure will be a shame, though, for her to witness you shot dead today," he answered squinting his narrow eyes.

"I agree, Officer," came a voice from behind the policeman. "I'm not too handy with a gun, but, as you say, at this range I don't think I'll miss."

Officer Dandridge froze in his steps suddenly aware that he was trapped. "I'll kill her! I'll kill her!" he shouted.

"Well if I actually believed that you intended to kill her, you'd already be dead, sir. But you see, that's my daughter you've dragged out here, and she's wearing a fine new dress that I'm sure she doesn't want stained with your blood, so I've decided to give you just one chance to throw down your gun and surrender," replied the General.

Officer Dandridge's head lurched forward as the barrel of the General's gun was pressed squarely against the back of his head. The policeman's eyes grew wide with disbelief. Time seemed to stand still as Garrett gazed first at Abby and then at her captor. Dandridge winced just before he reluctantly tossed his gun down in the dirt. Seeing the man was no longer armed, Garrett rushed forward to pull Abby to safety. Then he turned back towards the man who had dragged her from the courtroom.

"You son-of-a-bitch! I ought to kill you with my bare hands," Garrett said making certain that Abby was out of the man's reach.

"You don't have the stomach for it, blue belly," he taunted in response.

Garrett stood fuming in front of the man who had threatened the woman he loved. In an instant he replied with his fists, punching the man in the abdomen with his left, and following up with an uppercut to the man's jaw with his right. He stumbled back a few steps before Garrett followed up with another shot to the man's face. Officer Dandridge fell to the ground in a heap, coughing and spitting blood that gushed from his nose.

Abby called to Garrett, and reached to draw him back from any further confrontation. She clung to him, holding onto him for dear life. By that time, several other policemen came running to assist in Officer Dandridge's capture.

"I don't see what all the fuss is about anyway," he said as he was lifted from the ground and handcuffed there in front of the gathering crowd. "Dorothy was nothing but a greedy whore. The world's a better place without the likes of her."

Abby pulled away from Garrett, her damp eyes burning with fury. "How dare you say such a thing! She was a decent woman caught up in an awful situation. You had no right to threaten her, much less take her life."

Officer Dandridge scowled back at Abby who moved closer to him defiantly challenging him. "You're nothing but a troublemaker, woman. Too bad those drunks didn't really teach you the lesson you needed."

Suddenly General Randolph took the two strides needed to face Officer Dandridge, and in almost the same movement, smashed the man's face nearly snapping the man's neck backward. The policemen standing on either side of him were the only reason Officer Dandridge was able to remain upright. He yelped in pain with blood continuing to spew from his face. The two guards had to assist him in trudging back towards the jail. The General simply brushed off his knuckles, turned back towards his daughter, and escorted her over to Garrett.

Tears streaming unheeded down her face, Abby grabbed her father and hugged him tightly, while the General patted Garrett on the shoulder.

"Good job, son," he announced as the trio were joined by Roger, Helen, and Lt. Morgan. The afternoon air was unseasonably warmed by a radiant sun, somewhat unusual for the time of the year. Relief poured over the group like a fresh rain shower. Garrett's plan had worked, and Roger was now a free man again. With this final crisis resolved, they all headed back to Fort Douglas.

CHAPTER

24

Supper that night at the General's residence was a celebration. General Randolph had previously arranged for a catered dinner from the Officers' Club so neither Helen nor Abby would have to prepare the meal. They all sat around the table like the family they had grown to become. Helen snuggled close to her husband, unafraid of a public show of affection for the man she had been separated from for over a month now. Though she had seemed out of breath most of the afternoon, she was radiant, a combination of joy over his acquittal and the natural beauty of an expectant woman. Roger, too, obviously enjoyed the closeness of his very pregnant wife. Though he had seen her regularly in the stockade when she had come to visit, he had announced earlier nothing compared to sitting next to her at this moment.

Abby sat next to Garrett at the table, refusing to be separated from him either. Though not as demonstrative of affection as the married couple sitting across from them, Abby made it plain she was in love with the man who sat to her right. She felt she would burst with admiration for the man who had saved her friends. A military man, no less. Imagine that.

Lieutenant Morgan sat across from the two of them, next to Roger, and General Randolph took his place at the head of the table sitting between his daughter and Helen, who had grown to be like a sister to Abby. The General looked across at the sea of happy faces, and he beamed with delight. He admitted to them all his home had never felt this full before tonight, though there had been moments in the fall when Abby and Garrett had begun their courtship which came close. No, it was this shared trauma that had brought them all closer than he could have imagined possible. After they had all finished their meal, he stood and a hush fell over the dining room.

"I lift my glass to salute all of you. You all worked together to achieve this outcome, and we're all the better for the effort," he said raising his wine glass.

The others all followed suit, and clinked glasses to demonstrate their common bond.

"I know this has been a difficult journey for all of us, but here we are together, a family of our own making, enjoying this fine meal and each other's company. May we always remember this moment, especially in times of trouble. There's nothing we cannot overcome when we strive together as a family." He saluted them again, and drank the contents of his glass and sat down.

"Here. Here," rejoined the rest of them.

Then Roger stood at his place at the table and lifted his glass first towards the General and towards Garrett and the Lieutenant. "Gentlemen, thank you for your support. Thank you, General, for believing in my innocence. All your visits to the stockade, and arranging for Helen to visit so regularly, sir, I never could've gotten through those days without knowing that you believed in me." Roger raised his glass and said, "To General Randolph." and a chorus rang out at the table, "To General Randolph."

The General nodded in response, then modestly said, "Now, son, I didn't do all that much."

Lieutenant Morgan's jaw dropped open before he asserted, "Not much? Not much? Garrett never could have pulled off what he did so easily today if you hadn't convinced Joe Little to come to court."

"How did you do that, sir?" asked Garrett.

"It wasn't much," replied the General.

"He won't tell you, so I will," announced Lt. Morgan, leaning onto the dining room table. "We found Joe in the same spot you and I first found him last month, Garrett, but as much as he wanted to help us, he was more concerned that people wouldn't let a colored man into the courtroom.

"So the General took action. He took Joe to a Chinese bathhouse. Had to pay extra 'cause they didn't want a colored man bathing there. Then he took Joe to Johnson's, and the General bought him a new suit. That was a mess, too, you know, 'cause the store clerk didn't want Joe to try on the suit before he bought it. The General had to assure them he would buy whatever Joe tried on. That's why we couldn't get there until after 1 P. M. But I really thought we would make it before the afternoon session began, though."

"You probably would have if I hadn't asked for an early recess this morning," replied Garrett nodding. "I stalled as long as I could. Then Matthew Broadnax broke down on the stand when he testified about his wife dying. He was much too sympathetic a witness at that point, so I had to request a recess. Otherwise, the judge would've stopped my interrogation at a critical time, and there's no telling how that would've turned out." The others at the table nodded in agreement.

"But Chet, you were right about that small amount of blood. I spoke with Jacob Moore after court today when you'd all left. By that time, Officer Dandridge had made a complete confession. He told me Officer Dandridge had gone to Dorothy's room to threaten her. His intent was to scare her into leaving, just like Broadnax said on the stand. He admitted to losing his temper and fighting with her. When she threatened to go straight to the newspaper with the story, he hit her hard enough to knock her into the bedpost. He said she fell down dead from the impact. So you were right; she was dead before Broadnax shot her with Roger's gun."

"Apparently, when he realized what had happened, he put her body on the bed and left to find Broadnax. At first the two of them were just going to leave her and hope that no one tried to solve her murder. After all, their problem was solved by her death. But Broadnax was worried because he didn't want anyone to suspect him of the crime. They both agreed they needed to find someone who could take the blame."

"That's when Officer Dandridge saw Corporal Davis in Connor's; Broadnax was there, too, in the crowd, and he followed the two of them down to Dixon's. According to Broadnax, Roger, you actually won a few hands at the poker table before Officer Dandridge handed you a drugged glass of whiskey. Once you passed out, they carried you upstairs, and that would've been the end of it if Broadnax hadn't foolishly fired your gun."

"I am so relieved that my Roger's back home for good," Helen said, "but let's not forget how much help Abby was in solving this mess."

"Me?" replied a surprised Abby. "It's my fault that all of you got mixed up in this mess in the first place. If I hadn't insisted on trying to participate in the Women's Housing Association, and if I hadn't tried to find Dorothy that night, maybe none of this would've happened at all."

"Nonsense," Garrett said. "You're the reason that we were able to connect her with Matthew Broadnax in the first place. If you hadn't talked with her and learned about her situation, we would never have known how Broadnax was related to Dorothy. Without that crucial information, I wouldn't have known where to look. I might never have been able to get Roger off.

"You insisted that her husband was responsible for her death from the very first moment you figured out his relationship to the victim. And you were the one who found that campaign poster that showed Broadnax running for office. That's how we knew that Broadnax was at Dixon's when Roger was there. That proved to me that he was involved with the cover up." He put his arm around her shoulder and hugged her.

"And let's not forget, you're the only reason that I agreed to take this case at all. I was all ready to leave Fort Douglas when you pleaded with me to stay and defend Roger. Don't get me wrong, folks, I care a lot about all of you, but Abby was the only reason I agreed to stay." He reached over and kissed her gently on the cheek. "I love you, Abigail Randolph; don't you ever forget that."

"Well, I want to thank each of you for the part you played in solving this case," continued Roger. "Helen and I have decided that we're going to name the little one after you. I'm really hoping this baby's going to be a boy. If so, we want to name him Thomas Jackson Davis, with your permission, of course, General. We thought we'd give him your first name and Garrett's middle name, and we'd call him 'Jack' for short. If this baby turns out to be a girl, Helen wants to name her after you, Abby. She'd be called "little Abby" around here, of course." Roger laughed.

Abby smiled and nodded. Then she stood up in her spot at the table. "I want to thank all of you for making me feel so very welcomed here. Since my grandparents and my mother died, I've not felt a part of a family. I kept searching for purpose and for a sense of belonging. I've never had such good friends before I came here. I can't imagine my life without all of you in it."

Looking at her father, Abby grinned, "And you, Father, I've never been as happy as I am right now knowing that I have your love. I finally understand why you were away all those years now, but when I was a little girl, I often thought it was because you didn't want me. Until just recently, I didn't know what emptiness I was trying to fill."

"When I came out here, I was so afraid I'd do or say something that would make you not want me, just like I had felt as a little girl. I still miss Mother, but knowing I am truly your daughter, too, has filled the empty spot I had inside for so long. I'm so very glad I got the chance to come to Fort Douglas."

Everyone nodded and uttered their agreement while Abby turned from her seat and embraced her father impulsively. Holding her at his side, the General replied, "Yes, we've got so much to celebrate tonight." He looked over at Helen, and added, "Roger and Helen are back together and soon there will be a little Davis in the household."

The General reached for Garrett and continued, "In another month or so I plan on walking my daughter down the aisle of the little chapel across the street, so she can be married to this fine soldier here."

He smiled and shook Garrett's hand, then placed his daughter's hands in Garrett's. "And I finally have the family I wasn't able to have as a young man," he answered gesturing towards all of those assembled in the room. "God has truly blessed me by giving me all of you here in my home."

Turning to his daughter again, "Abby, I want you to know how proud I am that you are my daughter. And to hear how your example of sacrifice influenced some of those women in town, well, to say the least, I was overcome with pride knowing those women credit you with saving their lives. I'm sure Garrett'll agree that you should continue helping out with that organization when you can," the General said looking over to see Garrett nod his approval.

"See what you did by coming to Fort Douglas? You wanted a purpose; well, you achieved it. You made all of this happen when you came here," replied Garrett as he squeezed Abby towards him.

"Oh! That was a strong one," Helen exclaimed. Then looking at Abby, she beckoned her to come feel for herself.

Abby placed her hand on the spot, and within moments, she could feel Helen's baby punching at his mother's side. New life safely carried within her friend's body. A new life for me, too, Abby thought, as she beamed contentedly. She couldn't imagine any better place to be than here with her family. All her questions about her own life had been answered. Her relationship with her father was stronger than she could have ever imagined. She had been able to provide hope to those women in Salt Lake City, and now both her father and Garrett approved of her desire to help those less fortunate than herself. Reaching to gently grasp the locket around her neck, Abby thought of her mother, and felt warm all over.

"Oh! That one's different," Helen cried.

Abby looked at her friend and saw a look of fear wash over her face.

"It's never felt like that before," Helen said as she turned towards her husband. "Something's wrong, Roger. I know it."

Abby grabbed her friend's hands and squeezed to get her attention. Looking in her eyes, she said, "Nothing's wrong, Helen. Nothing's wrong. I won't let it." She turned to her father and asked, "Can someone go get the doctor?"

Immediately the General got to his feet. "Garrett, you and Chet go get Dr. Nash. Tell him to come right away. Roger, help me carry Helen to her bedroom. It may be that your child will be born tonight, and we need to make sure his mother is as comfortable as possible."

Abby watched as her father and Roger lifted Helen from her seat. The chair was wet where she had been sitting. Her water had broken. Abby pursed her lips and sighed. <u>It may be too soon, but this baby is coming tonight.</u>

Abby sat rocking Helen's baby boy while his exhausted mother slept. Born just after midnight, Jack seemed healthy and strong in spite of arriving a few weeks early. After learning that his wife and son were fine, Roger held his infant son for a few minutes while the General, Garrett, and Chet congratulated the parents. When the four of them left Helen's room, Doctor Nash and Abby washed and dressed the tiny infant, and after Helen had fed her baby for the first time, he had drifted off to sleep. Abby had taken the boy from his mother's arms with the intention of putting him in his cradle, but she couldn't resist the opportunity to rock the tiny baby in her arms. It had been several hours now, but Abby was still enchanted by this little boy whose face wrinkled up often as he slept. She wondered if he were dreaming of heaven or just his next meal.

"It won't be long, Abby, before you have one of your own," Helen said as she eased herself up on her pillows.

"I know. But right now, your little baby is the most wonderful treasure on earth," Abby replied. She got up from the rocking chair and placed the sleeping infant in his new cradle. She stood there a moment gazing at the peaceful child.

"He's quiet right now, Abby. But it won't be long before he'll announce his displeasure at being wet or hungry."

"I know. But right now in this quiet, isn't it wonderful?"

"Yes, it is, isn't it. Where's Roger and your father?"

"Asleep. I convinced Roger to take my bed, and Father agreed to try to get some sleep himself. They both cleaned the dishes and all. I think they were just glad to have something to do while you were in labor."

"Men are a little useless during this, I know," Helen said smiling. "Where's Garrett?"

"Asleep in the parlor, I think."

"He didn't go back to the barracks?"

"No. I spoke to him once in all the confusion. He said he wasn't leaving either of us until he knew for certain you were okay. When Jack was born, he couldn't stop grinning. I think he's really pleased that you're planning to name this child after both him and Father."

The bedroom door opened just slightly. "How's Jack?" asked Garrett.

"Still asleep," answered Helen. "Come on in, Captain. We were just talking about you."

Garrett stepped into the room and quietly eased over to the cradle. "Can I hold him, Helen?"

"Of course."

Garrett bent over the cradle and carefully slid his hands under the bundled infant. He slowly brought the child up into his arms, and gently rocked him. He seemed to know exactly what to do.

"I was just telling Abby that it won't be long before the two of you have one of your own."

"No doubt he'll have red hair and be headstrong like his mother," Garrett added.

"I just hope she is smart and brave like her father," Abby said as she edged closer to him. She put her cheek against his upper arm and smiled down at the sleeping child in Garrett's arms just as the first rays of daylight streamed in through the window. Jack crinkled up his nose and yawned. He opened his eyes and stared up at Garrett, but he didn't seem alarmed. Perhaps he sensed he was safe within a family that would love him and protect him. Abby thought so. This little baby would be surrounded by parents and friends who would always look out for him. And in time, Abby knew there would be other little babies who would fill their hearts just as Jack did now. She reached up and lovingly patted the locket with her parents' pictures. She was truly at home with her family here at Fort Douglas.

The End

www.ingramcontent.com/pod-product-compliance
Lightning Source LLC
LaVergne TN
LVHW041757060526
838201LV00046B/1035